CABARET MACABRE

CABARET MACABRE

A JOSEPH SPECTOR LOCKED-ROOM MYSTERY

TOM MEAD

THE MYSTERIOUS PRESS
NEW YORK

CABARET MACABRE

Mysterious Press
An Imprint of Penzler Publishers
58 Warren Street
New York, N.Y. 10007

Copyright © 2024 by Tom Mead

First Mysterious Press edition

Interior design by Maria Fernandez

Library of Congress Control Number: 2023922769

ISBN: 978-1-61316-530-0
eBook ISBN: 978-1-61316-531-7

10 9 8 7 6 5 4 3 2 1

Printed in the United States of America
Distributed by W. W. Norton & Company

To the current locked-room masters:
Yukito Ayatsuji, Paul Halter, and Soji Shimada.
In memory of Seishi Yokomizo (1902-1981) and,
once again, John Dickson Carr (1906-1977).

CONTENTS

AUTHOR'S NOTE

The quotation on page 70 is taken from "Backbone Flute" (1915) by Vladimir Mayakovsky.

The quotation on page 180 is taken from *A General View of the Law of Property* (1895) by James Andrew Strahan and James Sinclair Baxter.

DRAMATIS PERSONAE

Justice Sir Giles Drury, QC
Leonard Drury, his son
Ambrose Drury, his other son
Sylvester Monkton, his illegitimate son
Lady Elspeth Drury, his wife
Jeffrey Flack, her son from a previous marriage

Peter Nightingale, Leonard's secretary
Ludo Quintrell-Webb, a revolutionary
Arthur Cosgrove, a civil servant
Horace Tapper, a film producer
Thomas Griffin, a hospital orderly
Dr. James Findler, a police mortician
Mrs. Runcible, a housekeeper
Becky, a housemaid
Alma, a cook
Dr. Jasper Moncrieff, an experimental psychiatrist
Byron Manderby, an explorer

Victor Silvius, a madman
Caroline Silvius, his sister

"The Edgemoor Strangler"
"The Ambergate Arsonist"

Inspector George Flint, of Scotland Yard
Sergeant Jerome Hook, his second
Joseph Spector, a professional trickster

DRURY FAMILY TREE

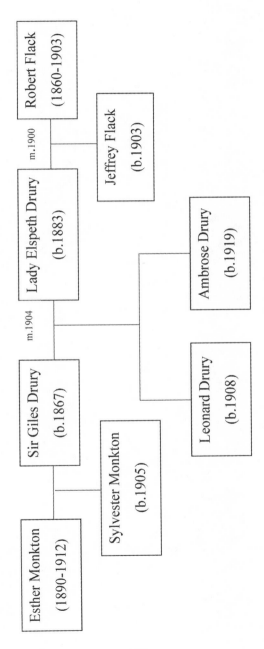

Esther Monkton (1890-1912) — Sir Giles Drury (b.1867) — m.1904 — Lady Elspeth Drury (b.1883) — m.1900 — Robert Flack (1860-1903)

Sylvester Monkton (b.1905)

Leonard Drury (b.1908)

Ambrose Drury (b.1919)

Jeffrey Flack (b.1903)

MARCHBANKS GROUND FLOOR

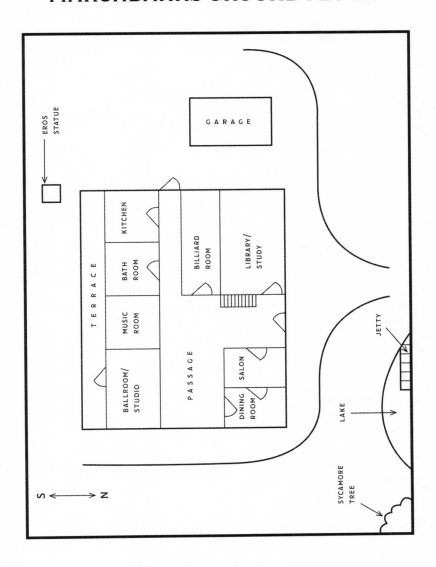

MARCHBANKS FIRST FLOOR

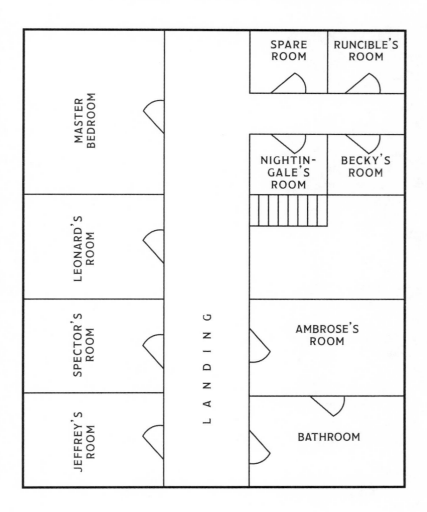

PART ONE

THE FACELESS MAN

December 13-15, 1938

He shall not live
To see the moon change.
—*The Revenger's Tragedy*, **act 4, scene 2**

There is pattern but no logic in criminality.
—**Ellery Queen,** *The Greek Coffin Mystery*

CHAPTER ONE

THE STEAMER TRUNK

Tuesday, December 13, 1938

I.

The steamer trunk had leather handles, brass fittings, and a dark, hardboard shell. As such it was like any other steamer trunk. You might say its only notable feature was its location: washed ashore on Rotherhithe beach, where it lay looking soggy and pitiful alone on the pebbles in the chilly morning sun. Nine-year-old Fred Lindsay and his seven-year-old sister Enid were bickering and laughing as they crested the dune and got their first glimpse of it on the flats. Benny, their beloved Jack Russell, bounded over with his tongue flapping, and commenced an exhaustive investigation with his probing nostrils. But the children were cautious.

They glanced at one another and Enid, the braver of the two, made the first move. She skipped toward the trunk, her head brimming with fantasies of pirates' treasure. This was the sort of thing that happened to little girls like her, she thought. They found treasure and got whisked away on adventures.

As she drew closer, the stench rolled over her like the tide. It rooted her to the spot and made her gag. It smelt worse than anything the Thames had ever spewed up before.

"What? What's the matter?" said Fred. Then the stench hit him too.

Once they had got over the initial shock of it (Benny the Jack Russell was still frolicking around the trunk), the siblings decided they'd better try and crack it open. They didn't *want* to, not really, but they felt it their duty.

Careful to breathe through his mouth, Fred dropped to his haunches and examined the brass clasp. It was caked with clumpy sludge from the bottom of the river, but otherwise seemed to be in decent working order.

"Pass me that, would you?" he said, indicating a chipped bit of slate on the ground.

Enid brought it over to him; the slate was heavy, so she needed both hands. He took it from her and swung for the clasp. The edge of the slate struck with a thump. Fred swung again. This time, some of the dried mud came away like clay. One more swing, he thought, and they were in.

It actually took about six more swings, but finally, with an eerie sigh of escaping air, the buckle snapped and the trunk lid splayed open. It made Fred and Enid jump. Even Benny was a bit suspicious. The three of them stood to examine what was inside.

Neither of the children screamed, though both wanted to. Eventually it was Enid, the brave one, who broke the silence.

"What have they done to his face?" she said.

II.

Inspector George Flint gazed out at the iron-grey surface of the Thames from beneath the brim of his slightly-too-large bowler hat (a gift from his wife, who often overestimated his dimensions) and sighed. He chewed his unlit pipe philosophically, then forced himself to look down at the mess inside the trunk.

Sergeant Jerome Hook, who was younger but steelier about such matters, hadn't taken his eyes off the tangle of limbs and torso.

He said, "Somebody didn't want us to identify him."

"Looks that way all right. Only reason I can think of for smashing his face into mush like that. But what I'm wondering about is his *hands*."

The body in the steamer trunk was male and had dark hair. As for distinguishing features, that was about it. The trunk had been in the water for at least a week. The body had the creamy, greenish tinge of old tapioca. It was mottled with mould and bruises.

"Hallo there," called a voice through the wintry river haze. The bulky outline of a greatcoated man with a doctor's bag came slowly into view.

"Dr. Findler," Flint said by way of greeting, "you're a sight for sore eyes."

"I might say the same of you," answered Findler through a yawn. "Why've you brought me to this godforsaken spot?"

"See for yourself."

Findler was a year or two younger than Flint, and it showed. He was clean-shaven and his face lacked Flint's ruddiness. Nonetheless, he was capable and well-versed in what he referred to as the "dark arts." He had built his life around death, and so neither life nor death held much terror for him. Findler was a strict Darwinian when it came to murder, with little sympathy for the victim who had failed to run fast enough, or picked a fight with the wrong man, or got in the way of a stray bullet. He was unmoved by the contents of the trunk, and peered at them in the way a window shopper might peer into Debenham & Freebody: with the measured curiosity and mild distaste of finding last season's suits still displayed behind the glass.

"What can you tell us about him?" said Flint.

"Nothing we haven't seen before. I'm tempted to call it a gangland killing. Quasi-professional. Except for one thing."

"Which is?" But Flint already knew the answer.

"His hands."

III.

Back at Scotland Yard, Flint shut himself in his Thameside office to read and reread the scant details he had scribbled in his notebook.

Today's discovery offered little scope for interpretation. Dark-haired male, aged between twenty-five and forty-five.

And what of the trunk itself? It was depressingly ordinary. The sort that might be purchased from any local shop. No travel badges or labels. Attempts to trace it would lead precisely nowhere.

But Flint kept coming back to the hands. If this were a gangland killing, and the victim known to the law, Scotland Yard would most likely already have his prints somewhere on file.

That's what troubled Flint. It made him wonder if maybe this wasn't a gangland killing at all.

The window frame rattled and he looked up from his papers to see spatters of rain on the glass. A fierce wind whipped against the side of the building. He briefly debated whether or not to light his pipe (chewing it unlit helped him to concentrate, though a puff of tobacco might stave off the chill) but was snapped from his reverie by a knock at the door.

"Come," he said, and Hook stepped inside.

"Sorry to disturb, sir," said the sergeant.

"It's all right, Hook. Any news?"

"No, sir."

It was a vain hope, but cases like the Rotherhithe trunk murder sometimes produced witnesses and informants. *Somebody* knew the dead man. He had come from *somewhere*.

"Well, what's it about, then?"

"Woman to see you, sir," said Hook. "Name is Miss Caroline Silvius."

"What does she want?"

"Won't talk to me I'm afraid, sir. Wants you and only you."

"Is it to do with the trunk business?"

"Don't know, sir."

Flint thought for a moment, finally decided to light up his pipe after all, then said, "All right. Bring her through. And brew some tea while you're at it."

IV.

"Inspector Flint?"

"That's right, how d'you do. Miss Caroline Silvius, is that correct?"

"Quite correct." Caroline Silvius's manner was polite but officious. She was a young, prim, schoolmarmish sort, dressed comfortably and frugally.

"Please come through. Sergeant Hook will bring you some tea in a moment."

He offered her the most comfortable chair. She sat in it willingly and seemed at once to lose some of the inhibition that had hung about her shoulders like Le Fanu's phantom monkey. She relaxed, the muscles in her narrow shoulders slackening.

"Hope you don't mind my barging in like this," she commenced. "Most out of the ordinary, I'm sure."

"Not at all," said Flint. "Now what's this about?"

Hook came in with a tray of tea, and Flint played mother.

"Well . . . it's to do with my brother."

Flint immediately pictured the contents of the steamer trunk. "Oh yes? And what's his name?"

"Victor."

"Victor, eh? What about him?"

"Well," she said, "I'm afraid somebody is trying to kill him."

Flint had just taken a mouthful of tea, and almost sputtered the whole lot across his desk. "Kill him?"

She scrutinised him, as though seeing him for the first time. "Can I trust you?"

"Of course," he answered, striking a match to ignite the tobacco in his pipe bowl.

She paused. "All right. It started some ten years ago, or thereabouts. I was only twelve. My brother was nineteen. He was—still *is*—an artist. He has a fiery, passionate soul, you see. He never was a fellow to do things by halves. So, when he fell in love with Gloria Crain, he fell very far indeed. He grew obsessed with her. Convinced that they would be married and live 'happily ever after.' The poor boy."

"So," Flint put in, "this Miss Crain didn't reciprocate his affections?" *Spurned romance from over a decade ago?* The inspector sighed inwardly. "Victor" was not the faceless man in the steamer trunk after all.

"Oh but she did. She was a year older than Victor, and secretary to an important fellow, a judge. Perhaps you know him—Sir Giles Drury?"

Flint nodded without comment. Everybody knew Sir Giles Drury. "Forgive me for being presumptuous—but may I take it their courtship did not end happily?"

Caroline Silvius cradled her teacup in her lap. "Indeed."

"She spurned him?"

9

Caroline gave a sharp, involuntary laugh. "I wish it were that simple. No, Inspector Flint. Gloria's love for my brother remained as strong as ever until the day she died."

Flint's moustache twitched a little. He waited for her to elaborate.

"Gloria died suddenly, ten years ago this Christmas. She was Sir Giles's private secretary, as I've said, and she had gone with him to his country retreat, a place called Marchbanks, to spend the festive season. The rest of the Drury clan was there too. Sir Giles is—as I'm sure you know—a gentleman ill-inclined to let a little thing like the Yuletide get in the way of his work. So he brought Gloria out there with him, and while the rest of the family was telling jokes and playing games, he and Gloria would be in his study, hard at work. She stayed with the family as their guest. And it was on Christmas night—after dinner . . ."

"Yes?"

"Gloria was taken ill. She was dead before dawn."

"How did she die?"

"Strychnine. A suicide, according to the official verdict."

Flint frowned. *Suicide by strychnine?*

"But there were certain *rumours*," Caroline continued. "They'd been fomenting for a while. Specifically, rumours that Sir Giles was unfaithful to his wife, Lady Elspeth. And when Gloria died, my brother lost all reason. He became obsessed with the notion that Gloria and Sir Giles had been having an affair, and that Sir Giles had killed her."

"What did *you* make of it all?" Flint inquired.

"I was just a girl. And though I loved Victor with all my heart, I think even then I knew that he'd come to grief. Men like Sir Giles Drury make powerful enemies. And poor Victor . . ." she spoke haltingly now, clouded by emotion. "Poor Victor never stood a chance."

"What happened?"

"Victor went mad. Really and truly mad. He attacked the judge. Waited outside his chambers and stabbed him. The judge survived, as you are no doubt aware. But there is nothing quite so momentous as the vengeance of a powerful man. Victor was taken and quietly committed, to avoid further scandal. Condemned as insane which, in a way, I suppose he was—though it was the judge that drove him to it. Gloria's death was hushed up and the whole mess was forgotten about. And my brother was left to rot. Our parents never spoke of him—they were embarrassed, and fearful Sir Giles would make life difficult for them. As far as they were concerned, Victor simply ceased to exist."

"Then what changed?" asked Flint.

She bowed her head. "Our parents died two months ago. As soon as I was able, I went to visit him. And my God, Inspector Flint, what a sight he was. Half-starved, with a beard down to here—a real Count of Monte Cristo. I scarcely recognised him at all. But he still had the same kind, loving eyes."

"And now you claim that somebody is trying to kill him," Flint prompted.

"It's the judge," she affirmed. "It has to be."

"But why? And how, for that matter?"

"Victor is an inmate at a private sanatorium owned and run by one Dr. Moncrieff. The doctor and the judge happen to be members of a curious drinking club known as 'The Tragedians.' Thick as thieves since their university days. Sir Giles pulled strings to ensure that Victor ended up at Moncrieff's clinic."

Flint's writing hand was getting tired. He let his pencil fall from between his fingers and clatter on the desk. He studied Caroline Silvius very carefully. This story of hers was fantastic, but he knew at least part of it to be true. Sir Giles Drury, the famous (and infamous) hanging judge, had indeed been attacked outside his chambers some years ago. Though Flint had been on the force at the time, he'd not been involved in the ensuing investigation. The incident briefly made headlines before being swiftly shunted in favour of more palatable fare. Another of the judge's chums pulling strings, no doubt. A fellow "Tragedian."

Flint had never heard of Gloria Crain. He would need to look into the fateful dinner party that had served as the backdrop to her untimely demise. And as for Dr. Moncrieff, he too was known to Flint. An "experimental psychiatrist" with a line in lobotomising promiscuous debutantes. That he and the judge were old friends did not come as a surprise.

But this Victor Silvius was an enigma.

"What makes you think Sir Giles wishes to hurt your brother?"

"There have been certain incidents. Naturally Moncrieff and the thugs he calls 'orderlies' have denied everything. But I've seen the truth for myself. They started with slivers of glass in his mashed potato. Oh Mr. Flint, they would have cut him to ribbons. I ask you, what's that if not attempted murder?"

"Very nasty," said Flint. His gaze twitched toward the window, which was now slick with sleet, dribbling down like a spent candle. "All due respect, Miss Silvius, but . . ." he chose his words carefully. "Can we be sure of the *veracity* of your brother's version of events?"

Her eyes narrowed then widened, as though she had been about to snap at him but thought better of it. "There's nothing wrong with my brother."

"No, no. Of course not."

"You don't believe me, do you? If you'll let me, I'll prove it to you."

"What did you have in mind?"

"Why, you must meet him and see for yourself."

"I'm afraid that won't be possible," said Flint, fatuously shuffling a few papers, "not without reasonable grounds for an investigation . . ."

"Please," she said, her eyes gleaming in the lamplight. "There may be more than one life at stake."

Flint exhaled resignedly. "When did you have in mind?"

"As soon as possible."

"Next week, maybe?"

"All right. I'll telephone you this afternoon with the details."

Flint got up from the desk and went over to the window, where he stood gazing out contemplatively with his hands folded behind his back. He glanced back at the mound of papers awaiting his attention on the desk. The thankless pursuit of the faceless man in the steamer trunk.

"Very well," he said.

V.

Leonard Drury studied the fellow from the agency with an appraising eye. Well-dressed but not too well-dressed. Good posture. Handsome but, most importantly, not *too* handsome. Leonard tried to guess his age and put him in the early thirties, rather like himself.

The two men were in the study of Leonard's opulent London townhouse, which he liked to think of as an encapsulation of his boisterous personality. He lived there alone (at least in theory), and his long-suffering servants tolerated him with saintly stoicism because he paid them well. But there was also the little matter of his celebrity. Leonard had just emerged triumphant from a year treading the boards at London's Alhambra Theatre in *By Twilight, My Darling*, a theatrical tour de force that had afforded him a swift ascent to the upper echelons of the acting fraternity.

"Remind me of your name?"

"Nightingale, sir. Peter Nightingale."

"Ah yes—I have it here. Nightingale. Good name—sounds like a film star. All right Nightingale, let's say I offer you this post. When could you start?"

"As soon as you like, sir."

This was the correct answer.

"I see you were with Byron Manderby, gallivanting about the Congo and what have you. I can't promise you anything as exciting as that, you know. It'll mainly be answering letters, forging my autograph, et cetera."

"Oh, that's quite all right. You'll forgive my candour, but a chap does get tired of gallivanting eventually." Nightingale gave a wan smile and a flicker of his left eyebrow.

He would not look out of place in a Noël Coward play, Leonard thought. This was going to be interesting.

"You know, I've often wondered about that Byron Manderby. Must take an odd sort of fellow to climb mountains and frolic with natives and suchlike. You must tell me about him some time." There was an unpleasant smirk on Leonard's face. He was testing the applicant, seeing how easy it might be to make him talk.

"Perhaps, sir."

Leonard continued to study him carefully. And Nightingale, in turn, studied his prospective employer.

"All right," said Leonard, "I think I'm going to like you, Nightingale. I shall telephone the agency this afternoon. You may start in the morning. I shall expect you to take the attic room. Does that suit?"

"Perfectly, sir."

"And I presume you haven't much in the way of personal belongings?"

"Just a few clothes and trinkets, sir. Nothing to concern yourself with."

"I assure you, I wasn't concerned."

He was plainly a gentleman, though there was nonetheless a tang of foreignness to him. It was evident that he had been away from his motherland for some time, and was studiously reacquainting himself with its more refined customs. He smoked, but he did not smoke any tobacco that Leonard recognised. Not even Turkish. When he extinguished one cigarette and swiftly lit another, Leonard noted the brand name on the packet. It was Sampoerna: "Dji Sam Soe." That was the scent that clung to him, that prickled in Leonard's nostrils.

"Everything seems in order," said Leonard, who really had no inkling whether everything was in order or not. "You've got the job." But further effusions were cut short by the jangling doorbell. "Ah. That'll be my brother. Let him in, would you, there's a good chap. Then you can see yourself out."

Peter Nightingale got obediently to his feet and loped for the study door.

Leonard watched him go, smoking thoughtfully. Young Ambrose (he was nineteen) had been oddly keen to procure an appointment with his brother for that evening. Evidently there was something he wanted to discuss.

"Who on earth was that who answered the door?" Ambrose demanded as soon as he set foot in the study.

He was trying to grow a beard, a drastic undertaking that took up most of his waking hours. He was an artist these days, and like his elder brother he knew it was important to look the part. And so the tufts of downy reddish hair plumed out from his chin like thin wisps of mist, and he dressed almost exclusively in haute couture kaftans with baggy, sultanesque trousers and a floppy straw hat. This look had worked wonders for him on the Continent, and he had travelled around the glorious capital cities of Europe making many impecunious bohemian friends along the way. Inevitably, he had drifted back to London when he ran out of spending money. Now he spent his days in coffeehouses, thinking about things, and his nights in cocktail bars, *not* thinking about things.

Ambrose was briefly in thrall to Dada, which seemed primarily to entail the impish procuration of household appliances. But Duchamp had the market cornered, and Ambrose couldn't get a look in, so he had returned to his first love—painting. When he turned nineteen he entered a prolific period that produced what he considered to be his most challenging and mature work. Each was a mad blur of shocking colour: electric blues, salmon pinks, ice whites. But the lines were bold, black, and—ultimately—naive in their execution. *The Tulip Field* was, Ambrose himself laughingly admitted, a nightmare. *L'Oeuf* was an Oedipal confabulation best left undescribed. *Eve* depicted a tree with female genitalia and, instead of leaves, eyeballs dangling from stalks.

Occasionally he paid a visit to his mother and father, when his coffers were uncomfortably depleted. Sir Giles, who had initially shown enthusiasm for his youngest son's artistic endeavours, was chilled to the bone when he looked at them, and whenever they were brought up in conversation he hastily changed the subject.

"His name is Peter Nightingale. My new secretary. What did you think of him?"

Ambrose flung himself into the chair that Nightingale had occupied moments ago. "Bit stiff. More like a butler if you ask me."

"Well, you should have seen some of the other hopefuls. Abysmal. I don't know where that agency finds them. All frustrated actors, no doubt."

"No doubt. Anyway, were your ears burning? I've just been discussing you with a mutual friend."

"Really? Dare I ask for a name?"

"Horace Tapper."

"Horace! Good God, whatever were you doing with that old reprobate? Some party I wasn't invited to?"

"Oh no," Ambrose responded laughingly. "As a matter of fact, I went to see him out at Shepperton."

"Is that so?" Leonard was immediately suspicious. Horace Tapper was the producer who had been so dazzled by Leonard's charisma onstage that he had signed him up for a motion picture almost immediately. The thought of idiotic Ambrose meeting Horace without Leonard's advance knowledge was disquieting.

"Yes," Ambrose answered tartly, "it is so. Matter of fact, dear old Horace thinks I might have what it takes for a certain picture he's preparing."

Leonard guffawed. "Oh, is *that* all! Going to act, are you? Failed as a novelist and a painter, so you're going for the hat trick?"

But the smirk did not leave Ambrose's face. "Horace says I have presence. A unique charisma."

So this was why Ambrose had been so keen to stop by. To gloat. Well, Leonard would not take the bait. "Care for a spot of billiards?"

"If you dare," Ambrose grinned. "I've been practising."

Leonard led the way through to the billiard room and started setting up the game. Ambrose seized a cue and began to chalk up.

"Leonard?" Ambrose spoke his brother's name with a childlike upward inflection. Difficult questions afoot.

"What is it, squirt?"

"Do you think there's any chance Father might die soon?"

"Possibly. He *is* hellishly old. Why?"

"I've been thinking about things lately. I'm going to be twenty soon. I need to buy so many things, cars and suits and the like. I won't be able to do it with the pittance he's got me on at the moment."

"I thought you were going to be an actor?"

"I am! I am. But all the same, it's important to keep one's options open."

Leonard lined up a shot. "What makes you think dear Father's demise would leave you any better off? You won't get a penny. I'm the eldest; I'll get the lot. Murdering the old man won't change that."

"You're not the eldest," put in Ambrose.

"Sylvester, you mean? He doesn't count. He's a bastard, and thus even further down the pecking order than you."

There was a pleading expression in Ambrose's eyes. "You'll look after me, won't you?"

Leonard shrugged. "I might. If you make it worth my while. If I were you, I'd make a concerted effort to be entertaining."

Ambrose looked out the window sulkily. "I never said murder."

"What's that?"

"I never said anything about murdering father. I was merely wondering aloud what the odds are on him dying soon."

"Oh, spare me. I know full well what you meant. Cigarette?"

Ambrose took one from the gold case and leaned forward so his brother might light it. "Stranger things have happened, of course."

"Stranger than what?"

"Than old judges getting murdered."

"Well, don't get any funny ideas. If you were going to murder Father, I bet you'd make an awful hash of it and get caught immediately."

Ambrose eyed his brother slyly. "Ever so sure of yourself, aren't you, Leonard? You know, I went to tea with Mother yesterday, and she happened to let slip a piece of information that I found awfully interesting. Something that might wipe the smile from your face."

"Which was?"

"Father was out . . . having lunch with Struthers."

Leonard swallowed. "Struthers? What the hell does Father want with him?"

"Obvious, I should have thought. He's changing the will."

"Don't be ridiculous," snapped Leonard. But they both knew there was nothing ridiculous about it. Here was the *real* reason for Ambrose's house call. Desperate measures were called for. "There's no reason at all to suppose he's planning to change the will," Leonard said soothingly. "There could be any number of reasons for him to meet with his solicitor."

But he struggled to come up with any. "Do you know," he continued, with a theatrical yawn, "I'm suddenly very tired. I think I'm going to turn in. Early start in the morning, and all that."

"Yes, all right, I get the message," answered Ambrose, dropping his cue onto the table with a dour thump. "Besides, I got what I came for."

Leonard escorted his younger brother out, pausing only briefly in the corridor outside the study, where the curiously strong aroma of Sampoerna tobacco prickled noisomely in his nostrils.

CHAPTER TWO

POISONED PEN

I.

Bit by bit, Joseph Spector's world was shrinking. He was an old man now; his friends were dying off one by one; his legs and back ached. A new decade—the 1940s—was scarcely a year away, but to Spector this felt less like a new beginning than an eked-out ending.

However, time had left two of Spector's attributes mercifully unharmed. The first was his mind, which was as quick and devilishly brilliant as ever. The second was his hands, which had lost none of their spindly dexterity. In the distant past he had been a music hall conjuror, and he still dressed like one in a suit of black velvet, with a cloak lined in red silk. He brought a touch of old-world flamboyance into the murky twentieth century; he walked with a silver-tipped cane and dabbled in the occult. He was out of step with his era, and yet he was an indelible product of it; an embodiment of the baroque, the Grand Guignol.

Spector was on his way back from a meeting of the London Occult Practice Collective when he first realised someone was following him. The meeting had been out in Greenwich. It was a pleasant trip with good food, good conversation, and one or two amusing tricks into the bargain. Spector waited for the train back into the City feeling fat and happy. But as he perched on one of the metal benches that lined the platform, he felt eyes on him.

It was midafternoon, and already dusk was closing in. The platform's overhead lamps flickered to life and clutches of travellers chatted, smoked, and stamped their feet to stave off the chill. Spector sat motionless with his bare fingers twined around the handle of his cane.

Once he realised he was under scrutiny, he waited a moment or two to make sure it was not simply his imagination, or a trick of the gathering dark. But it wasn't. Somewhere among the little clusters of waiting travellers, somebody was watching him.

Very slowly, Spector turned, and with a sweeping glance took in the entire vista of the platform. There were a few lone commuters, but only one viable suspect: a tall man whose head was now hidden behind a three-day-old *Herald*. Spector studied the man's lower half, which was all that could be seen of him. Smart, tailored trousers and impeccable patent leather shoes; a poor choice for this weather. Whoever the man was, he was certainly no professional.

Soon enough, the train arrived in a shriek of steam, and Spector smiled to himself as he boarded.

He disembarked at Paddington and took a gentle amble through the crowds. He was in no rush to get back to Putney. And once again, the eyes were on him. The man followed him along the central concourse, past the various concession stands, as he threaded his way through the bustle and toward the stone steps down into the Underground. Before he began his descent, Spector cast a quick glance in the man's direction, just to check that he had not lost him.

He hadn't. There the fellow was, loitering in the shadow of a nearby pillar beneath the clock. Spector headed down the steps, and the man followed.

His pursuer maintained a careful distance on the Tube, but even though he frequently employed his out-of-date newspaper, Spector got a good look at the man's face. He was younger than Spector had first thought, which went a considerable way toward explaining these idiotic *Boy's Own* antics. He had a merciless Gwynplainian grin, but there was a vacancy in his eyes that told of both ignorance and arrogance. He was convinced that he had the upper hand.

Stepping off the train at Putney, Spector ascended the steps to street level and wondered briefly how best to go about dealing with this fellow. There were two places in which he was truly comfortable. The first was his home in Jubilee Court, a weird ramshackle dwelling crammed with decades' worth of macabre bric-a-brac.

The second was the nearby public house, The Black Pig, an ill-lit, low-ceilinged Elizabethan tavern. To step through its door was to step back in time. Spector was as much of a fixture there as the brass beer taps; it would not be the same without the grey fug of his cigarillo smoke choking the atmosphere, or his skeletal, cheerily funereal figure seated by the fire in the snug. From time to time he gave impromptu displays of legerdemain: cardistry or coin manipulation to bamboozle the regulars. The Black Pig glowed warmly at the other end of the street, its painted sign swinging in the icy breeze.

The young man halted. The magician had pulled off some kind of vanishing act—the street was empty. The young man continued at a slower pace, his brow creasing. He tilted his trilby back, as though he might find Joseph Spector hiding behind the brim.

"What in the hell—" he said, before his words were cut off by a sudden, sweeping motion at his feet. The silver-tipped cane clipped his ankles and sent him sprawling, his hat scudding off into the darkness.

The young man rolled onto his back with a groan, and Joseph Spector towered over him.

The old conjuror smiled. "I don't believe we've met."

The young man propped himself up on his elbows and laughed. "Well," he said, "it seems as though your reputation is well-earned."

Spector did not demur. "Your name, please?"

"Flack. Jeffrey Flack. Sorry, didn't mean to put the wind up you. The truth is, I'm simply an emissary."

"Oh yes?" Spector gripped this Mr. Flack's hand and hauled him to his feet.

"It's my mother," said Flack, picking up his hat and brushing the grime off his suit. "She's a nervous sort, didn't want to come herself. But the fact is, she wants to hire you."

"I'm afraid I no longer perform in public."

"Ha! No, it's not that. She wishes to hire you privately . . . as an enquiry agent."

"For what purpose?"

"Honestly, perhaps it's better if she tells you that herself."

Spector was a little nonplussed. "Your mother knows where to find me," he said.

"Oh, she wouldn't be caught dead around here," Flack grinned. "She's a snob through and through. But I can personally guarantee her money is just as good as anyone else's."

"Very well," said Spector. "You're lucky to have caught me between engagements."

"Good," said Flack. "Will you come now?"

"This instant? I had thought we would make an appointment . . ."

"No time. She wants to see you tonight. And what Madre wants, Madre tends to get. Now, where might one find a cab in this godforsaken spot?"

II.

Once a cab had been procured, the two men clambered into the back and Spector got a better look at the young man.

By rights, Jeffrey Flack ought to have been handsome. He was even-featured and smooth-skinned, with a decent jaw and high cheekbones. And yet there was a steeliness to him that, combined with the vacancy in his eyes, robbed him of whatever charisma he might have had. And then there was that permanent smile.

They rode in silence.

Their destination was the Savoy, where the lady in question waited in a penthouse suite. Flack strode purposefully across the foyer with Spector trailing behind. The magician scanned his surroundings, met the gaze of disapproving doormen, and finally stepped into an elevator that slithered shut with disconcerting finality.

A frock-coated concierge met them on the top floor. Or rather, he met Flack; he neither looked at, spoke to, nor in any way acknowledged the presence of Joseph Spector. Flack escorted them into the suite, where the lady reclined on a fainting couch. Spector estimated her age at about fifty. She wore an evening gown of clinging crepe de chine, her hair was swept back in a velvety chignon, and her white throat was noosed with pearls.

"Here he is, Mother," said Flack cheerily.

"So I see." She took in Spector with a sweeping coup d'oeil and evidently found him lacking. Nonetheless, she gestured toward a seat, which Spector accepted.

"Mrs. Flack, I presume?"

"No," she said, "though that *was* once my name. Jeffrey is my son from a previous marriage. My husband is Sir Giles Drury, the QC. I am Lady Elspeth Drury."

Spector looked from mother to son. He had taken an instant dislike to them both, for different reasons.

"No doubt you're wondering why I wish to retain your services," the lady continued. "Well, I have it on reliable authority that you had a great deal to do with the Dean case.* Perhaps you were not aware, but my husband was the presiding judge when the case came to trial. Naturally I followed the details of the investigation in the press with some assiduousness, but your

---

* For details of the Dean case, see *The Murder Wheel*.

name did not appear in the newspapers. Therefore, I take it that you are a man of discretion."

Spector nodded. "When I have to be. Now, perhaps you'd care to tell me the nature of the present problem?"

Lady Elspeth glanced at her son, then back at Spector. "The problem," she said, "is that somebody is out to murder my husband."

"Is that so?"

"You do not seem shocked. Good. Giles has received threats in the past; poisoned pen letters and suchlike. But nothing like this. You see, I know who's responsible."

Spector reclined, warming to his role in this turgid chamber piece. "Then it sounds as though the case were better off reported to the police."

"No, no, no," she insisted. "We can't have any more scandal. That's why I've come to *you*, Mr. Spector."

"Let me get this straight," said Spector, "your husband has been receiving death threats. What do they say?"

She glanced away from him. "Awful things."

"Such as?"

"The letters make threats on my husband's life. That is all you need to know."

"And who is making them?"

"That is part of the problem. It makes the whole matter considerably more difficult. This is where I expect you to assist. The man who has been writing the letters is a fellow named Victor Silvius. Have you heard of him?"

Spector shook his head.

"Silvius is a dangerous man," said Lady Elspeth. "He tried to murder my husband nine years ago. And now, evidently, he's decided to resume his campaign of terror. I want you to put a stop to it."

"Me? How?"

"Mr. Spector," she said through taut lips, "do not force me to plead with you. If you don't wish to take the case, very well. But don't continue to waste my time."

Spector offered a placatory smile. "As a matter of fact, I *am* interested in what you've told me. But there are ways of telling when people are holding something back."

Without another word, Lady Elspeth unclasped her handbag and took out a sheet of notepaper. It had evidently been scrunched into a ball and subsequently smoothed out. She placed it on the table and slid it toward Spector with manicured fingertips.

Spector leaned forward to read the message.

MURDERER, it said, YOU WILL GET WHATS COMING TO YOU. The handwriting was not particularly distinctive, though the ink was an odd darkish green.

"*Murderer?*" Spector read aloud, arching an eyebrow.

"Victor Silvius had a fiancée who died by poisoning while she was staying with us in the country. Since then, Silvius has convinced himself that my husband is responsible."

"I see. And you naturally believe this to be false."

"Oh no," Lady Elspeth permitted herself a flicker of amusement, "as a matter of fact I know it's true. You see, the case is not as simple as it might appear. I am utterly convinced that my husband killed that girl. By rights I should let Victor Silvius have at him."

"Justice can take many forms," Spector commented. "But I wonder why it's taken this Victor Silvius so long to seek his revenge?"

"Because he's a lunatic. He's been in an asylum for nine years."

"Then how could he be sending the letters?"

Lady Elspeth pursed her lips. "I rather think that's for *you* to find out."

CHAPTER THREE

VALENTINE'S DILEMMA

Wednesday, December 14, 1938

I.

B eneath Scotland Yard, the police mortuary is as dank and ill-lit as the tomb it so closely resembles. Striding through the parade of shrouded slabs, George Flint felt as though he had stepped back in time and into the depths of some subterranean pre-Christian temple, where fresh sacrifices had been laid out for his inspection and approval. He extinguished his pipe and removed his hat as a mark of respect, and now he felt cold and vulnerable. Even without its grisly inhabitants the place was stifling and oppressive, thanks mainly to the paucity of natural light. A few bare bulbs overhead sent misshapen shadows slithering as Flint walked.

"Findler?" Flint took another echoing step. "Findler, where are you, man?"

The place was as still and cold as the corpses it housed. No movement. Not even a flicker in the darkness.

Flint approached the centremost slab. He flipped up the bottom end of the shroud and examined the corpse's feet. The right big toe bore a handwritten tag. Flint squinted at it in the dim light.

UNIDENTIFIED, it said.

Slowly, he took hold of a top corner of the shroud and lifted it. The face beneath (it had once been a face, at least) was unrecognisable. Somebody had hated this man very much indeed. Hated him enough to bludgeon him repeatedly, till his skull caved inward and his nose, mouth, and eye sockets splintered and turned to pulp.

"Two weeks," said a stentorian voice. The pathologist liked to make an entrance when he was on home turf. "Startled you, did I? I'd have thought you were made of stronger stuff than that, Flint. Anyway—dead two weeks, I should say."

"Cause of death?"

"Strangulation. Though I doubt the prolonged facial bludgeoning helped matters. It looks as though someone set about him with an iron bar—caught him a single blow to the back of the head, likely intended to stun—then strangled him to death. Finally, he had another go with the bar, this time focusing on the face. Must have struck the victim over forty times. Whoever did this is most certainly an individual to be avoided, Inspector Flint."

"Any notion as to identity?"

"Not yet. But I'm sure it won't be long. I've taken a nice set of fingerprints."

"Nothing identifying in his clothing, then?"

"No, his pockets were emptied."

"Where are his clothes?"

"Here." Findler held open a burlap sack and Flint leaned over to get a look inside. "Sorry," said Findler, "should have warned you. It does pong a bit. He was wearing a gingham suit. Three-piece."

Flint swallowed a gullet full of bile. "Anything else you can tell me about him?"

"Well, there's the trunk he was found in, which I'm sure you recognise." Findler pointed to the corner of the room, where the steamer trunk stood upright. "Killer had to fold him in half to fit him inside, cracking a bunch of ribs. Also snapped his ankles and dislocated both shoulders."

"Killer, singular? I'd have thought this more likely to be the work of a gang."

"Mm," Findler shrugged, "you may well be right. Now, if you'll excuse me a moment, I must complete preparations for the post-mortem." With that, the pathologist scuttled away.

Flint took a deep breath and looked around him at the sea of shrouded slabs. He glanced down at the dead man again and felt a wave of melancholy sweep over him. That was when a shroud at the far end of the mortuary began to twitch.

Flint watched. He had heard stories of things like this. Muscular spasms giving the uncanny appearance of life after death. These things happen all the time.

Nevertheless, a shudder ran through him. When the corpse sat up, he almost screamed.

The shroud fell away and Joseph Spector's smiling face greeted him. "What in hell is wrong with you, Spector, giving a chap a fright like that . . ."

"Well, I do find it rather peaceful here. I mentioned as much to Dr. Findler and he suggested I catch forty winks. He says he does it all the time."

"That doesn't surprise me. Now will you please tell me what you're doing here in the first place?"

Spector swung his legs round so they dangled a foot or so off the ground. Then he eased himself upright and padded across the chilly tiled floor to shake hands with his old comrade.

"I'm looking into a case. I doubt you'll know it, it's ancient history. A murder disguised as suicide, by all accounts. The victim's name is Gloria Crain."

Even behind his thick moustache and bushy eyebrows, Flint's face registered acute surprise. "What the hell do you want with Gloria Crain?"

Spector grinned. "So you *do* know it."

"Has somebody been speaking to you about the case?"

Findler reappeared, now whistling the hymn "Rock of Ages." "Ah, I see you've found each other." He headed over to a metal trough, where he twisted the tap and rinsed his hands under the ensuing deluge.

"Findler, I want to ask you about something."

"Let me guess: Gloria Crain. Spector's already given me a thorough grilling. But what do you want to know?"

"She died by strychnine poisoning, is that so?"

Findler nodded. "I was just a junior in those days. Valentine was the chief examiner. You remember Keith Valentine, don't you, Flint?"

Flint did. Keith Valentine was that rare creature, a celebrity medical examiner. Over the years his involvement in some of England's most notorious trials had made him famous, and fame was always dangerous. His career had come to a somewhat humiliating end a few years ago and was seldom talked of these days.

"All the indicators pointed to suicide," said Findler. "There seemed to have been no conceivable way for anyone to slip that poison into her food or into her drink. She was at a dinner party, you see. Everybody ate and drank the same things. Besides, no trace of the stuff was found on any of the dishes, nor in the wine glasses or bottle. But that left another awkward question: why strychnine? Strychnine poisoning is a particularly nasty, painful way to go. I find it hard to believe anyone would inflict that on themselves willingly. Yet even if we accept the suicide hypothesis, no container of the stuff was found on her person or in her room. Just the liquid in her stomach, which implies murder. And so the cycle continued. That was Valentine's dilemma. Part of his modus operandi—and the reason for his success—was in piecing together the chain, of which the death itself is merely a link."

"I remember," said Flint. "He told the newspapers once that he didn't think like a scientist, he thought like a detective. Fat lot of good it did him."

"A veritable Dr. Thorndyke," Spector commented. "So the Crain case proved an insoluble puzzle."

"It was a real knock to his ego," agreed Findler. "The first failure of his career. But he'd been slipping for a while. Truthfully, he should have gone before then. He'd begun to believe he was truly infallible, which is never wise. And it cut no ice with me. I saw him for what he *really* was: an intolerable old bore. But Gloria Crain was the turning point. That unanswerable question—why strychnine?—put Valentine on a downward spiral. He went round in circles. A young woman committing suicide? Wouldn't be the first time. But a young woman committing suicide with *strychnine*? Exceedingly rare. Strychnine is harder to come by than cyanide or arsenic, and it's also a slower, more painful death. Which suggests murder. And so, Valentine went back to the statements given by the dinner guests. He went through them repeatedly, obsessively, trying to pinpoint a gap in the timeline where the poison might have been administered. But he couldn't do it. He felt as though he had failed her. As if he'd come tantalisingly close to the truth, only for it to slip just out of reach."

"What happened to him?"

"Had a breakdown the following year," said Findler matter-of-factly, "and the high-ups forced him into retirement. I couldn't tell you what happened to him after that. Now, if you'd be so kind, I'd rather like to begin cutting up this unfortunate fellow." He nodded toward the faceless man from the steamer trunk.

Spector, however, was examining the dead man's toe tag. "Who wrote this?" he asked. "You, Findler?"

"My assistant. Not here today, he's come down with flu. The last thing I need is him coughing all over my corpses."

Spector shook his head gravely. "'Unidentified,'" he said. "One of the most poignant words in the English language, I reckon."

"The tags are only temporary, Spector. Just so I know who's who. You've seen how crowded it gets down here—it can be hard to keep track. Now, may I proceed?"

"Don't mind us," said Spector.

But Flint had no intention of hanging around to watch. "Come on," he said to Spector, "I'll buy you lunch, you old ghoul."

II.

After lunch, they walked along the Thames.

"This is a strange thing," said Flint. "So the madman's sister wants *me* to investigate, and the judge's wife wants *you* to investigate. A little much to be coincidental, wouldn't you say?"

"Absolutely. And there are still so many unanswered questions surrounding the death of Gloria Crain."

"I had a look at the case file," Flint commented. "If it weren't for the fact that she died by strychnine poisoning, there wouldn't be much more to say of it. It would be suicide, plain and simple. But get this—she was found to have a bottle of sleeping tablets in her handbag. None in her system, though. Just the meal she ate with the Drurys, and the strychnine."

"I begin to see," Spector observed, "why Professor Valentine grew obsessed with the case."

"And Victor Silvius. Though I've yet to make up my mind about him. I told the sister I'd go with her to visit him next week. Hear his side of the story."

"He was most unwise to fall foul of the Tragedians," Spector observed.

"Yes, that's what Caroline said. Tell me, Spector, who exactly are the 'Tragedians'?"

"Well," Spector began, "membership is an open secret, but the focus and substance of their activities remain largely sub rosa. Naturally this engenders a certain mythification, but really there's much less to it than meets the eye. It's a drinking club first and foremost, and ordination is based on heredity—nothing else. So all the present members are descendants of the original Tragedians."

"Sounds like a waste of time."

"Yes, it does, doesn't it? By and large, I think it is. But the Tragedians are noted for their staunch loyalty. Favours are their currency. In that respect, they are like any other secret society. They look after their own."

"So," Flint leaned in confidentially, "how do you spot a Tragedian? Secret handshakes? Signet rings?"

Spector laughed. "Nothing as colourful as that. But their emblem is a pair of crossed scimitars. You'd do well to keep an eye out for it."

By now, they were back at Scotland Yard. Before parting company, Spector said, "You must tread very carefully, Flint. Digging up the past can be a dangerous business."

"What about you?" said Flint.

Spector answered with a grin, "I'm *always* careful."

THE DEATH OF IDA COSGROVE

The death of Ida Cosgrove was a pathetically sad affair.

Ida's husband, a civil servant named Arthur, sensed something amiss the very instant he set foot in the house on his return from work. A kind of emptiness. Something absent that should have been there.

Ida was a perennially neat person, and yet a vase of hyacinths that had sat on the wooden hall table was now in bits on the floor. No doubt it had made a tremendous racket when it fell. And yet no effort had been made to clear up the mess, dead flowers and broken pottery making a pitiful heap on the patterned linoleum.

What had caused the vase to fall? It was a sturdy piece, a wedding gift from Ida's late mother that had been in the same spot for some fifteen years. Longer, in fact. Why, after all this time, should it suddenly topple to the floor like a soldier felled by a firing squad?

The weather outside was particularly savage, but nothing that might have shaken the vase free and sent it tottering across the tabletop toward the edge. Eventually Arthur settled on the only possible—albeit decidedly improbable—solution: Ida had toppled the vase herself. But Ida loved that vase; it was one of the few gifts her mother had ever given her.

Ida's mother had been a hard woman who never showed affection. She had hated Arthur and made no secret of the disdain she felt for the union between him and her daughter. And yet appearances were very important to her. Mrs. Lacey had a pathological abhorrence of attracting attention and criticism. Typically she adored gossip, except when the glare of scandal happened to shine on *her*. And so, she had put on a decent front when the wedding rolled around, and given a passably convincing performance as a mother who did not entirely detest the man her daughter loved. Hence the vase, which now lay in shattered fragments at Arthur's feet.

He began calling his wife's name, though he was already convinced she would not answer. Something in his heart told him she was there, that she was upstairs somewhere, but that she would not answer him.

"Oh Ida," he said when he saw her.

Just as he had predicted, she did not reply.

She had downed half a bottle of sleeping tablets and then simply lain down and let her eyelids flutter shut. She had left a note for him on her dressing table. Like much of her correspondence, it was neatly calligraphed but ultimately insubstantial. It told him nothing that he really wanted to know.

But when he sat down on her side of the bed for the first time in who knew how long, and felt a slightly uncomfortable lump in the mattress, he was compelled to investigate. The letters were bound by a red ribbon. Each one was written in a fluid, unfamiliar hand and signed "Jeffrey."

Jeffrey, Jeffrey . . .

Arthur could not place the name. He read on, and with each letter he read, another piece of the puzzle slotted into position, forming a hideous mosaic of ignominy.

The affair between Ida and Jeffrey had begun in the summer. Arthur began to remember certain brief incidents from the last few weeks. Ida had developed a tendency to wear the same outfits and jewellery. Arthur went to her jewellery box to confirm his suspicion. He was right: her collection had dwindled considerably. And there was no reason for it, was there? There could be only one explanation: Jeffrey had the jewels. She had given them to him. To silence him. He had blackmailed her into it. And when she ran out of trinkets to keep him quiet, Ida had felt herself cornered. She had scrambled desperately for a way out, and found none.

Arthur Cosgrove did not know who Jeffrey might be. But he would find out. He would scour the earth if he had to. This man had murdered Ida as surely as if he had slipped her the pills himself.

CHAPTER FOUR

SPECTOR AT THE FEAST

I.

Sir Giles Drury could not wait to get out of the city. Fatigued and irritated by London, the judge had begun counting down the days until his Chelsea townhouse could be closed up for Christmas and he and Elspeth might resume their rightful place among the squirearchy. But first there was dinner to be got out of the way.

A gathering of the clan was always fractious, but Elspeth had once again barracked him into it. She was inviting an "old friend" of hers, she claimed. Fellow with a foolish name straight out of a Saturday morning serial: Joseph Spector.

There came a sharp rap on the door of his poky little study (how glorious it would be to bask in the splendid oak-panelled library of Marchbanks once again!) and the judge's stepson, Jeffrey Flack, slipped unbidden into the room.

The judge had a superb set of moustaches that more or less covered his mouth, and one of his most distinctive features was his half-moon spectacles. Often, when delivering a particularly harsh sentence, he would peer unblinkingly over the frameless lenses, into the very soul of the prisoner. In moments like that, he was an awesome and terrifying sight. These days he was portly, but had been an active sportsman in his youth. An archer and a rower, he had in fact rowed for Cambridge in both 1886 and 1887, years in which they won the fabled Boat Race from Putney to Mortlake. But over the ensuing decades he had come to realise there was more to power than mere physical strength. This epiphany had started him on his eventual path into the heart of the criminal justice system.

Now he was stronger than he had ever been as an athlete. Voices grew hushed in corridors as he ambled past. People knew that he was somebody. He was a man who had faced up to every challenge the years had thrown at him, and could now justifiably retire in triumph, like Turner's *Fighting Temeraire* with the sun at its back. Sic transit gloria.

And yet he could not bring himself to do it. Increasingly, his hours in court became the highlight of his waking life. Bit by bit he had begun to lose whatever joy he had once had in the simple things. His sons were, by and large, a disappointment. He did not care for wine or tobacco, though he was a prolific consumer of both. He had lost the knack for reading after decades of tedious court reports. He was slightly deaf, and music these days seemed a screechy and unintelligible mess. He gambled from time to time—and lost.

So the prospect of retirement terrified him. He hated to admit it, but he did not wish to become just a tedious old husk, losing his faculties one by one. He wanted to be a judge until his dying day. And by God, he would do it.

It was in that spirit of stubborn cussedness that he continued to occupy the one function he had been put on this earth to fulfil. He would never relinquish it. Never.

Now he peered at Jeffrey Flack with the brutal malevolence he typically reserved for the worst kind of rogue in the dock. Flack of course was oblivious, slumping recumbent into a chair like a sullen adolescent. All the while his familiar smirk did not leave his face.

"Mother tells me you want a word before the others get here."

"Indeed I do." The judge had perfect, almost Shakespearean diction. His *d*'s were daggers; his *t*'s inevitably accompanied by a hail of spittle. "I should like you to inform me what the hell you've been playing at."

"In reference to what exactly?"

"Don't tell me you haven't heard. A woman is dead. Ida Cosgrove. One of your conquests, I understand?"

Jeffrey's smile widened. "Oh, Ida," he lamented. "I told her to burn the letters."

"Well, she neglected to do so. And when she killed herself yesterday, her husband found and read every single one of them."

"I see. Most unfortunate. Enough to put a chap off his dinner."

The judge growled. "The husband is a civil servant, as you well know. He wishes to see you charged with blackmail, fraud, theft, and just about any other species of malfeasance his dullard brain can conjure up. Luckily, I found out in time and was able to nip it in the bud. I did this not out of any affection for you, Jeffrey, but out of love for your mother, whom I know would be devastated to see you receive your just deserts."

"Lucky me, eh?" Jeffrey beamed. "I suppose if Mother weren't around you'd let the husband have at me?"

Sir Giles did not take his eyes off his stepson. "Perhaps I would."

Jeffrey got to his feet and began to pace the carpet. "This *does* sound rather troubling, though. I mean, what if the Cosgrove fellow decides to come after me?"

"I'm afraid that's your own affair. I've done as your mother asked me."

"Yes, yes," Jeffrey snapped, "but what about *me?* Do you think I ought to lie low for a while . . . ?"

Sir Giles shot Jeffrey an unpleasant look. "If you think I'm going to subsidise any more of your mendacious antics, you've another think coming. Understand?"

But Jeffrey would not be drawn into an argument. Instead, he remained pensive. "You and Mother are heading to Marchbanks for Christmas, isn't that so?"

Grudgingly, Sir Giles admitted that it was indeed so.

"Well there you are," said Jeffrey, clapping his hands. "I shall come with you. A spell in the country is good for the spirit. And it will allow me to keep my head down until the Cosgrove business blows over. Well, Pa? What about it?"

II.

A cheerless housemaid admitted Joseph Spector to the Drurys' Chelsea townhouse with a curt bob before ushering him through to the drawing room.

"Mr. Spector," said the unsmiling judge. "My wife tells me you are an old friend of her family."

"How do you do?" said Spector. "Are we three for dinner?"

"No," said Sir Giles, "we are six. My wife's son Jeffrey is making a telephone call, I believe. Leonard and Ambrose are keeping us waiting, as they are wont to do."

Spector nodded politely, computing the new names. His knowledge of Leonard and Ambrose Drury came primarily from gossip. Leonard was making a name in the motion picture business, having distinguished himself onstage thanks to his upright posture and crisp locution.

Ambrose, meanwhile, was still in the throes of that awkward adolescent phase where one doesn't know quite what one wants to be. Currently, he was an artist. He'd spent the previous summer pottering around Europe, getting drunk and leaving a slew of upturned tables, shattered glasses, and fist-shaking publicans in his wake.

Leonard, whom Spector had seen in the West End, was the next to arrive. Sir Giles introduced them, and Spector studied the young actor carefully. Leonard, in turn, seemed to be giving Spector a thorough once-over.

"A conjuror, is that it?"

"In the old days, yes," Spector informed him. "Now more or less retired, though."

That was when Jeffrey Flack came into the room. He still had that uncanny smirk, but for the briefest flicker of a moment there was something else there too: a kind of primal dread, like a cornered animal. In an instant it was gone, and Jeffrey was shaking hands with Leonard. Though they were only half brothers, there was a marked resemblance between the two young men. Leonard was slightly fatter, and his mouth lacked the sardonic upward tilt of Jeffrey's rictus, but it was obvious the pair shared at least one parent.

The maid returned with aperitifs, and Spector nursed his while soaking up the curious atmosphere of this unhappy household. Leonard and Jeffrey sat at opposite ends of the room, each man's body language curiously and unconsciously mirroring the other's; when Leonard crossed his legs, Jeffrey did likewise. When Jeffrey folded his arms, so did Leonard.

Finally, Ambrose Drury arrived. "Mr. Spector," he declared, "how d'you do? It seems as though Madre's been keeping you in a cupboard with all her other skeletons."

"How do you do?" answered Spector.

Skeletons? He knew that before she was Lady Elspeth—even before she was Elspeth Flack—she had been Elspeth Renard, and sung soprano in a couple of minor operas. When she married she was quick to forsake the stage. Now she was able to live the life of a diva without the exertion of actually being one.

"Please," said Sir Giles, "no skeletons. Not tonight. Let's talk of more pleasant matters, shall we? Until after dinner, at least."

"Ambrose is an actor now," put in Leonard. He said it sardonically, and it was unclear precisely what reaction he expected from his parents. "Matter of fact we're currently vying for the lead in a new picture. It's hotly contested, you know, but he's the front-runner."

"Really?" said Spector politely. "And what's the picture?"

"It's *Tarrare*," Ambrose informed him. "The life and loves of the French showman."

"Sometimes I wish you'd stayed a sportsman," Sir Giles grumbled at his youngest son.

"Not sportsmanlike enough, I'm afraid. Not since they outlawed fast leg theory."

But before they could discuss the news further, a gong sounded in the hall.

"Thank God," said Sir Giles under his breath.

III.

Dinner was served: exquisite pan-fried bream with lobster jus. Sir Giles tucked in heartily, failing to notice that neither Leonard nor Ambrose was eating. They were both watching their father closely, and shared an unpleasant glance. Spector, too, merely picked at his food and watched.

Having downed her aperitif with a flick of the wrist before promptly ordering another, Lady Elspeth seemed keen to indulge her propensity for malice.

"Leonard," she declared, "when are you going to stop pussy-footing around and give me a grandchild?"

Sir Giles almost choked on a mouthful of broccoli, but Leonard responded playfully.

"I'm doing my level best, Madre. The fillies find me a wee bit intimidating. Who can blame them? But it does tend to slow the process down somewhat."

"Got your eye on someone?" said Sir Giles, still chewing.

"Matter of fact I have. Sweet young thing."

"Oh yes?" The judge was interested now. "And where did you two meet?"

"Oh, you know, around and about. Dancing at the Palmyra Club."

"I see." Evidently Sir Giles was reserving judgement for the moment.

"What about you, Jeff?" said Leonard, turning his attention to Flack. "Any more conquests on the horizon?"

But before Flack could respond, Lady Elspeth swiftly changed the subject.

Spector watched and listened as the conversation devolved into the usual inanities. Leonard had recently engaged a new private secretary, though he was not yet convinced the fellow would cut the mustard.

"Quite the adventurer, old Nightingale. Adventurer's *assistant*, anyway. I was a Boy Scout myself," Leonard commented facetiously. "Master of the Monkey's Fist, they called me in those days. But most chaps tend to grow out of that sort of thing."

"Funny you should mention a Monkey's Fist," said Spector. All eyes were on him, for he had not spoken in a while. His right hand slipped into his pocket and produced a thin length of rope.

Brandishing it like a whip, he snapped the fingers of his left hand and a perfect silk knot appeared on the end of the rope. "An essential part of the magician's toolkit," he explained.

Ambrose, whom Spector judged to be sharper than his brother, though lacking finesse, remained unimpressed by the impromptu performance. "Funny that I've never heard of you before," he commented.

"Ambrose, don't be rude," said Lady Elspeth.

But Ambrose still had his eyes on Spector. "All I'm trying to say is, you obviously know what you're doing. One would think you ought to be a big name."

"I no longer perform professionally," said Spector, slipping the rope into his pocket.

"Oh? Then what do you do?"

Spector could sense Lady Elspeth's tension. "I'm in business," he answered.

"What sort of business?"

"Ambrose, *will* you behave?" Lady Elspeth punctuated her admonition with a slap of the tabletop, causing wineglasses to jangle and cutlery to clatter.

Sir Giles and Jeffrey turned in their seats to look at her, but Leonard and Ambrose did not. Instead they looked at each other; a look laden with meaning. Spector watched it with interest.

Regaining her composure, Lady Elspeth changed the subject swiftly like a good hostess. She coaxed Ambrose into talking more about his audition. He had been learning lines for his screen test at Shepperton. He was, he assured his parents, "doing it properly." That was when Jeffrey informed them that he would be accompanying his mother and stepfather to Marchbanks for Christmas.

This drew consternation and outrage from Leonard and Ambrose.

"You weren't planning to invite *us*, then?" Leonard asked pointedly.

Sir Giles just sighed. Before dessert, both Leonard and Ambrose had inveigled invitations.

"The Drury family seat," the judge explained to Spector. "There have been Drurys in that house for over four hundred years."

"And Mrs. Runcible has been in charge about as long," laughed Ambrose.

Marchbanks. The house, Spector reflected, where Gloria Crain was killed. And they would all be there, all the suspects, gathered under that roof ten years to the day since the unfortunate young woman met her fate.

As the dinner things were cleared away, Lady Elspeth began to complain of a headache. Before long, she retired to bed, leaving Spector at the mercy of the men of the house.

For the first time in a while the patriarch looked in Spector's direction. "Perhaps," he said, "while the others take coffee, you'd care to join me in my study, Spector? I believe we have certain business to discuss."

If this was an attempt to vex the magician, it failed. Spector accepted, and followed his host out of the dining room. But as he went, he cast a sideways glance at Ambrose, and saw that the young artist was eerily staring back.

CHAPTER FIVE

THE JUDGE'S SECRET

W hen the door to his moderately appointed study was shut, Sir Giles's manner and bearing changed.

"My dear wife," he said, "has never had a knack for keeping secrets. As soon as she mentioned this mysterious 'cousin' of hers, I guessed. You're an investigator, aren't you? No need to answer. I already know full well that you are. I'll be honest with you, Spector," he went on, "I'm *glad* that she's brought someone in. These threats are getting on my nerves. And you worked on the Dean case, didn't you? We never met, but I remember Flint mentioning your name."

"Everything you've said is correct, Sir Giles. Your wife is very concerned."

The judge nodded thoughtfully. "Mr. Spector, I will cooperate with your inquiry as far as I deem it convenient and prudent to do so."

"I can ask for no more than that," said Spector. Then he flipped open his cigarillo case and offered one to Drury, who declined. As

Spector lit up with a flourish, he said, "Now, I'd like you to tell me everything."

The judge gave a noisy, resolute sniff. "It goes without saying that nothing of our conversation leaves this room."

Spector waited.

"All right," Sir Giles finally said. He was not known for his prolixity but could nonetheless talk when the situation demanded it. "I'll tell you. There's a very good reason why I want to keep the whole Gloria Crain business under wraps. At the time, everybody thought it was suicide. That's nonsense, of course. No one would kill themselves with strychnine. It's a horrific way to go. And besides, she had sleeping tablets in her handbag. They would have been both easier and painless."

"So you suspected foul play?"

A lengthy silence hung between them.

Finally, Sir Giles broke it. "I can trust you, can't I? I mean, *really* trust you?"

"Of course."

The judge sighed. "My wife has always been a very jealous woman. And when she gets an idea into her head, it can be hard to disabuse her of it."

"She was jealous of Gloria Crain?"

The judge nodded.

"You believe your wife poisoned her, isn't that so?"

Whatever the judge was about to say, he only managed a single syllable. His sentence was cut off by a sudden whipcrack and gust of icy air.

Spector's gaze snapped toward the window, which he saw was now marred by a small round hole. The centre-point for a webwork of thin, pencil-line cracks.

The judge was on his feet in an instant, a whirlwind of papers swirling round him.

"Get your head down," snapped Spector.

But the second shot did not come. Slowly, gingerly, Spector crept toward the window. Peering out, all he could see was darkness. The gunman was gone.

"Bloody birds," the judge was saying. "That's what it was, Spector. Just a bird careering into the glass. Blown off course by the wind. Nothing more."

"This is a bullet hole," said Spector stubbornly.

"You're not listening. A bird did this. Understand?" The judge lowered his voice, his eyes scanning the street beyond the broken window. "My wife doesn't know it, but there have been other, similar . . . incidents. *Warnings* is what they are. That's all."

"From whom? And about what?"

"Somebody is trying to scare me. But I won't let them, Spector. For my wife's sake. Her nerves are in a bad enough state. The day after tomorrow we leave for Marchbanks." He fidgeted a little, drumming the desk with his fingernails. "Spector, will you come with us? Just to keep an eye on things?"

Spector noticed that the disturbance had knocked over a small framed photograph, which had been propped upright on the desk. Stooping to retrieve it, he saw it depicted a boyish Ambrose in cricket whites. Replacing it on the desk, Spector considered the image and found it decidedly poignant, though he was not sure why.

"All right," he said, "I'll come. But now, if you'll excuse me, I must see if our assailant has left any traces."

Spector left the study and headed through the hall to the front door. Stepping out into the night air, he glanced up and down the street and found it desolate, but it wasn't difficult to trace the gunman's movements. There was a narrow alley between the Drury house and that of the neighbouring property. A set of sprightly footprints emerged from the alley, assumed a position on the kerb across the street, and then swiftly retreated the way they had come.

Spector now stood alone in the snow at the mouth of the shadowed ginnel. The gunman was gone, but he could not have got far. The returning footprints terminated abruptly by a side window. So he had clambered out of the window, run around to the front of the house to take his shot, and then run back again. The footprints were men's shoes, leaving three suspects: Leonard, Ambrose, or Jeffrey Flack. A simple enough problem.

The conjuror went back into the house and made for the smoking room, which was only a couple of doors removed from the window in question. To his surprise, the card game had been abandoned as swiftly as it began. Jeffrey Flack now sprawled on a sofa, cigarette lolling between his lips and his arms behind his head.

"Looking for the boys?" he said. "They've gone to play billiards."

"Did you see anybody come through here in the last five minutes?" Spector inquired.

"No. Thought I heard a car backfire, though. Unless it was a gunshot."

Spector found his way to the billiard room, but to his surprise only Leonard was in there. "Where's your brother?"

"Upstairs," Leonard replied. "At least, I think that's where he went."

Leaving Leonard to finish setting up the billiard table, Spector returned to the hall. As he was making his way back to the study, a shape emerged from the shadows of the unlit passage. Spector squared his shoulders, bracing for an attack, but none came. The man stepped forward, and Spector was surprised to see that he was not one of the other male dinner guests, but a stranger.

"Have we met?" It was the young man who spoke first.

Spector's brow swiftly unknotted and he adopted his most urbane expression. "My name is Joseph Spector," he said. "And you are?"

"Sylvester Monkton," the man announced, but he didn't offer to shake hands. Instead he glanced distractedly toward Sir Giles's study. "I came in through the tradesman's entrance," he said by way of explanation. "Pa never likes people to see me coming or going."

"Pa?"

Monkton gave a slightly off-kilter smile. "By rights, my name ought to be Drury. But Pa thought it might complicate matters. Rather Shakespearean of him, don't you think? Disowning the bastard?" His hair was parted smartly at the centre of his cranium, and tapered to curiously ragged ends. His eyes were hidden beneath prominent, shadowed brows, and his lower lip jutted out. The criminologist Lombroso—a proponent of phrenology—would have termed him "atavistic," and a likely killer. But Spector was not so easily swayed.

"Yet here you are," the magician observed.

"I like to pop up from time to time, just to remind him of my existence. And to plead for handouts, of course."

"Did you see anybody outside the house just now?"

"Can't say I did."

Spector changed tack. "Lady Elspeth asked me to come. She wishes to hire me to look into something for her."

"Is that so?" Monkton spoke softly, evidently eager for his arrival to remain a secret. "Well, if it's about the letters I wouldn't waste your time. What would be the point in digging up a murky secret from his past? I *am* a murky secret from his past."

"Did you know Gloria Crain?" Spector launched the question without warning, but Sylvester answered quickly enough.

"No. Wouldn't put it past him, though."

"Put what past him?"

"What do you think?" said Sylvester, dark eyes twinkling.

"You believe your father killed her?"

Monkton was not about to let himself give too much away. "You know," he said, "when I heard that Victor Silvius had stabbed him, I laughed myself to tears. And felt a complete bounder afterward, of course. That's the lot of the bastard son, Mr. Spector. I love him—and I hate him, too. Love him for what he is, hate him for what he did." Without another word, Sylvester Monkton withdrew, ducking out the front door and traipsing off into the night.

Spector stood in the doorway and watched him go. That's when he spotted the footprints Sylvester left behind him. They were distinctive, one slightly deeper than the other. So Sylvester had a club foot. That ruled him out, didn't it, as a potential gunman? It meant he had not entered the house until *after* the shot was fired, or else Spector would have seen his footprints.

All these fresh uncertainties buzzed around in Spector's brain as he stepped back into the house and returned to the judge's study. He found that Sir Giles had wrenched the cover from an old book and used it to cover the bullethole in the window. Now he was hastily reordering the papers that had been disturbed by the wind.

"I think, Sir Giles, that it would be wise not to try and keep secrets from me."

"What the hell do you mean?"

"Secrets like Sylvester Monkton, for instance."

At once, the judge was on his feet. "Sylvester? What do you—?"

"He was here just a moment ago. I bumped into him in the hall."

The judge's eyes darted left and right. "Did anyone else see him?"

"I don't believe so."

Sir Giles heaved a sigh and headed for the window again. It was full dark now, but the streetlamps cast the snowy street in an eerie orange glow. "You don't need to worry about him, Spector. He's got nothing to do with any of this. He hasn't been sending me letters."

"How can you be sure?"

"You've seen one of the letters, have you? I imagine my wife has retrieved one or two of them from my wastepaper basket."

Spector nodded.

"Well," said the judge, "then you know they are written in green ink. Sylvester would not use green ink."

Briefly bemused, Spector soon had the answer. "I see," he remarked. "Sylvester is colour-blind."

"The red-green variety. Gets it from his mother," Sir Giles explained.

"But I doubt that would prevent him from using green ink. If anything, it might be a deliberate red herring." After a brief silence, Spector made another observation: "Green ink is an interesting choice. It has a certain significance in journalistic circles—apparently the most demented letters received by editors are often in green. It seems there is an assumption among cranks that the boldness of the shade reflects the gravity of the message." Another silence. "But our poisoned penman is no crank. I think the ostentation is an attempt to make us *think* he is a crank."

The judge opened his mouth to answer, but swiftly closed it again. He obviously wanted to argue.

Spector changed the subject. "You mentioned Sylvester's mother. What can you tell me about her?"

Sir Giles huffed. "She was a maid in the home of an acquaintance of mine. Her name was Esther Monkton. I was a bloody fool in those days—the early days of my marriage to Elspeth."

"Then Sylvester is your eldest son?"

The judge gave a nod. "A couple of years younger than Jeffrey, the child she had with Flack."

Spector considered this revelation. "And the acquaintance in whose home Miss Monkton was a maid—would he be a Tragedian, by any chance?"

"What do you know about the Tragedians?"

"Only that they are a club of which you and one Dr. Jasper Moncrieff are members."

"Another educated guess?" Sir Giles smiled. "Yes. But it won't do you any good. That particular Tragedian is long dead, I'm afraid. His name was Richmond Kessler."

"I take it he got rid of Miss Monkton?"

"He . . . removed her from his service, yes. It's my understanding that she ended her days in a home for unwed mothers. Which, of course, she was." Now the judge spoke coldly, as though passing sentence.

"You'll forgive me for saying so, Sir Giles, but that sounds like as good a motive as I have heard to commence a poisoned pen campaign. Your son wants revenge."

"And yet . . ." The judge was still looking out of the window. "I doubt the explanation is as simple as that."

"It's human nature to overcomplicate what is fundamentally simple," said Spector. "Magicians know that. We thrive on the knowledge. And so—in some instances—do killers."

CHAPTER SIX

THE CARD PLAYERS

Thursday, December 15, 1938

I.

G eorge Flint passed a troubled night. As soon as he got to his office he picked up the telephone and asked for the number Miss Silvius had provided.

"Inspector Flint!" she sounded surprised to hear his voice. "What is it?"

"Miss Silvius, I'd like to discuss something with you. May I come out and visit you this morning?"

"No!" she answered instinctively. "No, that is to say, I am a governess, living at the home of my employers. If a policeman arrived on their doorstep, they would inevitably ask questions . . ."

"All right, all right. Don't fret. Is there somewhere we can meet?"

She spoke cautiously: "Well, yesterday was my day off. I don't think I ought to . . ."

"Then bring the children. How old are they?"

"Three and four years."

"Bring them for a walk. We can meet and talk in privacy."

She pondered this. "Yes. Very well."

"By the way," said Flint, "I'd like to bring a colleague of mine. Someone whom I think may be able to help. Do I have your permission?"

"Yes."

"Good."

II.

Flint got to the Courtauld Institute in good time, though half-expecting Caroline Silvius to be waiting for him already. The Courtauld had been judged the most appropriate spot, being equidistant between the home of Caroline's employers and Scotland Yard.

He found the Long Gallery bereft of life—with one exception. The cloaked silhouette of Joseph Spector. He had his back to Flint, and was staring intently at a painting.

"I believe," Spector said without turning round, "that I've solved it."

Flint drew level with him and looked up at the painting. "Solved what?"

"*The Card Players*."

Flint himself examined the painting which—according to its accompanying card—was by Paul Cézanne and depicted two men in some Parisian hostel engrossed in a game of poker. "What's there to solve?"

"We can see neither man's cards, but we can tell enough from their body language to determine who holds the winning hand.

"The pipe is deceptive. A man with a losing hand will typically wet his lips or poke out his tongue. Therefore a pipe between his teeth is a useful foil.

"Both men are staring at their cards. This tells us nothing.

"We cannot see their feet. Unfortunate, for tapping feet are key signifiers.

"But look at the man on the left. He is sitting bolt upright, his pipe tight between his teeth. A common phenomenon in professional deception is to take up as much space as possible. In other words, when we are bluffing, we sit upright, we puff out our chests, we hold ourselves in a statuesque manner. But look at the man on the right. He is slumped and sullen looking, even his hat appears to have sunk in on itself. His fingers curl lazily around his cards. But the man on the left—his body has greater definition. You can almost see the tightness in his muscles. The fellow on the right could not look more relaxed. He's trying to convince his opponent to raise the stakes. *He* has a winning hand."

"All very clever," said Flint in a clipped tone, "but what's the point of it?"

"No idea." Spector gave a chuckle that sounded like clattering bones. "All the same, I'm glad you got here ahead of time, Flint.

There are one or two notions of mine which I'd like to discuss before I meet Caroline Silvius."

"Such as?"

"Last night I went to dinner with Sir Giles Drury and his family. There's something amiss there, Flint. Too many secrets. Sir Giles has invited me to Marchbanks, out in the country. I'm travelling there tomorrow."

"That's where Gloria Crain died," said Flint.

"Not only that, it also happens to be a mere thirty-minute drive from The Grange, the private clinic operated by Dr. Jasper Moncrieff. The place where Victor Silvius has been a permanent resident for over nine years."

"Oh, Christ," said Flint.

"So I need you to tell me everything you have found out so far about Miss Silvius."

Flint huffed. "Well, I did some digging into her past. But there's not much to see. Troubled relationship with her parents, so when they died they left their estate to charity. Which is why she has to work. But apart from that, nothing out of the ordinary. Perfectly clean record from the prep school she attended. Suitors, but nothing serious."

The sound of children's laughter resounded with eerie, tinkling musicality at the other end of the gallery. Both men turned, and there was the lady in question, Caroline Silvius, flanked by a pair of small children, one holding onto each hand. Caroline was smiling too, though it vanished from her face when she caught sight of Flint and Spector. She deposited the children on a wooden bench with a couple of sketchbooks and a fistful of crayons. Then she ambled over discreetly.

"Forgive me," she said, "but I can't risk my employers finding out about this."

"It's all right," said Spector. "We'll handle it as tactfully as possible."

"Miss Silvius, meet Joseph Spector," said Flint. "Spector has a remarkable brain for this sort of puzzle. We've worked together several times."

They shook hands, and Spector felt the warmth of Caroline's palm through her glove. She was nervous.

"Pleased to meet you," she said, glancing periodically at the two children on the other side of that vast gallery. "Thank you for coming."

"My pleasure," said Spector. "I've heard a great deal about you. And your brother, of course."

"That's what this is all about," she said. "I'm very frightened for Victor. I believe someone is trying to hurt him."

"Because of what he knows about Gloria Crain?"

"I suppose so."

"What do you remember about Miss Crain's death?"

She sighed. "I remember everything. It's burned into my memory, though a decade has passed since."

Spector considered her answer. "Lady Elspeth," he continued, "has asked me to look into a series of poisoned pen letters which her husband has been receiving. Letters which may or may not relate to the death of Gloria Crain."

Caroline's lips pinched tight.

"I don't suppose they're anything to do with you, are they, Miss Silvius?"

Spector did not take his eyes off her. She replied calmly: "The only thing I am interested in is seeing my brother freed from that wretched place where they're keeping him. What difference could tormenting the judge possibly make?"

"None, of course," said Spector, "but perhaps that's the point."

When Caroline spoke her voice was soft and crackly with emotion. "To think of my poor brother in that place . . ."

"It's all right, my dear," said Spector. But his pale eyes told a different story.

III.

"You a fan of romantic comedies, Nightingale?"

"Can't say I've seen all that many, sir."

"Well, not to worry. Because I can tell you now that you're smack bang in the middle of one. And I am the romantic lead. You shall be the Sancho to my Don Quixote. How does that grab you?"

"Quite nicely, sir," Nightingale smiled, his eyes fixed on the road. They were in Leonard's nippy little Austin Seven, Nightingale at the wheel weaving artfully among the slow-moving traffic. Leonard was paying a visit to Ambrose, whose putrid attic-cum-studio was in Soho.

The grubby side street that Ambrose Drury called home was almost unnaturally still as Leonard's Austin slithered to a halt. It was eleven in the morning, and the residents of this little Bohemia had likely either not yet slept or not yet risen. The only sign of life was a small, continental-style coffee shop with a scattering of chairs and tables on the pavement. Some seats were occupied, and the foetid tang of old coffee beans drew Leonard in.

"Wait out here," he instructed Nightingale, and ducked into the café.

Ambrose had snagged a small round table just inside the door where they could pretend they were in Paris rather than London in the depths of December. Leonard pulled up a chair, its metal legs shrieking on the floor, and sat opposite his brother.

"You wanted to see me?"

Ambrose beamed pleasantly. "I did. To resume our discussion from the other night."

"You have nothing to worry about," Leonard informed him. "No need to trouble your malicious little bones. Now, there's something else I need to talk to you about . . ."

"Oh, God," Ambrose breathed, his eyes latching onto something behind Leonard. "It's Ludo."

Leonard groaned. "Not one of your artists . . ."

Ambrose's cabal of Dadaists consisted of various performance artists whose "statements" frequently featured outlandish costumes in incongruous settings: a bearded man in a ball gown at King's Cross, for instance. Or a belly dancer on the steps of St. Paul's. But they kept Ambrose amused. Actually, he would often say, they were not such bad conversationalists as he'd been led to believe. He consorted with artists, composers, actors, photographers, writers, none of whom was especially burdened with talent, and most of whom supplemented their meagre income with a hefty inheritance or trust fund. These were the sons and daughters of the rich, and that was something Ambrose *could* relate to.

Ludo, an especially impecunious revolutionary, could often be found at Speakers' Corner in Hyde Park, calling for the summary execution of various illustrious persons, and often receiving a sound pelting with eggs, vegetables, and other projectiles for his trouble.

His argument was simple: the successful implementation of what he called "the communist model" in Russia had proved such things were possible. It should—nay, it *must*—happen here. We as a society had outlived the need for kings and queens. But he was ultimately a moderate. He didn't wish to see the royal family butchered like the Romanovs; he would quite happily permit them to live out their days in exile, perhaps on the Isle of Wight.

He was the son of a prominent Tory politician, and as such he was a young man of intractable opinions. In debates, this caused him to flounder. He was at his best when he had the crowd to himself, when he could fill the stage like John Barrymore essaying Hamlet's soliloquy.

"Ludo's a good sort, but inevitably prone to biting the hand that feeds him. He wants to dismantle the entire capitalist system, which is rather hard to do when you're living on an allowance from dear old papa."

Before Leonard could voice an opinion, Ludo Quintrell-Webb was upon them. He certainly dressed the part, with a long overcoat, cloth cap, and copious florid scarves.

"Comrades," he said, pulling up a chair.

They chatted for a few minutes, and Leonard was surprised to find that Ludo was not as tedious as Ambrose had led him to believe.

"Father has procured me a job with the civil service," said Ludo. "He wishes me to become a bourgeois lapdog."

"There are worse ways to make a living," Leonard observed.

"Are there?" The anarchist was unconvinced. "I'm a man of principle, you must understand that. I love and I hate in equal measure. And I never, ever compromise. Like Mayakovsky, I'll die before I compromise."

"Of course, Ambrose wants to murder Father," Leonard said.

"Capital idea," said Ludo. "In fact, it's the *only* idea."

"If I were to do such a thing," said Ambrose thinly, "the last person I would take into my confidence would be Leonard. He has a loose tongue."

Ludo laughed and began to roll a cigarette on the thigh of his khaki trousers. "'Whatever you do,'" he quoted, "'you cannot hide a corpse.'" With that, he produced a pack of cards from his pocket. "Care for a game of blackjack?"

"Not me," said Leonard. "This is just a flying visit, I'm afraid."

"Oh, why not?" said Ambrose. "What are we playing for?"

"You know full well I'm short on cash," said Ludo.

"All right—forfeits it is, then."

Leonard left the café as Ludo dealt the cards, disgruntled that his visit had been cut short. There was much he and Ambrose needed to discuss, but it must be handled delicately. Privately. It was, after all, a family affair.

When he reached the kerb he found the Austin Seven empty. Looking up and down the street, he eventually spotted Peter Nightingale loping toward him.

"I told you to stay with the car," Leonard snapped. "You know what sort of a street this is."

"Sorry, sir, but I spotted something which I thought may be of interest to you." Nightingale said this with a meaningful look, a look that could not be ignored.

"Really?" Leonard said at length, "then you'd better tell me as we drive, hadn't you?"

When they were back in the Austin, Leonard demanded, "Well?"

"Apologies, sir. But I think what I'm about to tell you may be of some use."

"Go on."

"Pure coincidence, sir, but I spotted somebody entering the Harcroft Hotel at the other end of the street." He pointed at a decidedly run-down establishment on the corner. "Somebody whom I recognised. And they were swiftly followed by a second person."

"And who *were* these two people?"

"The first was your mother, Lady Elspeth."

"Impossible. She's at her doctor this morning, in Harley Street."

"No, sir," said Nightingale, "she isn't."

Leonard turned in his seat to get a proper look at his secretary's face. "What are you implying, Nightingale?"

"Perhaps my inference will be elucidated by the appearance of the second person."

"Well? Who was it?"

"I did not recognise the gentleman, sir."

Leonard groaned.

"But," Nightingale continued, "I decided to slip into the hotel foyer to try and find out—keeping myself hidden, of course. And I happened to hear your mother call him by name."

"Which was?"

"Sylvester, sir."

Leonard continued to stare at Nightingale before suddenly, and in his most obnoxious theatrical tenor, he began to roar with laughter. "Nightingale, you've struck gold. Yes, you have. So my mother and Sylvester the bastard have been making the beast with two backs, is that the gist of your theory? How delightfully devilish. I wonder what on earth would happen if my father found out?"

Nightingale shrugged. "Not for me to say, sir, but I thought I'd better pass it on all the same." They were now drawing close to their final destination, and Nightingale eased the car to a stop.

"You're a good little spy, aren't you? Care for a smoke?"

"Well, don't mind if I do, sir." Nightingale took the offered cigarette and leaned over so Leonard could light it.

The two men grinned at each other over the shared match flame.

INTERLUDE

A CONVERSATION

"**W**ant a cigarette?" Leonard offered.

"No," said Sylvester Monkton. "Let's get this over with."

"Well, I appreciate you taking the time. A professional fellow like you." Like all good actors, Leonard Drury knew the value of a well-placed silence. Used wisely, the absence of words could be devastating. And so it proved. "You're having an affair with my mother, aren't you?"

Sylvester did not seem shocked. "What gives you that idea?" he asked lazily.

"You seem to forget that I have eyes."

There was another lengthy silence. "What happens now?" Sylvester said, running his index finger over his moustachioed upper lip.

"That depends. The way I see it there are two potential outcomes. Either you continue to enjoy the sordid delights of my mother's flesh, or else you permanently sever what meagre ties you have to the Drury family. Forego any claim you might have to the Drury fortune."

"What do you want?"

"Pragmatism: good. Well, in order to maintain your incestuous little ménage à trois, I will require the sum of ten thousand pounds. Should you decline to make payment, then I shall have no choice but to tell Father. And you can imagine what the shock would do to him—might even finish him off. The choice is yours."

Sylvester scratched his chin, which bore a hint of stubble. "You know, I've never been blackmailed before. I think I *will* have that cigarette."

Leonard grinned. "I thought you might."

"Ten thousand pounds is really a ludicrous amount of money, you know. It would bankrupt me entirely. I'd be out on the street."

"Oh, you're an industrious fellow. I'm sure you'll find a solution."

Unexpectedly, Sylvester returned Leonard's grin. "I'm sure I will. As a matter of fact, I believe I already have. You see, there's something you don't know. I was at the townhouse last night, Leonard. And I saw something I was not supposed to see."

PART TWO

INNOCENT VILLAINS

December 16-18, 1938

Was not this execution rarely plotted?
—*The Revenger's Tragedy*, act 3, scene 6

The criminal is the creative artist; the detective only the critic.
—G. K. Chesterton, "The Blue Cross"

CHAPTER SEVEN

MARCHBANKS

Friday, December 16, 1938

I.

S pector's first glimpse of Marchbanks was through the hazy, ice-threaded mist of early morning. This was perhaps the best time to see the place. It had a tranquillity that would melt away with the rising sun, and the landscape a Perigordian primitiveness.

Sir Giles had sent a car, which collected Spector promptly from the kerb outside his Putney home. The journey was smooth and gave Spector ample time for contemplation.

When the driver deposited him at the Gothic, gargoyle-flanked gateway, Spector dismissed him and made the last leg of the journey on foot. With silver-tipped cane in one hand and bulky canvas bag in the other, he commenced his trudge along the drive.

Marchbanks was more or less as he had pictured it: a Victorian monstrosity of neo-Jacobean design, with Tudor arches, white walls, black beams, and tall, wide ogee windows glowering down beneath a Gothic crocketed roof. Flat land sprawled on all sides, grass crisp with frost.

Spector approached slowly, feet crunching, taking in each aspect of the façade with an acutely critical eye. Sir Giles and Lady Elspeth had arranged for him to arrive early—before the rest of the party. He was to familiarise himself with the staff and the setting beforehand, so he would be able to spot anything unusual when the family arrived.

He passed an ovoid lake to his left, the surface of which was murky with ice. A puny wooden jetty jutted out like a broken tooth, with a small rowing boat roped to it. As he walked, Spector wondered if Leonard and Ambrose had learned to swim in that lake. Had the older Leonard plunged infant Ambrose's head beneath the water—all in fun, of course?

Spector was contemplating this when he heard a scream. He turned and advanced toward the house. But before he reached the porch he was met by a woman approaching in the opposite direction. This statuesque and oddly threatening figure was the housekeeper, Mrs. Runcible.

Needless to say, it was not she who had screamed. Spector perceived an almost uncanny air about her, as though she were not quite real. Like a chimera formed of fog.

"Mr. Spector, I presume."

"Correct. It appears my arrival has caused some distress?"

"The maid," said Mrs. Runcible by way of explanation. "She believes that she possesses 'second sight,' and is constantly assailed by spirits. I'm afraid the sight of a man in black in the morning mist was enough to give her the vapours." The housekeeper spoke with a pointed lack of sympathy.

But Spector was amused. "Marchbanks is haunted, then?"

"No," she told him, "it is not." Her hair was too neatly combed, her face too perfectly made up, to be real. The skin was a little too white; the lips a shade too pink. Her hair was the startling grey of polished iron. Her clothes were black and ageless. Her funereal countenance was unblemished and as smooth as one of Findler's slabs. She might have been fashioned from the same stone that built these walls.

Her gait was conspicuously upright, and she spoke with affected projection. Spector wondered if she had ever been on the stage. Perhaps he would ask her—or perhaps not. He followed her through the front door and into the cavernous hall.

There were a few concessions to the modern world here, like the fitted carpet in the stairway, but the predominant style was one of antique eclecticism, with faded old oil paintings and multicoloured wallpaper depicting unusual birds: dotterels, shrikes, honey birds, and hornbills, as well as numerous others that Spector was unable to identify. The focal point of the far wall was a pair of crossed swords, mounted on a thick wooden base. Ottoman scimitars, their crucible-steel blades curling skyward, their hilts peppered with turquoise and jade.

"I presume Sir Giles has told you why I'm here?" said Spector, discreetly examining his new surroundings.

"The master has informed me that you are to keep an eye on things."

"And an ear, too. You're here year-round, is that so? I mean, you don't accompany the family back to London."

TOM MEAD

"I do not. Marchbanks remains under my care permanently." She spoke as though she and the house shared a symbiotic kinship. "I am the one who keeps the lamps lit and the fires burning."

"And what do you know, Mrs. Runcible, about the reason for my presence here?"

Her jaw clenched, her lips scarcely moving, she said, "We recently had something of a problem with thefts among the house staff. A rotten apple in an otherwise acceptable bunch. He was swiftly disposed of, but I still like to keep a close eye on things. A *very* close eye. I count the cutlery myself."

Spector could well believe it. "No," he said, "that's not it. At least, not entirely. Tell me, when were you first engaged here, Mrs. Runcible?"

"Some time ago, sir."

"You were here ten years ago on the night a young woman named Gloria Crain died under this roof?"

"I see," she said, disapprovingly, "so it's *that*."

Spector offered her a cigarillo which, to his surprise, she took. "What can you tell me about that night?"

She smoked the exotic cigarillo as though she had been enjoying them all her life. "Your room is just up here, sir," she said, ushering him toward a wide, curved mahogany staircase. They ascended side by side and the housekeeper moved with elegant swiftness on silent feet. "I'm afraid there's very little to say of it, sir. She was taken ill and she died."

"Had you met her before?"

"Never, sir. That was the first and only time Sir Giles brought her to Marchbanks."

Spector cast a discreet up-and-down glance at Mrs. Runcible as they traversed the upstairs corridor. "Did you speak with her the night she died?"

"I'm sure I couldn't recall a thing like that after ten years."

"And what about when she died? It happened in one of these bedrooms, isn't that so?"

On cue, they came to a halt outside a door. Mrs. Runcible unlocked it with a long key she produced from her sleeve, then ushered Spector inside.

"Indeed. *Your* room, to be exact, sir. In that very same bed," she said, gesturing at the looming four-poster. "Don't you worry though, sir," she said with something akin to a smile. "I've changed the sheets."

The room seemed to have remained untouched for considerably longer than ten years. Its look was decidedly Victorian: all wine-dark velvet and tassels, oriental rugs, with a candelabra looming rigor-like on the chestnut bureau. The bed was a four-poster, hung with patterned drapes that matched the Anaglypta on the walls.

Spector spoke severely. "Were you here when it happened?"

She did not take her eyes off him, and spoke in a low, almost sultry voice. It was as if she were trying to hypnotise him. "I was in bed—my room is at the end of the corridor—not ten minutes when I heard her scream. The whole household came running. This door was locked. It was Sir Giles who managed to shoulder it open. And she was on the bed, Miss Gloria Crain."

"Did she say anything?"

"She screamed, sir. Screamed and clutched at her belly. Twisted and rolled like an eel, she did."

"Dear God," Spector commented under his breath.

"Shocked, sir? It was poison, they said. Strychnine. Such a nasty way to die."

"How did she come to be poisoned?"

"Not for me to say, sir. Nothing that was cooked in *my* kitchen though, I can tell you that. I was there with cook, and I served the meal."

"Was there anything she ate that the others didn't? Or perhaps drank?"

"No, sir. I always keep a close eye on that sort of thing. But then, you already know that, don't you sir? Wouldn't be much of an investigator, would you, if you didn't know that." There was a slyness to the woman that deeply disturbed Spector.

"I know it's what the records say. But I want to hear the truth."

She studied him, unblinking. Impasse. "You'll excuse me, sir," she said, "but I must see to the linens." And she swept away, leaving only a chill in her wake.

Spector stood in the middle of his room, which faced out onto the driveway. He closed his eyes and pictured Gloria Crain on the four-poster bed, writhing—as Mrs. Runcible had grotesquely put it—like an eel.

He was a sceptic, but he knew well enough that places, just like people, retain memories. And here was the inescapable presence of Gloria Crain. She lurked in corners, her gaze fixed on him like that of a painting on the wall, a portrait with moving eyes. He glanced around, almost expecting to see her standing there. The object of Victor Silvius's obsession. He got the uneasy sensation that she was hiding from him, keeping just out of reach.

II.

"Ah, Spector," said Sir Giles as the conjuror descended the stairs. The judge was still removing his overcoat, and Mrs. Runcible was assisting Lady Elspeth with her hat. "Been getting the lie of the land?"

"I wasn't aware," said Spector quietly, "that I was to be staying in the room where Gloria Crain died."

Sir Giles and his wife looked at one another, but neither remarked on this. "The weather report is threatening snow," said the judge. "That can be dicey around here. I've asked Runcible to brief the staff, shovels at the ready, that sort of thing. Leonard is coming the day after tomorrow, so we need to make sure the drive remains passable."

Jeffrey Flack appeared in the doorway leading from the salon, followed by Ambrose. "Nice to see the old place hasn't changed," the younger man observed.

Spector gazed from one face to the next, wondering what was really going on behind the glazed eyes of his hosts.

"Will you join us for tea?" asked the judge.

"Of course," answered Spector, following them into the other room.

Unlike the wood-panelled walls and chilly parquet of the hall, the salon was an arrangement of button-back armchairs and otto-mans, all draped in doilies, as well as tables and cabinets packed with vases, porcelain, glass, and assorted taxidermy—mainly rats and dormice. The creatures were positioned in disturbingly humanoid tableaux and wore little doll-like clothes.

Spector met the dead gaze of a rat in a blue sailor suit, complete with a jauntily angled straw hat. As he studied it, he wondered what the creature had done to deserve this obscene punishment.

In all corners were wall sconces adorned with Tiffany lamps, each with a forest green shade.

"Or perhaps you'd like something stronger? I ordered some absinthe in especially for you." Sir Giles indicated a tray of decanters and glasses atop a hip-high cabinet. Amid the amber and burgundy of more conventional beverages lurked the unmistakable gleam of *la fée verte*.

"Very generous," said Spector. "But before I join you, I should like to take a look around the grounds. Please excuse me." The truth was, he did not wish to spend any time making small talk with the Drurys if he could avoid it. He left them before they could protest.

Stepping into the bitter air, Spector headed for the large outbuilding that had been repurposed as a garage. Heaving open the double doors, he was confronted by a narrow, bold-blue Bugatti. Ambrose's car—not that it fit particularly with his image of the "starving artist."

At the other end of the building was a kind of storage space that housed shovels, hoses, lawnmowers, gardening tools, coils of rope and, on the wall, a couple of ornamental horseshoes. A curious mélange of decadence and practicality, where croquet hoops were propped alongside plant pots, it seemed an effective analogy for the Drury clan as a whole.

Closing the doors again, Spector looked up at the exterior of Marchbanks. It was a place of secrets, he thought. *Secrets, and death.*

III.

Horace Tapper was looking harried. At home he did not cut the same mercurial figure that stalked the soundstages of Shepperton.

He'd mislaid the rewrites for *Salome*, and was migrating lazily back and forth between lounge and study in search of the wandering screenplay. He spotted the corner of a sheet poking out from behind a pillow on the lounge sofa. What the hell was it doing there? Grumbling aloud about those children of his, who were always taking things that didn't belong to them and then hiding them God knows where, he went over and retrieved the script.

He was just reordering the pages—which were now hopelessly dishevelled—when the doorbell rang. There was a moment of silence, save for the rustling of paper, and then it rang again.

Tapper groaned, "Will somebody get the door?"

He heard children's footsteps skittering on tiles out in the hall, followed by snickering. Tapper traipsed out into the now-deserted hall and opened the front door himself.

"What are you doing here?"

"Telephoned the studio," said Leonard Drury, striding past him into the hall and removing his hat. "They told me I'd most likely find you here."

"Come through to the lounge," said Tapper resignedly. "Care for some tea?"

"I'll take something stronger if you don't mind," said Leonard, eyeing the drinks cabinet at the far end of the lounge.

"Does sherry suit?"

"Capital," Leonard breathed, collapsing in an armchair.

Tapper unstoppered the crystal decanter and filled two small glasses. "What's this about, anyway?"

"What do you think? *Tarrare*."

Leonard downed his sherry. Children's footsteps approached again from the hall. Tapper crossed one leg over the other and made a show of studying the script.

"I'm not in a position to discuss *Tarrare*. Not with so much work left to be done on *Salome*. We finish shooting on Tuesday, then I'm closing up Sound City for Christmas. Perhaps we can talk about *Tarrare* in the new year . . ."

When a small, laughing boy burst into the room, Leonard's eyes snapped toward the tot and he opened his mouth to let fly some acerbic comment. But he stopped himself.

Caroline Silvius came careering into the room after the child. "So sorry, Mr. Tapper, he just slipped away from me . . ."

"Well don't let it happen again," said Tapper, not looking up.

"Why Caroline," said Leonard, "what an almighty coincidence."

"You know one another?" said Tapper.

"I know her brother. Don't I, dear?"

Through all this, the boy was scuttling around the room, opening the cupboards and drawers.

"Miss Silvius," said Tapper, "kindly see to my son, if you please."

Caroline snapped from her daze and scooped the boy in her arms. "Of course, Mr. Tapper. So sorry. It won't happen again." She spoke over the child's sudden burst of crying, and whisked him toward the door. But she could not resist a final glance at Leonard. She gave him a pleading look, and was met with only the chilly blackness in his eyes as he smiled.

IV.

"I'd keep your voice down if I were you," Leonard instructed. "I doubt your employer would be too impressed if he found out about us." He had left the Tapper home a few minutes earlier, but had sneaked back in through the kitchen door, and bearded Caroline as she was coming out of the pantry.

"What the hell are you doing here?" she whispered hoarsely. "Can't you leave me alone?"

"Business to discuss with your employer," came the answer. "Though an excuse to see you is always welcome."

"Please," she said, "get out of here."

"Caroline, Caroline. You need to learn some manners, my girl. Perhaps I'll teach you. Or perhaps I'll simply spill the beans to old Horace. What do you think?"

"You know this won't end well for you," she told him. The words were a hollow threat, but she spoke with enough conviction to give Leonard pause.

He frowned at her. "I'm not sure I care for your tone," he said. "You seem to forget that *I'm* the one in charge. Not you. And not your wretched, murderous brother."

She raised her hand to smack him, but he caught her by the wrist. It was a tableau from a bad play—he had performed it often enough before, with a slew of ingenues.

But somewhat surprisingly, Caroline quickly relented. Her lip curled in profound distaste.

"Don't look at me like that," said Leonard.

But she did not stop. "Your father's son, I see," she said.

"Wrong. I'm much better at this than my father. And I have a simple enough proposition for you. No cause for alarm. All I want is for you to come to dinner with me tonight. Nothing more than that."

"Never. I'll die first."

"Don't be so hasty, my sweet. This isn't just about *you*, you know. It's about your brother, isn't it? Dear old Victor."

"Please," Caroline whispered, "leave Victor out of it."

"Well, that's up to you. Your lunatic brother tried to murder my father, yes? And you are still your brother's sister. I doubt Horace Tapper would take too kindly to the notion of you caring for his children if he found out about your brother's situation, don't you?"

She hung her head. "I need this job," she said. "I need the money."

"Well, you're in luck," said Leonard. "Because I have a proposition which will guarantee my silence. All you need do is come to dinner with me."

Peter Nightingale was waiting at the wheel of the Austin as Leonard sauntered cheerily away from the Tapper residence. "Nightingale, book a table for two at The Ivy for tonight, would you?" he said as he clambered into the passenger seat.

"Of course, sir."

"There's a good chap," Leonard beamed. As they drove away, he sang softly to himself:

"You made me love you, I didn't want to do it . . ."

V.

That evening, Spector found the judge sitting alone at his desk. Sir Giles had a drink in his hand and fixed his gaze on a framed portrait of himself as a younger man.

"I wonder sometimes if this is what I deserve," he said. "I mean, I'm not a bad man, Spector. But all the same I've taken lives. Many of them. Hundreds. Indirectly, of course, but no less irrevocably. Maybe this is my punishment."

"You believe in divine retribution, Sir Giles?"

"You must think I'm a damn fool for talking to you, a comparative stranger, in this way. I don't know you from Adam, do I? But all the same, I'm compelled to be honest with you. Mr. Spector, I'm . . . frightened." He sipped his drink. "For a man whose vocation puts him in such close proximity to death, I'm inordinately afraid of it. I see it in the eyes of condemned men and women in the dock. And it never fails to terrify me. It's a wretched, ugly thing. And yet it is my ally. It is a tool of justice."

"That's one way of looking at it," said Spector, producing one of his thin, black cigarillos from a silver case. "Care for a smoke?" he offered.

"Thank you, no. But don't let me stop you."

Spector, who had no intention of letting anyone stop him, lit the cigarillo and plumed smoke.

"Tell me," Sir Giles said, "what do you make of it? Who's behind it all? Who's the mastermind?"

"I've been involving myself in mysteries for a long while now," Spector answered, "and there's one thing I can tell you for a fact, sir: it's that those who fear death are those with the most reason to do so."

"What's that supposed to mean?"

"It means that I believe there's something you're not telling me."

"About Gloria Crain? But damn it, man, I already explained—"

"Yes," Spector cut him off, "you did."

There ensued an uneasy silence.

Finally, Sir Giles ventured: "My whole family hates me, Spector. Every last one of them. It pains me to admit it, but nonetheless I must. You know, the other day I met with my solicitor. I made no secret of it, and I imagine the boys know well enough. I was going to disinherit the whole lot of them."

Spector twitched an eyebrow. "That seems a drastic move."

Sir Giles rubbed his forehead, apparently battling a migraine. "Ingrates, Spector. I raised a family of ingrates. They hate me and, God help me, sometimes I hate them too. Fortunately my solicitor—chap called Struthers—was able to talk me out of it."

"Who benefits according to your present will?"

"The estate—everything I own—goes to Leonard. There are allowances in place for the others, but Leonard does the best of the lot."

For a moment, the only sound was the crackling of the fire.

"Do you think one of your sons may be responsible for the letters? And for the gunshot?"

"I don't know *what* to think," the judge snapped. He got to his feet and began to pace in front of the fireplace. "That's what I want you to find out."

Spector nodded and continued to smoke.

CHAPTER EIGHT

SOMEBODY ON THE LAKE

Saturday, December 17, 1938

I.

Overnight, it snowed. By dawn—what dawn there was—the land was deluged in white. But the sky was now clear. The snow lay pristine and unmarked, roughly a foot deep. Spector studied it from his bedroom window and could not escape the sensation that somebody, somewhere, was setting the scene for a tragedy.

It did not take long for the nature of the tragedy to reveal itself. It was the judge who spotted it; Spector came upon him standing by the landing window, looking down at the long driveway leading to the front gate.

"Mr. Spector," he said, pointing, "there's somebody on the lake."

The lake, an ice-white ovoid, now bore a single blemish in the dead centre of its nacreous surface. The flimsy wooden rowing boat, which must have drifted free of the jetty during the night. But that was not all. Lying on his back in the curved hull of the rowing boat, his sleepy eyes cast heavenward, was Sylvester Monkton. He seemed typically aloof about his unlikely situation, no doubt on account of the chunky knife handle protruding from his chest.

Before long the whole house was effervescing with the new and gruesome story. Monkton was dead, stabbed during the night. How had he come to be there? Who had invited him?

Hasty telephone calls were made, and once again the grounds quickly filled with police cars and uniformed officers patrolling the perimeter. Nearby Benhurst had its own police station, but all the same Joseph Spector made a telephone call to George Flint. The Scotland Yard man had not even had breakfast before setting out from London with a retinue of investigators.

"I don't see how it can have happened," Flint confided, chewing lustily on his pipe as he spoke.

Joseph Spector stood like a thin, sinister shadow in the midst of the pristine white snow. He was studying the lake, where several uniformed constables were now endeavouring to pull the rowing boat back to shore. It bobbed in a rapidly shrinking circle of unfrozen water, the ice still creeping in on all sides. Their efforts caused this ice to splinter like a cracked mirror, snapping and crunching noisily.

As the boat drew closer to the shore, Spector observed the corpse's curious posture. He lay flat on his back, his legs bent and his arms outstretched in a sort of T shape so that the knuckles grazed the surface of the ice. His moustache was brittle with frost.

When Dr. Findler got his hands on the corpse he swiftly proclaimed, "Solid as a rock, as I expected."

Flint and Spector ambled over to join him and take a proper look at the dead man.

"What about time of death?" asked Flint.

"Ought to be easy enough to establish. Evidently he was killed and deposited in the boat before the lake froze, or else it couldn't have drifted away from the jetty like that. It should be simple enough to pinpoint the time at which the surface of the water would have been too stiff for the boat to drift. That'll give us a cut-off point for the murder."

"I don't suppose the killer could have carried him across the ice and dropped him in the boat?" Flint mused.

"Impossible. He'd have fallen straight through the ice. The water's frozen solid, but not solid enough to take the weight of two grown men."

"It's a unique problem," Spector said. "If Monkton's killer had carried him across the ice, it would have buckled beneath the weight and sent them both tumbling into the depths. And he couldn't have rowed out there without disturbing the ice. Which begs the question: why?"

"Why what?" said Flint.

"Why kill him out here at all, and leave him for anybody to find?"

"There'll be a reason for it," Flint huffed grumpily. "There always is."

Spector smiled. Flint was right. There always was.

"Then the assumption," Flint continued, "is that Monkton was killed early in the evening. Otherwise there'd be evidence of disturbance on the frozen surface of the lake."

"That's *an* assumption," said Spector, his pale blue eyes scanning the scene, "but not the only one."

"Well, what else is there? If he were killed later, there'd have been no way to get the body out there."

A thin smile spread across Spector's creased features. "It *does* seem that way, doesn't it? So either Monkton was killed earlier, ditched in the boat which was then shoved away from the jetty whereupon the surrounding water began to freeze, *or* he was killed later and his body somehow deposited out there in the middle of all that ice. Neither option is particularly appealing. But one of them must be the truth."

Findler was examining the knife. He extracted it from the wound (it took some effort, and the tight grip of both gloved hands) and showed it to the investigators with a curious sense of pride, as though it were a prize fish that he had just caught.

It was a steak knife from the Marchbanks kitchen. This was soon established by the discovery of a single empty slot in the wooden knife rack on the kitchen wall. But its disappearance had not been noted last night.

"Mrs. Runcible told me she counts the cutlery every evening because of recent thefts," Spector commented. "But she didn't report the missing knife. Assuming she went through her usual routine last night, that seems to indicate the knife was taken after she went to bed."

"Findler," said Flint, "is there anything you can tell us about the knife?"

"Of course," growled Findler, as though his professional integrity had been impugned. "I can tell you it was wielded by a man. And a strong man at that. Even with the blade slipped between the ribs, the breastplate appears to have been punctured at a single stroke."

Spector raised his eyebrows. "That seems rather unscientific, Findler. Downright antediluvian, in fact."

"Is that so?" the pathologist responded tetchily. "Then perhaps you'd care to give us the benefit of *your* expertise?"

"Well," said Spector, smiling down at the body, "I'd say he was stabbed on the north shore of the lake, and collapsed against the sycamore. There appear to be traces of bark on the back of his jacket. If you examine the tree trunk I imagine you'll find dried blood.

"With that in mind, I should say he approached via those trees there, and that he met with his killer at the foot of the sycamore."

The tree was examined and—to Findler's apparent chagrin—the dried blood found. The woods were duly searched, and as Spector had predicted, a frozen-over automobile was found parked in a shadowed glade. It was an unfamiliar, sturdy-looking Morris, and a single telephone call confirmed that a vehicle with that registration number had recently been rented in the name of Sylvester Monkton.

"Well, what have we got?" said Flint. "A corpse that appeared from nowhere with a knife in its chest."

"Indeed," said Spector, "and so it becomes a question of alibis."

II.

Each member of the household was interviewed in turn, and to Spector's perverse delight the true nature of the problem was revealed: up until midnight, they each had at least one person to vouch for them.

Mrs. Runcible had been supervising Becky in the kitchen (Alma the cook had long since gone home). They both went to bed at midnight; Becky had seen Mrs. Runcible counting the cutlery, and nothing had been amiss.

Meanwhile, Jeffrey Flack and Ambrose had walked into the nearby town of Benhurst to get blind drunk in the pub, The Old Ram. They were questioned anyway but had little memory of the previous evening. A pair of thumping hangovers rendered them largely incoherent. And besides, enquiries in Benhurst soon revealed that they had not left the pub until gone midnight, with Jeffrey propping up an especially sozzled Ambrose as they traipsed back through the snow.

Meteorological reports indicated that last night's rapidly dropping temperature would have caused a delicate sheen of ice to form on the outer edges of the lake long before then. It would have been nigh-on impossible for the killer to have gone about his wicked business without disturbing the ice, leaving visible traces that were not there the following morning. So the murder, it was hypothesised, took place *before* midnight.

Sir Giles and Lady Drury had been in each other's company throughout the evening, and gone to bed early, which Spector himself could confirm. But in spite of this, he made a point of interviewing the couple separately.

Sir Giles, decidedly sanguine about the death of his bastard son, did not seem especially eager to assist the investigation, but he nonetheless affirmed that he and his wife had taken their evening stroll around the lake at roughly half past eight the previous evening.

"Why?" asked Inspector Flint.

"I beg your pardon?"

"I said, why? It was freezing outside. Why on earth would you go for a stroll on a night like that?"

Affronted, Sir Giles answered hastily: "All part of the rest cure for my dear wife. A turn about the lake each evening before bed. She suffers with insomnia, you see, and the treatment is calculated to tire her sufficiently."

"In all weathers?"

"In all weathers."

"I see, thank you sir," said Flint, noting this down in his dreadful shorthand. "And do you accompany her every night?"

"Not every night. But most. What's good for the goose is good for the gander."

Flint opted to let this slide for the moment. "Did either of you pay much attention to the surface of the lake?"

"We both noted the boat in its centre. In fact, my wife commented on it. She said it looked so lonely and desolate. The lithium works wonders, though it does make her wax lyrical from time to time."

"Of course," put in Spector, "the water wasn't yet frozen."

"And neither of you noticed Mr. Monkton lying there?"

"Certainly not! What do you think we are, imbeciles? He wasn't there. If he were, we should have seen him."

"All right. And at what time did you return to the house?"

"I should say around half past nine."

"Very good."

This helped to narrow the window of time in which the murder might have been committed. So the boat was last seen unoccupied at nine thirty the previous evening. And Monkton could not have been killed later than midnight, as the ice creeping out across the water would have spread too far by then. And yet there was the inconsistency of the murder weapon. The knife was in the rack until gone midnight—both Mrs. Runcible and Becky confirmed as much. But after midnight, it would have been impossible for the body to have been dumped in the boat without disturbing the ice.

"Did you invite Mr. Monkton out to Marchbanks?" Flint asked.

"No," was the swift answer from Sir Giles. "I did not."

"Then how did he come to be here?"

"Not as my guest, I can tell you that much."

"You didn't arrange to meet him under cover of darkness, or anything like that?"

"I ask you, why the hell should I?" The judge's face was pink with righteous anger. He seemed to be bracing himself for a tirade. Spector had no especial inclination to hear it, so left the room pursued by a forlorn, pleading look from Flint.

A suitably deathly air hung about the house now. As he made his silent way along its downstairs corridor, listening to the moans of various floorboards beneath the weight of roving policemen, watched by the dead eyes of the oil paintings, Spector wondered if perhaps Becky the maid was right. Perhaps Marchbanks was haunted after all.

He found Lady Elspeth on the terrace, sitting on a stone bench to watch the investigators circling the lake. Her sharp shoulders were draped in the flesh of some dead animal, and she seemed almost hypnotically immune to the cold as she stared at the men who were making such a mess of the garden.

Spector sat beside her unbidden. She did not look at him when he spoke.

"When did you last see Sylvester Monkton?"

"I believe it was . . . August," she answered crisply.

"Really? You haven't seen him at all since then?"

"No."

"And under what circumstances did you see him?"

"I couldn't say."

Spector lit a cigarillo. "I think you're lying. In fact, I think you saw him considerably later than August. I'm right in thinking that you and he were having an affair, weren't you?"

She gave him a venomous glare. "Just who do you think you are?"

"A humble conjuror, no more, no less. But when I came to dinner at your Chelsea townhouse, I bumped into Sylvester Monkton, who had just crept in via a side door. He claimed he was there to borrow money from his father, yet he didn't even set foot in his father's office. And you somewhat conspicuously retired early, didn't you? You had something important to discuss, isn't that so? It must have been, for him to take such a risk. Particularly with *me* in the house. I think he was there to see you."

Summoning up all her dignity, arching her back with feline grace, she said, "I would ask that you keep this matter secret. That you not breathe a single word of it to my husband."

Spector inclined his head. "As you wish. But you must understand, Lady Elspeth, that it was very unwise of you to try and deceive me. I always, always find the truth."

She did not comment on this. Instead she began to speak in a low, measured tone, almost as if her voice were running away from her.

Spector had seen such behaviour in fraudulent psychics, but this was no act. As a young man Spector had travelled widely, once crossing paths with a Haitian *bokor*, a practitioner of Vodou magic. The *bokor* was able to induce the deepest trances in his subjects, and was known in some cases to raise the dead. Lady Elspeth spoke now like one of those subjects, like a zombie.

"There was a change of plan," she said. "It was supposed to be just the two of us at Marchbanks, and then the boys were going to come down on Christmas Day. But because of Jeffrey and his little indiscretion . . . Sylvester and I arranged to meet at 1:00. I slipped a sleeping draught into Giles's evening tincture. He went out like a light. The house was utterly still and quiet. So I dressed and went to the meeting place."

"Which was?"

"The statue of Eros on the south lawn."

"So you didn't pass by the lake at all."

"Why should I? We were meeting on the opposite side of the house."

"Why meet in such unsociable circumstances? Surely it wasn't an assignation?"

"You are correct," she said, "it wasn't. There was something we needed to discuss."

"How did he appear to you? What was he wearing?"

"Well, he was bundled up in scarves and things. It was very cold indeed, as you know."

"And how did he sound?"

She looked at Spector a little suspiciously. "Like Sylvester. Much as he did when we spoke on the telephone."

"It never occurred to you that it might not actually *be* Sylvester?"

She seemed mortified at the very idea. "It had to be Sylvester," she said. "He was the only one who knew about our meeting that night." But she seemed to be trying to convince herself as much as Spector.

"What did he say? What words did he use?"

"He . . . he called me by a name which . . . which only he and I knew. Only he would ever have called me that . . ." And all at once she seemed to experience a flood of emotion. She did not cry. In fact, her facial expression did not even change. But her eyes grew wide and seemed to darken.

Spector felt almost sorry for her, but not quite.

"And what did you discuss?"

"Some things must remain private, Mr. Spector, even in the face of death itself."

Spector got up and wandered over to the edge of the terrace. Not looking at her, he said, "You and he were conspiring, weren't you?" She didn't answer, so he continued, "*That's* the real reason that he came out to your townhouse three nights ago. Not to beg for money from his father, as he claimed, but to see you. You pretended to retire to bed with a headache when in fact you telephoned him from the upstairs extension, didn't you? And you informed him that your three sons would be at Marchbanks for Christmas, and you suggested that it might be worthwhile for him to put in an appearance, too. You and he were partners in crime. Sylvester knew well enough that Sir Giles had disinherited him. But he hasn't disinherited *you*. You were going to split the inheritance with Sylvester, weren't you, in exchange for him ridding you of your troublesome husband."

Lady Elspeth was on her feet. "This is an appalling, unconscionable allegation—"

"It's why you hired me, isn't it?" Spector persisted. "I was to be the independent witness, wasn't I? You would bring me out here on a pretext of investigating the letters, but in so doing you would remove yourself from suspicion. Perhaps, when the deed was done, you would even confide to me your 'suspicions' regarding Sylvester. Once he was in the frame, it would be your word against his. And of course, yours would be believed. Sylvester Monkton would hang, and the entire inheritance would be yours—"

"That's enough!" snapped Lady Elspeth. "This is all pointless conjecture. The fact is, nobody has tried to hurt Giles. And yet Sylvester is dead . . ."

"True. Which is the only reason, Lady Elspeth, that I haven't yet reported my 'pointless conjecture' to Inspector Flint. But there's something else I must ask you. I have a feeling it may be the crux of the whole messy affair. Did you poison Gloria Crain?"

This proved to be the limit of Lady Elspeth's endurance. She was on her feet without another word, marching toward the house.

Spector simply stood and watched her go.

III.

Slowly, thoughtfully, Spector did another circuit of Marchbanks, stopping at the garage. Now, the doors were wide open, and Flint's men were ransacking the place. Spector strode over to observe.

Flint had stepped out for some air after his interview with Sir Giles, which had evidently proved unexpectedly blistering. "Where'd you disappear to?" he asked Spector.

"Nowhere particular."

Drifting toward the workbench, the conjuror quickly scanned the clutch of outdoor items. Naturally, they had been moved about a bit. But there also seemed to be a few missing. Hadn't there been a coil of rope here previously? His eye was caught by a small object. He grabbed it and held it up to the light.

"Excuse me," he said to one of the constables, "where did this come from?"

Flint himself came over and scowled at the object as though it were some nasty little creature that had bitten him. But it was in fact a cricket ball. What set it apart from any ordinary cricket ball was the round hole, roughly two-thirds of an inch in diameter, that went right through the centre.

"Nothing to do with me."

"It seems to have been drilled at this bench."

"Must have been a small drill bit," Flint pointed out.

"Indeed," said Spector, pocketing the ball. He pulled out a drawer in the underside of the bench and examined the pair of drill bits that lay there. One was an inch in width, the other two-thirds of an inch. "This one, I'd say."

Whether the cricket ball was significant remained to be seen, but there could be no denying that it was *interesting*. And Spector was a collector of interesting things.

"What do you reckon it means?" said Flint.

"Nothing at all," Spector replied, "but I suppose that's the point."

"I've taken a room at the pub in Benhurst," said Flint, changing the subject. "The Old Ram."

"I think that's wise," said Spector. "I've a feeling this is not the last death we shall see here. And no doubt Sir Giles will not take kindly to the idea of policemen staying on his property. He would find it rather uncivilised, I think."

"Funny," said Flint, "I happen to find *murder* uncivilised."

The two men were strolling the grounds, while clutches of uniformed officers scoured the icy turf inch by inch for some trace left by the killer. Spector knew they would not find anything, and of course they did not.

A thin wind had got up now and sent ripples of gooseflesh down Flint's spine. "What about Leonard?" he asked.

"I believe Sir Giles telephoned him this afternoon to break the news."

"Irritating," said the Scotland Yard man. "That'll have given the lad plenty of time to come up with an alibi."

Spector stopped. "You think he's responsible, then?"

"Well," Flint said, "I don't see who else it can have been. All the others have alibis before midnight. And if Monkton was killed after the lake froze, how in the hell did the killer get him out into that little boat?"

"Indeed," said Spector, "you might even call it impossible."

The word sent another chill through Flint. "Well, every other suspect is accounted for. The ice was solid and undisturbed. If it's not Leonard, then it's hopeless. There's no possible answer."

"I rather believe that's what the killer hoped we would conclude," said Spector. He was thinking now. Thinking of sacrifice, of ancient altars in fretted stone. There was something ritualistic in it. A living game of bagatelle, with the pins falling one by one. "He's wrong, of course. And so are you, Flint. There *is* an answer."

They went into the house and made for the judge's study, which Flint had appropriated as a makeshift base of operations. Before resuming their discussion, Flint picked up the telephone and made a call to his office at Scotland Yard. While he spoke discreetly to Sergeant Hook, Spector waited and listened.

Then he heard it: the faintest of creaks. Somebody was outside, out in the hall, eavesdropping at the door.

Spector silently caught Flint's eye and raised a finger to his lips. Then he moved across the carpet with startling agility for his age—positively spiderlike. In a single motion he threw open the study door, revealing the housekeeper.

"Mrs. Runcible," he said, "good of you to drop in. Would you please bring Inspector Flint and me a glass each of that delicious absinthe?"

Utterly unashamed at being caught in such a potentially compromising position, Mrs. Runcible simply said, "Yes, sir," and went.

When Spector resumed his seat, Flint put down the phone. "Bad news," he said.

"Let me guess," the conjuror offered, "Leonard Drury has a watertight alibi up until midnight?"

Flint nodded. "The Ivy! The Ivy, of all places. It doesn't get much more conspicuous than that. Hook has checked up on it, interviewed the maître d' and everything, so he can confirm it. Leonard was at The Ivy till gone midnight."

There came a knock at the door and Mrs. Runcible slipped wordlessly into the room bearing two glasses not of absinthe, but

of sherry. Spector took his without complaint and sipped it gratefully. Flint, who was still reeling from the latest revelation, barely
noticed the housekeeper's presence at all.

When she was gone, Spector spoke. "If we're going to fit all
the pieces together," he said, "we will need to compile a credible
chronology. It's there that the killer has played his cleverest trick.
Because either Sylvester Monkton was killed before midnight and
his body deposited in the boat, which simply drifted to the centre
of the lake and froze there, *or* he was killed *after* midnight and his
body deposited in the centre of the frozen lake by unknown means.
If we pursue the former theory, then the man Lady Elspeth met
beneath the Eros statue was simply impersonating Monkton. If
that's the case, we need to determine how the impostor came to
know the 'secret name' that was hitherto known only to Elspeth
and Sylvester. We also need to determine who had the opportunity
to murder Sylvester, because up until midnight all our suspects have
fairly solid alibis. Look at it this way, Flint: up until midnight,
our killer had the means but not the opportunity or the weapon.
After midnight, he had the opportunity and the weapon but not
the means. A conundrum, don't you agree?"

Flint agreed, but didn't feel like saying so.

"Let's talk about the lake," said Spector.

"What about it?"

"Well, it's one hundred feet in diameter, and approximately
fifty feet deep. Therefore, we are looking at roughly three hundred
and fifteen feet in circumference. The boat is, I would say, six feet
long. And while it is impossible—that word again!—to pinpoint its
precise location, and although the lake isn't uniformly frozen, the

boat—and thus the body—has approximately thirty feet of sheer ice all the way around. The jetty is ten feet long, so even standing on the edge the killer would have had to lob the corpse around twenty feet. I don't see that happening, do you?"

The only solutions Flint could come up with were at best wildly impractical, and at worst comical. The least ridiculous of them required a trebuchet. But Spector, he reflected grudgingly, was right. There was no way any of their suspects could have committed the crime before midnight. It was impossible.

CHAPTER NINE

THE WRONG ROOM

Sunday, December 18, 1938

I.

It snowed heavily overnight. Once the investigators had with-drawn for the day, the household retired early, and Spector sat up as long as he could before sleep overcame him. Now he woke in that ill-fated bed of his to the glow of ethereal whiteness beyond the window. But the sky was clear. It was going to be one of those beautiful winter days when the ground is soft underfoot and the sun pale and beneficent.

Spector observed through the glass as an Austin Seven coasted expertly up the snow-caked drive, then came to a crunching halt outside the house. The driver, a tall fellow with a sharply hewn chin and close-cropped blond hair, was a stranger. But the passenger was Leonard. The actor rubbed his gloved hands and approached the front door.

When Spector descended the staircase, he saw the Drury parents embracing Leonard—who was, after all, the favourite son. Ambrose and Jeffrey were nowhere in sight. The blond driver carried the bags.

"Made it in one piece, anyway," Leonard was saying.

"Oh darling," said Lady Elspeth, "thank God you're here, we've been having the most *awful* time of it."

Leonard didn't acknowledge this. "I take it there'll be room for my man Nightingale?"

"Plenty," Sir Giles assured him.

"Well, you had better get ready," said Lady Elspeth. "We are leaving for church in half an hour."

"Church!" Leonard sighed. "One forgets these provincial pastimes so easily. I suppose there's no way out of it? In light of . . . you know, *what's happened?*"

"None," said his mother. "The reverend and the others will be expecting to see you there."

Leonard was about to protest again when his father said, "It's important for us to show the community a united front. Of course, they all know by now about what happened here yesterday. Gossipmongers will be on the prowl. If we stay holed up here, we'll only add fuel to their fire."

"Very well. Needs must. I had better put on a clean suit, hadn't I?"

Lady Elspeth looked him up and down. "Yes, you better had."

Mrs. Runcible materialised with a young maid in tow. The maid bore a heavy suitcase, monogrammed "L.D."

"I'll take that if you like, miss," Nightingale offered.

"No you won't," said Leonard, "you'll go and park the Austin in the garage. It's had enough of a pasting in this snow as it is."

"Right you are, sir."

The driver, the maid, and Mrs. Runcible all went their separate ways, leaving Spector with Sir Giles and his wife.

"Good morning to you, Spector," said Sir Giles formally. "I hope you'll be accompanying us to church in the village as well?"

"With pleasure," said Spector, "I shall join you in a few moments."

He left them and headed out via the front door, following Nightingale's footprints. He reached the garage just as Nightingale was parking the Austin.

Spector strolled over as Nightingale clambered out of the car.

"You're Leonard Drury's factotum, is that so?"

Nightingale smiled politely. "That's the sort of thing, sir. I was engaged as a personal secretary. Though that seems to incorporate the duties of a valet, driver, and dogsbody. Peter Nightingale."

They shook hands. Nightingale's grip was warm and pleasant.

"Have you been with Mr. Drury long?"

"Not long at all, sir. Less than a week. I only arrived in England at the beginning of the month."

"Is that so?"

"Before that," Nightingale explained, "I was with Byron Manderby. The explorer. I accompanied him on his latest sojourn along the Ulanga River in his Javanese junk, the *Shamshir*."

Spector had travelled himself, albeit not as widely. "The Ulanga River," he said, "that flows through several unexplored territories, isn't that so?"

"Quite right, sir," said Nightingale, pulling shut the garage door and heading back toward the house.

Spector kept pace with the younger man's long, loping steps.

"It must have been very dangerous at times. I know Byron Manderby has found himself in mortal peril on more than one occasion. I read his book about that disastrous Antarctic expedition. *The Demons of Winter*, I believe it was called."

"It was my privilege to serve as his right-hand man on the Ulanga expedition. Unfortunately, it was cut short when he contracted malaria."

Spector drew a little closer to Nightingale and spoke confidentially. "I can't help but wonder how Leonard Drury compares to Byron Manderby as an employer."

Nightingale smiled. "Indeed, sir," he said. "Well, there is one thing I will tell you: Manderby, for all his virtues, has little comprehension of the value of money. I'd been a private secretary before joining the British Battalion, so I thought why not? I went back to my former agency, and they accepted me with open arms."

Spector stopped and placed his hand on Nightingale's arm. "Peter," he said, "are you aware that a man was murdered here the night before last?"

Nightingale sighed. "I'm afraid I am, sir. Mr. Drury explained the situation to me yesterday after receiving a telephone call from his father."

"The victim was a man named Sylvester Monkton. Did you know him?"

"No, sir."

"Did Leonard ever mention him to you?"

"No, sir."

"I see. Now I'm going to be up front with you, Peter. You and I are both outsiders to the Drury family, but it's important for you to know that I'm investigating Sylvester Monkton's death. So I must ask: Where were you the night before last?"

Nightingale did not seem offended by the question. "You'd like my alibi, sir? Well, I drove Mr. Drury to The Ivy for his dinner appointment at 8:00."

"And after that?"

"There's a pub I go to, The Crescent Moon, they do a rather nice meat pie. So I headed there for my evening meal."

"Alone?"

"The regulars know me. And the landlord. I lodged there for a while when I first arrived back in England."

"I see. And then?"

"I stayed and chatted for a while, played a few card games. Then I went back to The Ivy to pick up Mr. Drury at a little after midnight."

Creating a conspicuous alibi for Leonard, thought Spector. "Thank you. And I hate to labour the point, but during your employment with Leonard Drury have you encountered anything at all that you would consider unusual?"

"What did you have in mind, sir?"

"Anything," said Spector, "anything at all. Whatever the term suggests to you."

Nightingale shook his head, but said, "If you think there's danger here, sir, just say the word. After all, once a man has traversed the Ulanga all the way from the Eastern Rift to the mouth of the Atlantic, a house party in the country holds few terrors."

"I understand the Ulanga can be . . . deceptive," Spector commented.

"Oh, yes. All those swamps, channels, and tributaries to lead one astray."

"Then you know how to spot a deception when it plays out in front of you," said Spector, smiling.

"A deceptive river, but a populous one, too," Nightingale continued. "Plenty of friendly souls, human and otherwise. The puku, the lapwing, the red colobus monkey. Watch out for the hippopotamuses, though."

"I believe they can be very deadly," Spector agreed. "They happily slaughter humans for the sheer pleasure of doing so, isn't that right?"

"Uncivilised beasts," Nightingale said with a chuckle. "Fortunately the Ndamba harpooners kept them out of our way."

"Your relations with the locals were cordial?"

Nightingale nodded. "When Manderby fell ill, we took him up to Mahenge, to the Franciscan friary there. They were able to care for him through the worst of it."

"Mahenge," Spector repeated thoughtfully. "Near von Hassel's coffee plantation?"

Nightingale grinned. "You know what you're talking about, don't you, Mr. Spector? Most people's knowledge of the region comes from C. S. Forester. *The African Queen* and whatnot. Perhaps you've travelled there yourself?"

Spector affected modesty. "I have a memory for such details."

"Must be useful in your line of work."

"Oh, it's vital." Spector said nothing more. He simply waited.

Nightingale, too, seemed unsure what to say next. He fumbled with a cigarette case and slipped one of its contents between his lips. Spector, smiling slightly, lit it for him, then lit one of his own cigarillos.

The two men smoked peacefully for a moment, looking out across the snow-carpeted lawn.

"Have you ever heard of Gloria Crain?"

Nightingale kept on looking dead ahead. "Can't say I have."

Spector gave him a sideways glance. "You surprise me. Her name was rather famous some years ago."

Nightingale gave a measured sigh, creating a cloud of smoke. "I think I'd better take my leave, sir. It seems I've already spoken somewhat out of turn." He gave a little bow and disappeared back into the house.

Spector took a deep breath of the crisp morning air, stubbed out his cigarillo, and walked on. He did a quick circumnavigation of the house, examining each façade from the outside. When he passed in front of the French windows that opened onto the ballroom, he saw Ambrose hard at work on his latest canvas. But the magician paused only briefly before crunching away, leaving behind him a set of shadowed footprints in the fresh snow.

Somewhat incongruously, a statue stood atop a solid stone plinth in the middle of the lawn. Spector had spotted it yesterday, but this was the first time he had troubled to examine it up close. Eros, the Greek god of desire. He carried his customary bow and arrow, and his back bore a set of splendid wings. But the look on his face was one of singular consternation. The smooth, pupilless eyes stared down at Spector with undisguised hostility. This was where Sylvester and Lady Elspeth had met under cover of darkness.

Spector glanced around in all directions. He pictured the location as it would have looked on the night in question, swathed in fog. He had encountered plenty of "identity tricks" in the past. Could Lady Elspeth really have recognised the man she spoke with? Could she be *sure* it was Sylvester Monkton?

Heading back round to the front door, he passed beneath the window to the master bedroom and was surprised to see that it was open. He recognised the silhouette of Lady Elspeth, and her distinctive voice that had made the briefest of ripples in the opera world all those years ago.

"For God's sake, Runcible, are you blind? I said my *emerald* brooch . . ."

Not waiting to hear the housekeeper's mumbled apologies, Spector pressed on.

When he re-entered the hall, his nostrils flared slightly at the familiar scent of smoke. He followed the scent to an ashtray on a decorous little table, in which an envelope had blackened and burned.

A curled sheet of notepaper lay in the bottom of the ashtray, and for a moment Spector thought it might be another of the fabled poisoned pen letters. But when he retrieved it, he saw that the paper bore a company letterhead, which was still partially legible:

PPER PROD

Tapper Productions, thought Spector. The film studio that was producing *Tarrare*. Unable to make out any of the message itself, he left the note burning precisely as he had found it.

From there, he headed into the ballroom—Ambrose's studio. Though the room still oozed old-world grandiosity, it was now bare save for the canvases heaped along the walls, and the easel in the centre.

Ambrose himself was jabbing violently at his latest canvas with a brush, producing wild swathes of colour.

"Good morning, Ambrose," said Spector.

"Ah, good morning," Ambrose answered without looking up from his work. He was wearing a paint-smeared smock and—ludicrously—a beret. "Saw you wandering past the window a minute ago. Off to church with the others, are you? I'm afraid I'm a bit of an ungodly sort, so I'm keeping Runcible company here."

"I've been meaning to ask you," said Spector, "about Gloria Crain."

Ambrose gave him a look of almost beatific nostalgia at the mention of the name. "I never saw Gloria that night ten years ago," he said. "Past my bedtime, you understand. I was only nine. And I wasn't allowed to eat with them either. I stayed in the kitchen with Mrs. Runcible. Lucky me, I got to watch cook prepare the feast." He smiled absently. "So I never saw her the night she died."

"Did you hear the screams?"

He nodded. "Her room is usually closed up. Nobody ever goes in there. You're honoured, Spector."

"Who killed her, Ambrose? You must have come up with a theory in all the years since."

Ambrose's voice was almost childlike. "Whoever it was, it wasn't me. I didn't know her. Mother didn't like her, though. Thought she had *designs* on the old man. But she was wrong. If Gloria Crain was after anyone, it was Leonard. Leonard loved her. Or thought he did. He was at an impressionable age."

By Spector's calculation, Leonard would have been the age that Ambrose was now. Nineteen; a year younger than Gloria herself.

Ambrose indicated the painting. "Do you like it? It's a portrait of my brother. Can't you see the likeness? I'm only in the early stages, but if I work quickly I may get the whole thing done today. Done, and ready for hanging!"

Spector studied it. *Ready for hanging, indeed.* The paint itself seemed to have curdled and coagulated. Whatever this piece might be called, it was most assuredly not like any portrait Spector had ever seen.

"I've captured his avarice, don't you think? You see, Leonard has to *have* things," said Ambrose. "It's got him into trouble before. There was a girl once . . . anyway, he's dreadfully jealous of me, you know. I do believe that's the only reason I bothered with *Tarrare*. I don't care for films. I never really wanted to act. I couldn't care less. But I wanted to show Leonard. That's all. Isn't that pitiful?"

Pitiful; yes, that was the word. And now the painting and the burnt letter made sense. Spector said, "I take it you no longer have the part."

"That transparent, am I? Yes, I heard from Horace Tapper this morning. Had his secretary type it up for him. Couldn't even muster the energy for a telephone call. And so, Leonard gets his way once again." Ambrose grinned, but it was the kind of melancholy, mirthless grin Spector had seen on Jeffrey Flack. "That maid, Becky . . . she believes she can see ghosts. She says that Gloria Crain is still here. That she never left Marchbanks. Do you believe in ghosts, Mr. Spector?"

"The only ghosts that concern me," said the conjuror, "are those that live in our heads."

"I know just what you mean. But all the same I find myself glancing over my shoulder as I walk the corridors. There is something here all right, Mr. Spector. You take my word for it."

Spector stood, stolid and unsmiling in the centre of the room. "I think . . ." he said at length, "that if you know anything, you ought to tell me."

Ambrose Drury stared back at him for what felt like a long time. And then he said, "Better hurry now, Mr. Spector. Wouldn't want to keep Mother waiting." And the spell was broken. "Be sure to say a prayer for my immortal soul, won't you?"

Spector promised that he would, and wandered out of the studio and back toward the main hall feeling bemused. Almost as though that strange, brief glimpse behind Ambrose's mask had not happened at all.

"Where are those damned boys?" the judge grumbled.

"You know full well that Ambrose has sworn off the church," said Lady Elspeth, adjusting her emerald brooch as she descended the stairs. "And Leonard is . . . I don't know where Leonard is."

Sir Giles continued peering irritably at his watch for a couple of minutes or so before Jeffrey Flack and Leonard appeared.

"At last," said Sir Giles. "Now perhaps we may head off?"

The motley band of residents spilled out of the house and began a gentle amble along the drive, down toward the gate. Sir Giles and Lady Elspeth were arm in arm, Leonard and Jeffrey Flack kept more or less equal pace. Spector trailed behind with careful, unhurried steps.

They had almost reached the gate when Lady Elspeth stopped.

"Oh!" she cried. "My gloves, how silly of me. I believe I left them in the salon. Would one of you be so kind . . . ?"

"I'd be happy to oblige," said Spector.

"Most kind of you," said Lady Elspeth.

Jeffrey and Leonard did not exactly sigh with relief, but there was a kind of shared loosening of the shoulder muscles, an easing of tension.

Spector traipsed obediently back to the house. He eased open the front door quietly and slipped into the hall. Truthfully, he wanted to see what really went on within the walls of Marchbanks when Runcible was in charge. As he crept toward the staircase, a sudden, heavy thump overhead caused the chandelier to shake. Spector frowned and headed up the stairs.

Pausing on the landing, he peered along the corridor and saw what had made the sound. Mrs. Runcible was again chastising the young maid, who had evidently dropped a suitcase. She was in the process of heaving it from one room to another a few doors down.

"I'm sorry, Mrs. Runcible."

"Just buck your ideas up, that's all I ask."

Spector advanced on them. "Somebody moving out?" he said casually. Of course he had already spotted the familiar monogram on the side of the case: L.D.

"Indeed, sir," answered Mrs. Runcible. "It seems that Master Leonard was originally put into the wrong room."

Spector tutted. "A rudimentary error."

Mrs. Runcible did not reply but simply glared. She watched the maid struggle with the case and snapped, "Quickly, quickly."

Spector retreated downstairs but halted halfway. Ambrose had surfaced from his studio to use the telephone on the hall table. He now stood with his back to Spector, studying the intricacies of the ornamental brocade that hung from the opposite wall.

Spector crouched slowly so that he was hidden behind the banister. He waited, and listened.

"Ludo? It's you-know-who," said Ambrose, his voice low. "Ready for your forfeit, old man?"

Spector strained to hear the voice from the receiver, but it reached him as little more than a tinny murmur.

"Good," Ambrose said, and hung up the telephone. Spector watched unseen as Ambrose went back the way he had come and disappeared into his studio.

Spector descended the remaining stairs quickly and toyed with the idea of picking up the telephone to ask the operator for that number. But the others were waiting for him. Instead, he went into the salon, where Lady Elspeth's gloves were waiting conveniently on the glass-topped coffee table.

Becky the maid was in the hall now, making a meal of dusting the architraves in case Mrs. Runcible happened to be watching. But when she saw Spector, she scampered over to him.

"Please, sir," she said, "I'd like to speak with you. In *private*."

"Come this way," he said, leading her back into the salon. "What's this about, Becky?"

"I had to tell *someone*," said the maid, "and it may as well be you. It's about the girl who died, sir."

"Gloria Crain? What about her?"

"Sir, it's just . . . oh, I don't know if I ought to say anything."

"You must." Spector's voice did not rise, but it carried sufficient gravity to send a chill fluttering over the housemaid's skin.

"It's . . . Mrs. Runcible, sir. Lately I've been wondering if *she* might be the one who . . . who poisoned Gloria Crain."

"Why?"

"Something I heard, sir. A while ago, it was. But it sort of makes sense with everything that's happened."

"Go on," prompted Spector.

"It's a telephone conversation I happened to overhear, sir. A few months ago now, back in the summer. The master and mistress were in London, so there was only a skeleton staff about the place. The fête was on in Benhurst, and Mrs. Runcible gave me the afternoon off. But I forgot my purse, sir, and I knew there'd be candy floss and toffee apples and bits I wanted to buy. So I came back. But I came in quietly, sir, because I didn't want Mrs. Runcible to hear me. She's a one for 'little jobs,' sir, and I knew if she caught me she'd have me doing some dusting or some such, and then I'd *never* get away.

"So I slipped my shoes off and crept in through the front door. I took it for granted that she'd be in the kitchen, or in her room. I didn't think she'd venture out into the main house when she had the place to herself. But as soon as I opened the door, there she was.

She had her back to me and was speaking on the telephone—that's how come she didn't notice me. So I pulled the door to again, so that it was only open a crack, and I . . ."

"You listened. It's all right, no need to be reticent. I shan't give you away. But who was it that she was talking to?"

"Now that I *can't* say. But it was someone she knew well, sir. *Very* well, if you get me."

"You oughtn't speculate, Becky," Spector chided. "Tell me what you heard."

"Yes, sir. Sorry, sir. This is what she said: 'I'm sorry,' she said. 'She was so young and I regret it now. I wish I could tell her I'm sorry.' And then she went quiet for a bit, like as though the person on the other end was talking. Then she said: 'He's the one who broke her heart, but if it weren't for me she'd still be alive today.'" Becky stopped, her eyes ablaze. "I didn't put two and two together until people started talking about Gloria Crain again, sir . . ." Her voice had grown louder as she convinced herself that she was onto something.

"Becky, calm down. Are you positive those were the precise words you heard?"

"Positive, sir. Ten times over. That's what she said."

"All right." Spector slipped her a coin. "You did well. Now get back to work before Mrs. Runcible notices."

"Oh sir, do you think it's safe for me to be alone with her . . . ?"

"You're not alone. You have Master Ambrose and Peter Nightingale here to look after you."

Reassured, Becky took a deep breath, steeled herself, and returned to work. Gloves in hand, Spector proceeded thoughtfully down the drive.

Lady Elspeth made a perfunctory show of gratitude and the group continued into the village. She looped her arm around Leonard's and drew herself close to him as they walked. The favourite son, indeed. Spector remained at the rear of the party, noticing that the breeze was blowing in his direction, carrying with it the susurrant voices of the others. Jeffrey had moved in front and was now conversing with Sir Giles, who looked a bit pink in the face. Either the cold air was getting to him, or else the subject of their tête-à-tête was decidedly distasteful. Money, no doubt.

II.

The market town of Benhurst was perhaps half a mile along the ragged country lane leading from Marchbanks. The stroll was a leisurely and pleasant one. By the time the group reached the church, Sir Giles and Jeffrey Flack seemed to have reached détente.

The church itself was unprepossessing in the way only English village churches can be. Its spire was stumpy, its stained glass dark in places, faded in others. The organ was shrill and a little off-key. Spector kept his eyes on the Drury party as they filed into the building along with the other parishioners.

He did not hear a word of the sermon. Instead, his attention was fixed on the family beside him in the pew. He observed every single surreptitious movement, every glance that passed between them. He could not rid himself of a profound foreboding.

He thought about the poisoned pen letters that had started this whole affair. He had seen only one, and yet they had apparently been arriving for some time. What was the purpose behind those letters? Simply to instill fear in the judge's heart? Or did they serve another, more practical purpose? Were the references to Gloria Crain simply an old-fashioned red herring?

Then he thought about that half-hearted gunshot the other night. One of them—Leonard, Ambrose, or Jeffrey Flack—had crept out into the street to take aim through the study window. Then he fired, missed, and dashed back into the house. Not the most ambitious murder scheme the aging conjuror had ever come across. Rather, it was the impetuous act of a spoilt child.

But impetuosity was not a trait Spector would ascribe to the author of those poisoned pen letters. Rather, they were the product of a careful, calculating mind.

The service dragged on, and Jeffrey in particular grew restless. He fidgeted and rubbed his hands together and scratched his head and generally made a nuisance of himself to those around him. Finally, when the proceedings drew to a close, he practically bolted for the door. He didn't even pause to shake hands with the vicar.

Spector glanced around and tried to work out what had driven the young man to speed away with such alacrity. His eye was caught by a nondescript parishioner, a balding man with a dreary moustache. He was short, fat, and neither particularly handsome nor remarkably ugly. An ordinary man. But he was staring at Jeffrey with pure hatred. The church was a place of sanctuary, and yet this ordinary parishioner had the fires of hell in his eyes.

Spector opted to follow Jeffrey, while the others made their own way home at a plodding pace.

The uphill trek back to Marchbanks was considerably more demanding than the outward journey. Spector was out of breath when he finally reached the familiar iron gates, allowing Leonard to catch up to him.

"Spector," the actor said, "the other night you showed us a trick with a rope. It was untied, then you gave it a flick and the silk knot appeared."

"Did I?"

"You did. It was an impressive trick. Care to explain how you did it?"

Not taking his eyes off Flack, who trudged on ahead, Spector said, "It's bad form for a magician to explain the method behind his tricks."

Leonard grinned slyly. "Are you sure I can't persuade you?"

Spector chuckled. "Sleight of hand, that's all it is. The silk knot is tied in the *other* end of the rope, the end gripped in the magician's palm. The motion of flicking the rope confuses the spectator's eye, it allows the magician to grab the loose end between thumb and forefinger, releasing the knotted end at the same time. It creates the illusion that a knot has been tied in under a second."

In spite of himself, Leonard was impressed.

"Now," continued Spector, "perhaps you'd care to explain something to *me*."

"If I'm able."

"I should like to know where you were last night. It seems a little unusual that you didn't come to Marchbanks as soon as you heard what had happened."

"I had a few things to take care of in town."

"I see."

They continued walking, their feet skidding and crunching on the mildly perilous terrain.

"It was you, wasn't it, who took a shot at your father the other night?"

Leonard stopped suddenly, almost slipping into a roadside ditch. "What the hell are you talking about?"

"Keep your voice down. Do you want everybody to hear?"

"I want to know where you get off making that kind of accusation . . ."

"Your bluster only confirms my suspicion, Leonard."

There was little point in trying to deny it. Leonard had been caught totally off guard and had given himself away.

"Bloody clever fellow, aren't you?" he said bitterly.

"Not particularly. The more I considered the events of that evening, the more obvious it became that the attempt on the judge's life was a desperate act. You wanted to stop him from doing something. I learned afterward that he'd recently met with his solicitor to discuss altering his will. And then I realised *our* meeting that evening was based on a misunderstanding. When your father escorted me into his study to talk business, you concluded that the will was to be changed then and there, didn't you? You know that a change of will requires a witness, and you thought *I* was to be that witness. You needed to put a stop to that, didn't you? That was the rationale behind your actions."

"I don't see how you're so positive it was me. Could have been Ambrose or Jeffrey, couldn't it? Even Sylvester."

"Not Sylvester. I doubt *he'd* have made the mistake that you did."

"What mistake?"

"A gap in your legal knowledge. It takes *two* witnesses for a will to be changed."

Leonard gave a hearty guffaw. Falstaffian bluster in the face of his own ignorance. But he didn't deny it.

Spector resumed, "It couldn't have been Jeffrey Flack for two reasons. First, he knew the real reason I was there that night. And second, it would make no difference to him if Sir Giles changed his will; Flack is not recognised in it.

"Which leaves you and Ambrose. Between the two of you, I deemed *you* the likelier suspect because *you* had more to lose. You are your father's primary legatee. He's made no secret of it, has he? After all, he's an old-fashioned sort of fellow. Very keen on heredity, and the sanctity of the first-born. That's why you've always been the favourite. I'm right, aren't I?"

"Let's say you are. What are you going to do about it? Have me arrested?"

"No. At least, not yet. Because as you and I both know, there is very little in the way of tangible evidence to indict you. And if I were to tell the judge what I had learned, I'm sure you'd find some insufferable means of talking yourself out of it, wouldn't you?"

Leonard laughed. "I am the favourite son, after all."

"Besides," said Spector, "now that you know the *real* reason I'm here, you've no need to put an end to your father, do you. Now you know he has no plans to change the will."

"No plans *yet*," Leonard amended.

"But I'll be watching you, Mr. Drury. Very carefully. I want you to remember that."

The conjuror looked on as Jeffrey Flack reached the front door of Marchbanks and disappeared inside. By the time the rest of the party entered the hall, Flack was already bounding up the stairs.

"What's got into him?" Lady Elspeth said quietly, speaking to no one in particular.

The judge held his tongue and made for the stairs too.

"Spector, come with me," Leonard said. The old man's eyes were still tilted toward the landing where Jeffrey Flack had just disappeared from view. "Spector! Are you listening? Come with me. Something has just occurred to me. I think it may be important."

Spector followed Leonard into the music room, beside the studio where Ambrose was presumably still hard at work. The music room was somewhat sparse, with bare boards and minimal wall decoration in the form of friezes depicting musical notes.

The conjuror followed Leonard over to the window, where the actor hastily commenced, "Listen, I . . ."

But he got no further than that.

Time stopped.

A cataclysmic blast shook the very foundations of the house. It came from upstairs. Spector darted for the door and plunged into the hall. Lady Elspeth was at the bottom of the stairs, gripping the banister, apparently struggling to summon the courage for the ascent.

"Oh God," she said. "Oh, Christ. They've killed him."

"That was a shot," said Spector. "All of you, wait down here."

Ambrose had now emerged from his studio. Both he and Leonard comforted their mother.

As Spector mounted the first step, Becky the maid came running out of the study, her sensible shoes thundering. She pointed at the front door.

"He went that way!" she yelled. "I saw him coming round the side of the house. He ran by the study window!"

Leonard hurled the front door open, admitting a swirl of blustery air. From his vantage point on the first step, Spector could make out a black figure—scarcely identifiable as a man at all—bolting down the drive, little more than a humanoid blur against the grey-white land.

"After him!" Leonard roared, but Spector grabbed his shoulder to stop him.

"No," he said, "stay here. Telephone the police."

And with that he began to climb the stairs.

He found Sir Giles on the landing. Contrary to his expectation, the judge was alive and well, but the look on his face was one of extreme shock and agitation.

"Jeffrey," he said mechanically. "Jeffrey." He was looking down the hallway, and Spector followed his gaze.

Jeffrey Flack had been flung back into the corridor—*through* the flimsy wooden door of his room. That is, the room into which his things had recently been moved; the room that had previously been Leonard's. His chest was a mess of blood and tattered flesh. He lay on his back, more of the red stuff bubbling from his mouth.

"He's been shot," said the judge.

This was plain to see, but it was no mere bullet that had killed Jeffrey Flack. Both barrels of a shotgun had been emptied into his chest at very close range. The air was thick with smoke.

Spector and Sir Giles inched closer to Flack's brutalised body, which lay half in and half out of his room.

The conjuror plunged into the bedroom, and Sir Giles followed, shaking his head slowly.

"I don't understand," he said. "There's nobody here. I . . . I just can't fathom it. Somebody shot Jeffrey dead. I saw it happen. But where did the bastard go? He must have jumped out the window. Don't you think so, Spector?" Sir Giles traipsed over to the little bay window and gripped the latch to heave it up and open. But even with all his strength, the window wouldn't budge. He grunted and tugged at it.

Giving up, he began pacing the length of the bedroom. He tore the sheets from the bed and threw open the wardrobe. But the gunman was gone.

"Somebody killed him," he murmured under his breath. "*Somebody* killed him."

Spector was now standing over the corpse, whose problems were over. Jeffrey lay on his back, broken bits of door beneath him, an eerie, mirthless grin on his face, his half-lidded gaze fixed on the ceiling.

"Nobody came out of the room?" Spector said.

"Nobody. I was on the landing. I saw Jeffrey come in here. I heard him bolt the door. Then somebody shot him dead. The door buckled and he came flying out."

Spector dropped to his haunches to examine the doorframe's bolt housing. It had splintered, bits of broken wood now protruding messily. So Flack had indeed bolted the door behind him.

With his back to the judge, Spector permitted himself the slightest of smiles. It was the one thing the case had been missing. A locked room.

CHAPTER TEN

THE PERMANENT RESIDENT

I.

T he madman's hair hung from his wide widow's peak in greased-together cords of black. It was long hair that spilled over his collar and put George Flint in mind of a photograph he had once seen of Edgar Allan Poe.

Indeed, Victor Silvius had much in common with Poe. Those same sunken, haunted eyes, that same sallow complexion. The same obsession with a dead woman. But whereas Poe's look was one of morbid resignation—the face of a man who had confronted death—Victor had a wildness to him. He had a long beard streaked with grey; no effort had been made to trim or treat it. Like some hollow-eyed hermit he had forsaken his place in the modern world. He was a refugee from a distant past, or from a land of ghosts.

He looked down at his hands, which were surprisingly thin and delicate. The hands of an artist, not a killer.

There was something poignant in the way his shirt was buttoned all the way to his throat. He looked as though he had not dressed himself. Worse than that, this little detail gave him the appearance of a creature that was merely impersonating a human being. A man who had had the life drained out of him.

Before venturing out to The Grange, Flint had done a little digging. But the more digging he did, the less there was to see. Asking around his senior colleagues at the Yard had yielded nothing on Victor Silvius, to the point where Flint had almost begun to wonder if the fellow existed at all. But there could be no denying that Moncrieff's clinic was real.

In the decade following the Great War, Jasper Moncrieff had done sterling work helping to rebuild the shattered bodies of soldiers whose limbs and faces had been torn to shreds by shrapnel or scorched by firebombs. This earned Moncrieff considerable good will, plus a hefty wedge of money, from various high-society families whose sons had fallen foul of the Hun. But over the years Moncrieff had grown increasingly interested in the broken *minds* of his quarry. Shellshock, mania, melancholy; he pursued these beguiling phantasms with growing fascination. By the time the 1930s dawned, Moncrieff was running out of soldiers. This, coupled with the fact that his research had taken a singularly dark turn, pursuing a path of abnormal psychology, meant that Moncrieff himself was becoming more and more of a "fringe" figure. An eccentric and—increasingly—an embarrassment. His clinic had shrunk considerably since its post-war heyday, and now occupied a Georgian dwelling in the wilds of Hampshire, a couple of miles from the small market town of Benhurst.

These days the "clinic" was in fact a private sanatorium that offered occasional drying-out services to high-society drunkards. And with the revenue these treatments generated, Dr. Moncrieff continued his other research unhindered. Discretion was the byword here—to the point of almost sinister secretiveness. As far as Flint had been able to discern, Moncrieff's enterprise had rarely been subjected to even the most rudimentary checks and balances. The clinic functioned in a vacuum, outside of the petty bureaucracies that might have tempered the doctor's research. Moncrieff also cheerfully performed the odd lobotomy on troublesome sons or daughters of his high-society friends.

He was generous with his favours, and as such he was permitted to do more or less as he pleased with the remaining facilities at his disposal. The clinic housed only three "permanent residents," in a cloistered wing of reinforced doors and barred windows.

Flint had walked from The Old Ram to the Benhurst station that morning and been surprised to find Caroline Silvius waiting for him. He'd made a point of getting there at least thirty minutes before the appointed meeting time, and yet here she was, greeting him again with a curiously luminous smile. It was almost as if she felt a kinship with Flint that had not been there before.

"I took the earlier train," she explained.

He supposed he had taken a leap of faith in coming out here at all. She slipped her arm through his as they promenaded along the platform. It was eleven in the morning, but the sun had not fully risen. The sky had a kind of dusky greyness that matched Flint's curious mood.

"Thank you," she said to him as they walked.

"What for?"

"For listening to me. I didn't think you would come."

"Whyever not?" said Flint, feeling himself blush slightly and hoping the young lady did not notice.

"You'd be surprised how many people have turned a blind eye in the past."

Flint could well believe it. He spoke with the stationmaster, who telephoned for a car to take them out to Moncrieff's clinic.

II.

They were met by the head orderly, a mean-looking cove who wouldn't have been out of place in one of those Hogarth prints depicting the worst excesses of Bedlam. His name was Thomas Griffin. He had a square head, flat nose, and silvery muttonchops. His white uniform stretched tautly across a fat belly, and he towered a good eight inches above Flint.

Griffin had been a soldier; Flint could tell from his bearing. He wondered idly what regiment the deranged orderly had graced with his presence.

And that was when Flint got his first look at the madman, Victor Silvius.

Brother and sister embraced, and then Flint stepped forward to shake hands with Silvius. The Inspector ran through the story Caroline had told him the other day and tried to place *this* Victor Silvius in the role of lover and poet turned knife-wielding avenger.

Silvius gestured for his sister and Flint to sit on the bed. They did, and Flint felt the straw-filled mattress sink beneath his weight.

Silvius stood.

"What you must understand, Mr. Flint, is that I know full well that I am mad. I have, after all, had nine long years to consider the nature of madness. But surely we are all mad people, in one form or another?" He was softly-spoken and perfectly reasonable. And Flint could not fault his argument.

"You may well be right."

"The difference between myself and your average madman is that I know full well what has made me mad. My enemy has a face and a name. Giles Drury. He killed the one woman who ever meant anything to me. Apart, that is, from my dear sister."

Caroline looked at Flint pointedly.

"Perhaps," Flint said, "you'd better tell me the story."

"Very well. I first met Gloria at a dance, through a mutual friend. It was . . . love at first sight. And I flatter myself that it was reciprocal. We began courting. Unlike myself, Gloria came from rather a poor family. She had originally worked as a maid in one of the London hotels, and used the money to fund her secretarial studies. When I met her, she was a clerk in Drury's office. Soon afterward, he promoted her to the role of private secretary.

"Anyway, it wasn't long before I made my decision. I wanted her to marry me. To become Mrs. Silvius." He closed his eyes at the memory. A curious commixture of bliss and agony danced across his face. "When I asked her, bless her heart, she said yes. That was the happiest day of my life.

"We began our preparations in earnest. I for one was particularly glad she would finally be able to give up working altogether. I had my nest egg, you see, and we could comfortably live on that. But before she got the chance to hand in her notice to Drury . . ."

"She died," Flint finished for him.

"Murdered."

"Her death is recorded as a suicide."

"Ludicrous," Silvius spat. "She was murdered. And Sir Giles is the one who killed her." He spoke with such fierce conviction that Flint almost let himself be swept along by the madman's argument.

"So you decided to murder him in return."

"I did what any man would have done. I lost my mind. And now, I am as you see me. This place is full of lunatics. They surround me on all sides. You know who is the other side of that wall? The Edgemoor Strangler. Remember him?"

Flint did.

"He's surprisingly easy to get on with. We've spent many a night chatting through the wall, setting the world to rights. And what about the other side? Any guesses? No? Well, I'll tell you: It's the Ambergate Arsonist."

"Your sister," Flint said, as though Caroline were not sitting next to him, "believes that someone is trying to kill you."

Victor's eyes grew a little wider and he said softly, "They are in it together, you know. The judge and the doctor. What you must understand, Inspector Flint, is that they are both *Tragedians . . .*"

As though this last word were some kind of cue, the cell door swung inward and the orderly, Thomas Griffin, reappeared in the doorway with his arms folded. He was dressed in white from head to foot, including a pair of squeaky plimsolls. He was a hulking, statuesque presence.

"Time's up," he said.

"Just two more minutes . . ." Caroline pleaded.

"No. Time's up now."

Silvius scampered into a corner.

Flint squared up to the orderly, but the difference in height between the two men made the spectacle almost comic. "You know I'm from Scotland Yard?" Flint demanded.

"I do, sir," said Griffin, with the unspoken coda that he could not have cared less. "Orders from Dr. Moncrieff."

"Well," Flint concluded, not taking his eyes off Griffin, "then I suppose we don't have a choice."

"You'll come back soon, won't you? Won't you?" There was a pleading plaintiveness to Victor Silvius's voice.

Flint and Caroline filed out of the cell.

"Yes," said Caroline, "of course . . ." She tried to take a last look at her brother through the bars, but Griffin blocked her way as he pulled shut the door.

"I'd like a word with you, Griffin," said Flint, adding pointedly: "in private."

"This way," said Griffin, leading Flint and Caroline back along the corridor, through another door which he locked behind them, and into more recognisably administrative surroundings. Here, it might have been any other country hospital, somewhat spartan but functional nonetheless.

"I said *private*."

"This is the best you'll get," Griffin told him.

Caroline stood by as Flint drew Griffin aside. "Look here, what's the meaning of all this? The draconian measures? That man's no more dangerous than I am."

"Orders from Dr. Moncrieff," Griffin repeated, failing to modulate his voice, so Caroline could hear every word. "I do what I'm told, Mr. Flint. No more, no less."

"That's *Inspector* Flint," Flint reminded him, though he was not usually precious about such things. "All right, I'd like to see Dr. Moncrieff."

"He's in town today."

"When will he be back?"

"Couldn't say, sir. But until he *is*," Griffin could scarcely conceal his pleasure, "I'm in charge."

III.

"I don't like that Griffin fellow," said Flint when he and Caroline were out in the frosty air once again.

Caroline's voice cracked a little as she said, "It breaks my heart to think of my brother in the hands of that monster."

"Is there no legal means by which his situation could be reviewed?"

She shook her head. "Giles Drury holds too much sway over Moncrieff. As things stand, there's no way my brother will be certified as anything other than a gibbering lunatic. Drury's vindictiveness outweighs everything. There's only one possible way in which my brother might ever see the light of day again. And that, truthfully, is the reason I called on you to help me."

"Oh yes?"

"If you can prove that Sir Giles murdered Gloria Crain."

Flint did not reply straight away. When he did, he chose his words carefully: "You believe that if Drury were out of the equation, the medical establishment might be able to give your brother a fair hearing."

"Yes! That's it exactly. That's why I wanted you to see Victor for yourself, so that you'd understand the conditions they're keeping him in. They treat him like an animal, Mr. Flint."

They were almost at the gates. A porter stepped out of the gatehouse to let them go.

As Flint and Caroline retraced their steps toward Benhurst and civilisation, Flint spoke again. "Miss Silvius, I've no doubt that your brother's predicament is a very dire one indeed, but I'm afraid I've seen nothing to indicate that his life is in danger. And as such, there's very little Scotland Yard can do."

"You mean you're not even going to speak to Moncrieff?" She sounded desperate now.

"I will," he assured her. "But you must prepare yourself, Miss Silvius, for the likelihood that nothing will come of it."

Was there really a conspiracy on the part of the Tragedians? A plot to keep Silvius out of the way, so that his awkward questions about Gloria Crain's death would remain unasked?

Flint and Miss Silvius were walking back toward the station when a police car rolled up beside them and a voice from within called out, "Sir!"

Flint halted and peered inside. "Hook? What's the matter?"

"Lucky I caught you, sir. It's Marchbanks. Some more trouble to do with Giles Drury. A second man has been killed."

CHAPTER ELEVEN

A REASON FOR EVERYTHING

I.

W hen George Flint stepped out of the police car and into the shadow of Marchbanks, he felt a wave of palpable anguish roll over him. Like Spector he believed a place retained echoes, the shadows left by its residents. But unlike Spector, he also believed in ghosts. If he'd glimpsed Gloria Crain or Sylvester Monkton gazing down at him from one of the upstairs windows, he would not have been surprised.

Spector came out to meet him. The magician was irritable—not because of the murder itself, but its circumstances.

"A vanishing killer?" said Flint incredulously.

"A vanishing killer," Spector confirmed.

Flint gave a resigned nod. "All right then," he said.

Before Flint's arrival, Spector had conducted a sweep of the ground floor at Marchbanks. He started with the kitchen, where

Mrs. Runcible and Alma the cook had been when they heard the shot. Becky was dusting (read: snooping) in the judge's study when the shot came, peering out of the window as the man ran by. Now she was crying at the kitchen table as she recounted the tale. Spector listened patiently, but her account was lacking crucial descriptors that might help to identify the running man. Mrs. Runcible stood stoically by the small, net-curtained window, contemplating the small patch of garden that was visible. But there could be no question of alibis. She and Alma had been together—that was the end of it.

Next, Spector went out of the side door and toward the garage, where Peter Nightingale was in his shirtsleeves, in spite of the cold. He had a bucket of water and a sponge, and was in the midst of washing the Austin Seven. He had been in his room for an hour, taking care of his employer's correspondence, before coming out to perform a bit of maintenance on the car, followed by a wash. Not much of an alibi, as he'd been in nobody's line of sight for a long while.

Spector studied the Austin, which was unmistakably clean, but noticed a few wisps of steam rising from the bonnet. "Are you sure you haven't taken this car anywhere this morning?"

"I had to turn the engine over a few times," Nightingale responded without hesitation. "To keep it from freezing up."

Spector gave a slow—though not altogether convinced—nod. In contrast, the Bugatti's brash shade of blue was muted by dust and grime. Its bonnet was open, revealing the confusion of metal and cables that made up its engine.

"You've been working on Ambrose's car as well," he observed.

The secretary looked suddenly bashful. "As a matter of fact, no. I was curious, that's all. You don't see too many Type 35s these days."

Spector considered the engine in all its ugly functionality. Some people, he reflected, had an almost instinctive understanding of mechanics; they knew without being told the rightful place of every cylinder rod, piston ring, and sparking plug. Spector's technical knowledge was limited; he could just about spot the lime-green brake cable, twined like a wily serpent around the purple and grey petrol gauge connectors. He had a different sort of brain.

He strolled idly toward the wooden workbench at the far end of the outbuilding. To his moderate surprise, several items seemed to have been moved around since that morning. "Nightingale, did you touch anything here?"

"No, sir. Though I understand Sir Giles requested that the shovels be moved in readiness for tonight's snowfall."

Spector nodded. "I see. Well, I'll leave you to it. But if you happen to remember anything that might prove useful, do let me know."

From the garage, he headed round the rear of the house and entered Ambrose's studio, which was now empty. He looked out at the garden, taking in the vista of smooth, unspoiled snow. He went over to the French window and opened it, admitting a gust of glacial air. Then he stepped outside and peered up at the sealed window of the murder room. Whichever way the killer had gone, it was not this way. He was just ruminating on the problem when news reached him that Inspector Flint had arrived.

In a flagrant breach of domestic protocol, Mrs. Runcible was sitting beside Lady Elspeth on the divan in the salon. Lady Elspeth appeared to be in shock. She sat upright, her hands clasped in her lap, staring dead ahead with the troubling glazedness of a mannequin. Mrs. Runcible poured tea from a silver service and kept a close eye on her mistress. On his way through the salon to the study, Spector perceived a quiet sympathy between the two women.

Now that Flint was on the scene, things began to move quickly. The operation was undertaken with military efficiency—the occupation of Sir Giles's study, that is. It was indeed a splendid room, lined with oak panels and shelves of leather-bound volumes. Pausing to scrutinise some of the titles, Spector saw mainly esoteric legal tomes—very little to stir his colourful imagination.

They spoke with Sir Giles first. As the master of the house, this was only fitting. He paced the rug like a caged animal.

Spector sat in silence while Flint ran through his rigmarole. "I understand you saw the shooting take place?"

"I was at the top of the stairs. I saw Jeffrey go into his room and . . . come out again."

"He stepped into the room with the killer, bolting the door behind him. The killer fired both barrels of a shotgun, the impact of which took Mr. Flack off his feet and sent him *through* the door out into the corridor. Wrenched the very door from its hinges. And you never took your eyes from the doorway?"

"What do you mean?"

"Well, I'd like to establish whether or not a killer could have got out via the corridor."

"For God's sake man, do you think I'm a complete imbecile? What do you suppose I did when I heard that explosion and saw poor Jeffrey? I went running over."

"But you couldn't see *into* the bedroom?"

"Not from where I stood."

"And the killer couldn't have got out?"

"As I have said to you a hundred times, *no*, a killer could not have got out of that room past me."

"Then that just leaves the window."

"He didn't go out that way either."

"How can you be sure?"

"Because the window frame is warped."

"I see. Has it always been that way?"

Sir Giles huffed. "Strangely enough, Inspector Flint, I don't make a habit of memorising the various peccadillos of every single aperture in this wretched house. I haven't a clue. You'll have to ask somebody else. But the window is warped now. I tried it myself. And so did Spector."

Flint's gaze snapped toward the conjuror, who nodded. This was correct.

It was Flint's turn to exhale bemusedly. "Well, sir, if all this happened the way you say it did—and of course I've no cause to doubt you—then it seems to be something of an impossible scenario. The killer didn't leave via the door, nor did he leave via the window. You and Joseph Spector searched the room, so there's no way he could have been hiding in there. So where did he go?"

II.

When the investigators had the study to themselves once more, Flint said, "So you saw the man?"

"We saw *a* man. The shape of a man, running down the drive. Not the killer, of course. It couldn't have been the killer."

"Why not?"

Spector shrugged. "Because it makes no sense. The shooting took place in an upstairs room on the south side of the house. The man appeared a moment later on the *north* side, running down the drive. Peter Nightingale claims he saw him running round past the garage. But why would he take such a risk, when he could just as easily have made his escape across the south lawn and into the trees? Additionally, this presupposes that he escaped from the crime scene via a seemingly impenetrable window. We've yet to establish how he managed that."

Flint was flipping through his notebook. "Nightingale. That's Leonard Drury's secretary, isn't it? I must have a little chat with him," he said. "Well, Spector? How do you explain it? It's impossible, isn't it?"

"Not impossible," Spector reassured him. "A puzzle. An enigma. A conundrum. But never impossible, Flint. *Nothing* is impossible."

The Scotland Yard man, however, was unconvinced. "I'm going to see how they're getting on with the search." Then he left the room without waiting for the conjuror to comment.

"Hook," he said, bumping into the sergeant at the bottom of the stairs, "I need you to do something for me."

"Yes, sir?"

"Spector's already questioned the servants, but I need you to take their statements officially."

"Yes, sir."

"But there's something else. Leonard's secretary—one Peter Nightingale. He seems like a colourful character. And he's a stranger in the household. Do a bit of digging, would you?"

"Right you are, sir."

When Flint got outside, he saw that the light was already beginning to fade. Fortunately, his men had made considerable progress with combing the grounds. They had turned up a few bootprints in the mud and murky grass of the northern lawn. A man had indeed come this way.

But that was not all. In a ditch about half a mile north of Marchbanks, they found a shotgun. Examination showed that not only had it been recently fired, but it conformed almost exactly to the model that had inflicted those savage wounds on Sylvester. Of course, a shotgun is much more difficult to identify than, say, a revolver. One is much like another, and the ballistics of a shotgun cannot be pinpointed with the accuracy of a smaller calibre weapon. But the circumstantial evidence was enough for Flint.

This added yet another layer of complexity to the puzzle.

The few bootprints the intruder left behind him, as well as the location in which the shotgun had been found, seemed to indicate that he had indeed run across the north lawn, through the trees, then made off across the fields. So far, so good.

However, Flint did not find this altogether satisfactory. If the shotgun was the murder weapon, how did the killer escape from the room? And why take the shotgun with him at all, only to drop it in a ditch half a mile away? There could be little doubt that the weight and shape of the weapon would have impeded his escape. If he was going to drop the weapon, why not do so in the bedroom, the scene of the crime?

Then there were the bootprints themselves. Flint got down on his hands and knees to scrutinise them through a magnifying glass, but for the life of him could not pick out any distinguishing features. They were a size eleven; but then, so were a lot of people's. So were Flint's own. This told him precisely nothing.

III.

Seizing upon the lull in the investigation, Joseph Spector took the opportunity for another stroll around the ground floor rooms. Lady Elspeth was still in the salon, but she had forsaken the divan for the window, and now stood gazing forlornly out at the northern lawn, where numerous officers were still making careful surveys of the terrain.

Mrs. Runcible was back in the kitchen, and that's where Spector found her.

"I'd like to ask a question if I may," he said.

She glanced at Alma the cook, who was sitting at the kitchen table with a faintly amused expression.

"Very well," said Mrs. Runcible. "Out here."

She escorted Spector back into the corridor, glanced up and down to make sure they were unobserved, then said, "Well?"

Spector wasted no time. "Why were Leonard's things moved into Jeffrey Flack's room?"

Instantly defensive, Mrs. Runcible spoke through pinched lips. "They were moved at Master Leonard's request, and with the full knowledge of the late Mr. Flack."

"So they swapped rooms?"

"They did."

"Why?"

"I'm afraid to say that Master Leonard was inadvertently allocated the incorrect room."

"So he demanded his usual room when he arrived?"

"Nothing out of the ordinary in that, sir. When he got here and found he was in the wrong room, he asked to do a swap. So I got the maid to see to his things."

Spector considered her answer carefully. "This maid—Becky, isn't it?"

"That's right, sir. Been in service here three years or so. And with Mrs. Valdane some seven years before that."

"Ten years! But she's so young!"

"Twenty-six, sir. Old enough to know her job better than she does."

Spector spoke more to himself than to Mrs. Runcible now. "So Leonard had his things moved into Jeffrey's room . . ."

"If you'll excuse me, sir, I've the lunch menu to see to."

"Just one more thing," Spector persisted. "The window of that room—the wooden frame is warped. Can you explain that?"

She shrugged. "It's an old house."

"When did you last air out the rooms?"

"That's the maid's responsibility."

"And when did she do it?"

"Before the guests arrived."

"And was the window in working order then?"

Mrs. Runcible looked distinctly uncomfortable as she confessed in hushed tones, "I'm afraid, sir, that the unanticipated arrival of Jeffrey Flack meant that not all of the rooms were aired. Becky opted to put Leonard Drury into the room at the top of the stairs. This, in spite of the fact she *knew* his preferred room was the corner one. So she did not air the corner room. However, as Mr. Flack arrived *before* Mr. Drury, he was given his pick of rooms. Mr. Flack selected the corner one—Leonard's—because it has the best view."

"What about Ambrose?"

"Master Ambrose has his usual room. The same one he had as a boy."

Spector considered this new information. "So in other words, Mrs. Runcible, you don't know if the window was in working order."

She inclined her head. "As you say, sir."

Then, not waiting for his permission, she headed back into the kitchen, swinging the door shut in the magician's face.

When Spector came back through the salon, he found Lady Elspeth stretched out on the divan this time. Her eyes were fluttering, and a man was standing beside her—a man Spector had never seen before. Nor had he heard him arrive. He was handsome and well-dressed; "distinguished" was perhaps the word.

The man looked at Spector and raised a finger to his lips. "I've got her under sedation," he said softly, "but it's best if we keep quiet for the time being."

Spector nodded. "You are her doctor?"

"My name is Moncrieff, Dr. Moncrieff. Friend of the family."

"I see. A friend of Sir Giles, is that so?"

Moncrieff gave Spector a somewhat suspicious glance, but at that moment Sir Giles himself came into the room.

"There you are, Spector," he said. "Wanted to introduce Moncrieff, he's an old pal of mine. I telephoned him as soon as I could. He's a good sort, he'll take care of Elspeth."

"When convenient," Moncrieff said, "I would suggest relocating Lady Elspeth to her bedroom."

"Right you are. Scotch, Jasper?"

Throwing another awkward little glance at Spector, Dr. Moncrieff said, "Don't mind if I do."

Sir Giles did the honours, going over to the well-stocked drinks cabinet along the far wall. He did not offer Spector a drink.

"Dr. Moncrieff," said the magician, "am I right in thinking that Victor Silvius is currently in your care?"

Sir Giles signalled his disapproval with a theatrical clatter of glasses, but Moncrieff was candid. "That's right. Why do you ask?"

"He's been a permanent resident at your clinic for nine years, isn't that so?"

"Look here, Spector," put in Sir Giles, "what's this got to do with what happened to Jeffrey?"

"I wonder," said the conjuror thoughtfully.

At that moment, Peter Nightingale slipped surreptitiously into the room. "Forgive me," he said, "I believe I left my cigarettes in here."

"Dji Sam Soe," said Spector, retrieving the pack from the coffee table. "I noticed the scent earlier. An exotic brand."

"I have exotic tastes."

Moncrieff, who was looking quizzically at the newcomer, said, "I don't believe we've met, have we?"

"That's Leonard's secretary," explained Sir Giles. "Don't mind him."

But by the time he had finished speaking, Nightingale was already gone.

IV.

There was another person whom Spector had yet to question. He found Ambrose in his studio, still hard at work on his latest canvas, and still clad in his ridiculous garb.

"I see you haven't let this tragedy disturb your process," Spector observed.

"Far from it," said the young man. "In fact, I rather think it's helped." He spun the easel to show Spector his latest creation—the portrait of Leonard Drury that was formless and shockingly abstract. Just a blur of darkness.

Spector blinked at the bizarre, otherworldly composition. "Remarkable," he said.

"You like it?"

"It's . . . remarkable," the old conjuror repeated. "Is this what you were working on when you heard the shot upstairs?"

"Yes. It's come on since you saw it earlier, wouldn't you say?"

Spector stepped forward and leaned in close, examining the individual brushstrokes. He reached out and gently prodded them with his fingertips. To his surprise, Ambrose did not protest. "A truly startling piece of work."

A creak of the floorboards overhead made him jump. Ambrose looked at the ceiling. "They're moving him, I suppose."

Spector nodded. "That will be Findler. He's with Scotland Yard. Very thorough. He'll be going over every inch of the crime scene as we speak. So tell me, Ambrose, exactly what you heard and saw."

Ambrose shrugged. "It's all somewhat of a blur. But the shotgun blast gave me an awful fright. I ran for the stairs. Too late, of course. Jeffrey was already dead in the corridor. But then, you know well enough, don't you?"

"Yes," answered Joseph Spector. "I do. Did you see anyone on the south lawn?"

Ambrose thought about this very carefully. "I can't be sure," he said.

"Oh? Why not?"

Ambrose looked around, as though hoping somebody else might step in and rescue him. "I was working," he said. "I didn't see anyone."

Spector's next stop was the crime scene itself, where Findler was in the midst of examining the window.

"Ah," he said, "Spector. If anyone can make sense of this mess it'll be you. Come here, will you?"

Spector did as instructed.

"I've been trying for a good ten minutes," said Findler, "and I can't for the life of me work out what's wrong with this window. It's not locked. And it doesn't *appear* to be warped. Yet it won't open."

Spector ran his fingertips along the surface of the window frame. "This isn't warped at all," he commented. Then he placed his palms either side of the window. "As a matter of fact, I think it's the jambliner."

"The what?"

"The jambs are the vertical parts of the frame. And in order for the sash to slide up and down easily, there should be a strip of jambliner on each side that fits snugly round the outer edges of the sash. It's the jambliner, and not the frame itself, that's warped."

"What does that mean?"

Spector shrugged. "Your guess is as good as mine. But I think it's notable, all the same."

Just as they were examining the frame a little more closely, Flint came into the room.

"Well?" said Spector. "Any developments?"

"Plenty," answered Flint, though he did not seem particularly pleased. "Footprints for one. Shotgun for another."

"Shotgun? So you've found the murder weapon?"

"Possibly. Both barrels were empty, and it looked to have been fired recently. Any ideas, Findler?"

Getting to his feet with a groan, the doctor answered, "Well, there's no question the shot was fired from inside the room." He stepped about a foot away from the window. "I'd say from about *here*. Point-blank. Damn fool never stood a chance."

"Could it have been some sort of device? A booby trap?"

"Don't see how. I mean, in theory the idea is sound. But there would be traces in the room. Some sort of apparatus. Spector tells me he was in the corridor when the shot came, and that he was one of the first in the room. He'd have noticed, wouldn't he?"

"Moncrieff was here," Spector said, eager to change the subject.

"Here? What for?"

"To sedate Lady Elspeth. Sir Giles telephoned for him while you were out looking at the shotgun. You must have missed him by moments."

"This is a very messy case," commented Flint. "Whoever's behind it, they are out to make a fool of me. I don't care for it one bit."

"They're out to make fools of all of us," Spector reassured him, "and they are going to fail. Come with me, Flint. I must refill my cigarillo case, and then we may return to the study."

Before heading back downstairs the two men took a brief detour to Spector's room. While the conjuror refilled his silver case, Flint looked around.

"So this is where Gloria Crain died ten years ago?"

"Indeed."

Flint approached one of the walls and leaned forward so that his nose was almost touching it. He sniffed.

"It makes me wonder about the walls," said Flint. "I mean, we've all heard stories about arsenic in this Victorian wallpaper."

"Arsenic," said Spector, "not strychnine."

All the same, Flint ran his hand along the tactile surface of the Anaglypta, then gave his fingertips a sniff. "Odourless," he said.

"Hardly surprising," said Spector.

"But I wonder," Flint persisted, "if it *could* have been done this way? Some sort of poison seeping out through the walls?"

"You forget," Spector corrected him, "that the poison in Gloria Crain was ingested, not inhaled."

Getting a little irritable, Flint said, "I'm waiting to hear *your* theory."

"Then you'll have to wait a little longer. For now, let's focus on the murder of Jeffrey Flack."

They headed back down to the study, and once Spector had eased shut the door, Flint demanded, "What do you make of it, then?"

"Very little, I'm afraid."

"Oh, come now. You were here! You saw the whole thing!"

"I saw nothing."

Flint sighed, hanging his head. He felt exhausted. He scarcely had the energy to fish for his pipe in the pocket of his overcoat.

But Spector was smiling. "You misunderstand me, Flint. I saw nothing, but seeing nothing can sometimes be just as instructive as seeing everything."

Flint frowned. "What do you mean?"

But they were interrupted before the magician could answer.

The door swung open and Sergeant Hook barrelled into the study without knocking, shoulders heaving up and down as though he had been running.

"Sir. Mr. Spector," he panted. "It's all right. We've got him."

"Who?" Flint demanded.

"The killer, sir. Caught him in Benhurst. It's him all right, sir. We've had a tip-off."

"For God's sake, *who?*"

"Name's Arthur Cosgrove, sir."

Spector and Flint piled into the back seat of the waiting car, while Hook clambered into the front. Flint was struggling to mask his bemusement, while Spector remained silent and thoughtful as Hook explained the situation.

Cosgrove's wife, Ida, had committed suicide a few days prior, leaving behind a cache of letters that implicated Jeffrey Flack in a sordid blackmail scheme. Cosgrove had motive. The fact that he was in Benhurst presented a highly improbable coincidence. And on top of that, an anonymous telephone call had been made to the Benhurst police station, informing them of his location. He had surrendered without protest, and was now in one of the holding cells.

Arthur Cosgrove. It made sense in theory. But the method was impenetrable. Flint found himself returning to Valentine's dilemma: *How* was Flack killed in that particular way? And *why?*

The squat stone cottage that served Benhurst as a police station was thronged with people—constables from surrounding villages, and locals succumbing to the inevitable gossip about the murder up at the "big house." Village police were ill-equipped to deal with crime on the scale of the Marchbanks affair. But even if they *had* been, it would inevitably have ended up in the hands of Scotland Yard anyway. Fortunately, Spector's presence on the scene of both crimes had expedited matters.

Now, Hook led the way through the crowd, and a couple of camera bulbs flared. Reporters. They were quick off the mark. Almost as though someone had tipped them off. The same person, perhaps, who had phoned in the suspect's location?

"This way, sir," said Hook, escorting the two men through the front office and toward the cells in the rear of the building. Spector followed, his pale eyes taking in the blur of activity in the open-plan office—typewriters clacking, hushed conferences around desks.

Stepping through an ordinary-looking door, Spector felt as if he'd stepped back through time, to the era of the Inquisition. He was confronted by a row of grey stone cells with iron bars. Four cells in all, though Spector could not imagine the circumstances that might see them all occupied. Now, only one of them held a prisoner.

The squat, bald figure of Arthur Cosgrove sat alone and hunched in the end cell. A constable on guard in a creaky wooden chair leapt to his feet and saluted a little over-enthusiastically.

"This is Inspector Flint," said Hook, "and Mr. Spector. Here to interview the suspect."

"Yes, *sir*," said the constable, springing to unlock the cell door.

They filed into the cell and the constable discreetly pulled shut the barred door behind them.

Spector broke the silence. "Good afternoon," he said.

"Good afternoon," answered Arthur Cosgrove, with a thread of palpable despondency in his voice. His chin was downturned, his eyes were fixed on the floor. He looked almost as if he were collapsing in on himself, buckling under a great invisible weight.

"My name is Spector, and this is Flint. I presume you know why we're here."

"I have an idea. Somebody finally polished off that scoundrel Flack, is that it?"

Flint took over. "Why were you in Benhurst? What was your business?"

Cosgrove shrugged. "I had no business. I simply came to see the service."

"Then why did you travel out to Marchbanks?"

Cosgrove looked up for the first time, offering an ironic ripple of his eyebrows. "I didn't."

Flint changed tack. "I understand that you recently tried to have Jeffrey Flack prosecuted for his involvement in your wife's suicide. You claim he blackmailed her."

"He *did* blackmail her. He made her life hell. He convinced her there was no way out." Cosgrove said all this reasonably and with the quiet lucidity of a man who was beyond anger or pain. As though he were on a different plane of existence altogether, speaking from the depths of a trance. Like a golem; a clay man without a soul.

"And you hated him for it, didn't you." Flint did his best to match the suspect's tone.

"More than you'll ever know, Inspector."

Flint nodded slowly. "Did you kill him?"

"No," answered Cosgrove immediately. "No. I could have. I *would* have. But Ida would never have forgiven me."

"What if I were to tell you that you were seen running away from the Marchbanks estate in the aftermath of Flack's murder?"

"I would tell you that a man cannot be in two places at once."

"We have only your word."

Cosgrove shrugged. "My word is all I can give you."

Flint removed his pipe from between his tobacco-stained teeth and seemed about to say something further, but he restrained himself. Instead he got up, his chair shrieking on the stone floor, and left the cell.

Finding himself alone with Cosgrove, Spector said, "I saw you at the church this morning."

"Yes."

"Why did you go there? Were you waiting for Jeffrey Flack?"

"Nothing of the kind. I had no idea that Flack lived near the village. I simply went because I was invited."

"And who was it that invited you?"

Cosgrove smiled. "My wife." He seemed to ponder the two words, then continued, "She was no great beauty Mr. Spector. But look at me—neither was I. We suited each other. Oh, she was a lovely wife."

"I'm very sorry for your loss."

"Thank you. But at least I didn't have to watch her killer go unpunished for long. Not easy for a red-blooded type like me."

There was something tragicomic in the notion of Arthur Cosgrove as an avenging angel. He was squat, bald, and middle-aged, with a toothbrush moustache and small round spectacles. His gut strained against his waistcoat. But when he spoke there was such an earnest undercurrent to the measured timbre of his voice that Spector couldn't help but believe every word he said.

"You would have killed him, wouldn't you?"

"Oh, without a doubt. But only if I thought I could get away with it. I've no wish to rot in prison, you see. Ida wouldn't want that."

"*Did* you kill him?"

Arthur Cosgrove looked the old conjuror full in the face. "No, I didn't. I'm glad he's dead. But I swear on Ida's grave I didn't kill him. A man like Jeffrey Flack must have no shortage of people who wanted him dead."

Tacitly, Spector agreed. He studied Cosgrove thoughtfully. "You say your wife brought you to the village."

"Sounds absurd, doesn't it? The ramblings of a madman. Well, it's true. I wouldn't have come if not for her."

"Would you care to explain?"

Cosgrove smiled sadly. "I'm glad he's dead," he said. "I didn't kill him, but I'm glad he's dead." But he was no longer talking to Spector. He was talking to Ida.

Spector left the cell and the constable locked the door once again, sealing Arthur Cosgrove in with the memories of his deceased wife. The conjuror headed out into the main office, where Flint was conversing with a couple of uniformed officers.

"This is a waste of time," said Flint when he saw Spector approach. "That man obviously didn't kill Jeffrey Flack."

"I'm glad we can agree on that. I saw him at the church in the village this morning. He was still there when I headed back to Marchbanks. There's no way he could have beaten us to it on foot, and if he'd travelled by car or bicycle he would have left traces. He also ran the risk of being spotted."

"What about the man on the lawn? Could *that* have been Cosgrove?"

"I don't see how. If he'd approached the house from the north, he would have had to go all the way around, most likely through the trees. It would have taken significantly longer. The timing just doesn't add up."

"All right. So let me get this straight," said Flint. "Leonard Drury was downstairs."

"Correct, he and I were in the music room. And there's something else I need to tell you about Leonard, but it can wait until later."

"Right. Sir Giles and Lady Elspeth were with you, so that's them covered. Who else is there?"

"Becky, Runcible, and the cook. They were together in the kitchen. And there's Leonard's secretary, Peter Nightingale. He claims he was in the garage when the shot was fired. No witnesses."

"Aha," said Flint, "which reminds me: Hook? Where are you, Hook?"

The sergeant's head poked up from beneath a desk—he had ducked under to tie his shoelace.

"Did you get the chance to do any digging on Nightingale?"

"I made a telephone call, sir. Fortunately, most of it is a matter of public record. Bit of a daredevil, by my reckoning. Went out to Spain a couple of years ago and fought alongside the Tom Mann Centuria. Injured at the Battle of Jarama, and transferred to a field hospital in Córdoba. Eventually repatriated at the end of 1937, and it was while recuperating in a convalescent home that he crossed paths with Byron Manderby, the explorer. I understand they were treated by the same doctor. Anyway, Manderby was putting together a crew for his newest expedition, and Nightingale offered to tag along. He kept a journal of the trip, which was unfortunately cut short when Manderby contracted malaria. Nightingale arrived back in England at the beginning of December."

"Good work, Sergeant Hook," said Spector. "Thank you."

"But before you get too full of yourself," Flint went on, "I need you to check up on somebody else."

"Another suspect, sir?"

"No. At least, I don't think so. His name is Thomas Griffin. Chief orderly at The Grange, the sanatorium on the other side of Benhurst."

"Right, sir."

While Hook busied himself on the telephone again, Flint returned his attention to Spector. "There's somebody we haven't discussed yet. Brother Ambrose."

"He was in his studio," Spector explained. "Heard the gunshot and came running up the stairs. Looked somewhat green when he saw the corpse."

Flint rubbed his forehead, evidently battling a migraine. His eyes were red-rimmed and his skin sallow. He looked utterly miserable. "Then who was the man on the lawn?"

Spector gave a little sigh. "That remains to be seen. But whoever he was, he couldn't have fired the shot that killed Jeffrey. It's physically impossible."

"You're absolutely positive it couldn't have been Cosgrove?"

"Even if Cosgrove didn't have an alibi, that proves nothing. It doesn't explain how he was able to fire a shotgun into Jeffrey Flack at point-blank range without even setting foot into the house. It also doesn't explain what he did with the murder weapon. The *real* murder weapon," Spector swiftly extemporised, "not the rather obvious prop your men found in the woods. Somebody has made a ham-fisted attempt to frame him."

"I don't like this at all," Flint said quietly. He might have been speaking to himself. "The whole thing feels like a jigsaw with all the wrong pieces. They should fit, but they don't. It's all upside-down. Think about it, Spector. You're the killer. You've decided to finish Flack off once and for all with a shotgun blast at point-blank range. Right?"

"Right."

"That's not a discreet crime. It's the crime of a man who doesn't care who knows he's the killer, who doesn't care if he's caught or about facing the consequences of his actions. Still with me?"

"I think so."

"All right. In that case, why bother sneaking into the house like that? Why not simply wait for your victim to step outside and then blast him in broad daylight?"

"I think you're onto something," said Spector. "The weapon does not match the method."

"Why go to the trouble of engineering a disappearance like that, only to empty both barrels into the man in front of witnesses? And why let yourself be spotted running across the garden like that?"

"You seem to be forgetting," Spector put in, "that there's no evidence he was ever in that bedroom at all."

"No. No, you're right. But if he *wasn't*, then why was he there in the first place? He had no reason to visit the Drurys. And if he *wasn't* in the bedroom, who was?"

"Perhaps no one?"

"No, it won't do, Spector. I know you're an admirer of the remotely triggered murder device, but I don't see how it can have happened this time."

Spector closed his eyes. Unlike Flint, he relished the challenge. He had never encountered one quite like it. In a way, he admired the sheer backwardness of it. How every single interpretation had an equally valid opposing interpretation. The obvious suspect could not have committed the crime. But also, he could not *not* have committed the crime. An amusing paradox.

"I suppose there's no doubt that shotgun *was* the weapon?" Spector asked idly.

"We're as sure as we can be. Which, unfortunately, is not very sure. We can't examine ballistics for a double-barrelled job like that. It's not a matter of matching up calibres and serial numbers that it would be with a revolver."

"Interesting. Why do you think he did that?"

"What?"

"Used a shotgun. Such a loud and cumbersome weapon. It would have made more sense, wouldn't it, to procure a revolver for his wicked purpose? It would have made the whole thing easier all-round."

"Just another thing that makes no sense," said Flint.

"Yes," said Spector. "It has an almost Alice-in-Wonderland feel to it. None of it makes sense. And yet, I'm convinced there's a reason for everything."

That was the key to Spector's methodology. No matter how illogical or nonsensical the reason, there was nonetheless a reason for everything.

"All right," said Flint, "what about this: what's the *reason* that our eyewitness saw Arthur Cosgrove running away from the crime scene?"

"I'd have thought that was fairly obvious. He didn't."

"You think he's lying?"

"Not necessarily. But having seen Cosgrove for myself at the church several minutes prior, I can tell you that the only way he could have beaten the rest of us back to Marchbanks would be by motorcycle. A car would either have passed us on the country lane—and none did—or else it would have travelled across the fields. The fields were so treacherous that I am inclined to rule them out. No, I think that the eyewitness *did* see someone, but that it was an impostor."

"Someone pretending to be Cosgrove? Why, for God's sake?"

"To frame him."

Flint needed some air. It had ceased snowing for now, so he left Spector and stepped out of the main entrance to the station and lit up his pipe. Before he could even take a breath of the razorlike air, he was interrupted.

"Inspector," said a voice.

He turned. "Miss Silvius. What are you doing here? I thought you were taking the train back to London?"

"I telephoned my employer," she explained, stepping toward him. "And I told him the truth. He told me not to bother coming back. So," she continued, brightening slightly, "I decided to stay in Benhurst for a few nights. To be near to Victor."

Flint was appalled. "He sacked you? Miss Silvius, why on earth would you do a thing like that?"

"Knowledge is power," she offered cryptically. "I decided it was about time I seized the upper hand."

The tobacco had obviously stimulated Flint's deductive skills, for he instantly understood what she was alluding to. "Someone's been blackmailing you, is that it? Threatening to tell your employer about Victor?"

She gave him a becoming smile. "Not anymore," she said, and continued on her way.

ENCOUNTER IN
THE OLD RAM

"You wanted to see me?" Leonard Drury was smiling to himself, gently swirling the brandy tumbler in his right hand. His left held an open cigarette case, and he offered one to Caroline. She declined.

They were in the bar at The Old Ram, Benhurst's local hostelry. It was a run-down old village pub not all that different from Putney's Black Pig, and its popularity stemmed largely from the fact that it was the only place to serve beer for thirty miles in any direction.

"Yes," she said, sitting on the stool beside him, "I did."

"Well, I must say this is most refreshing. I'm pleased that you've begun to grow accustomed to your situation."

"As a matter of fact," she said, "I asked you here so I could tell you that I never want to see you again."

Leonard laughed. "Very droll. Of course, you know very well what will happen if you decide to sever our burgeoning relationship . . ."

"You'll tell my employer about Victor. Well, there's no need to concern yourself, Mr. Drury. I have already told him."

"You *what?*"

"So I think it's fair to say you have no hold over me anymore. And so I can tell you at last what I really think of you."

Leonard was aghast. His mouth was open but he struggled to form the words. He gulped once, then clamped shut his jaw. Finally, and at some length, he spoke.

"There's something you may not know about me, Caroline," he said. "I happen to lead a charmed life. Good things simply *happen* to me. Call it kismet, or whatever you like. But I always, always get what I want."

"Not this time."

His expression grew callous. He lowered his voice. "You'd be a fool to make an enemy of me," he informed her. "Women who make me their enemy tend to suffer the consequences."

She placed her hands on her hips. "Is that so?"

He smirked. "Oh, yes. Take poor Gloria Crain. She turned me down, and look what happened to her."

"*You* poisoned her, is that what you're saying?" Caroline was incredulous.

"Did I say that? I said nothing of the kind. And what about dear old Ruth Kessler? Only a year older than me—playmates since we were tots—but look what happened to *her.*"

"I've never heard of Ruth Kessler."

"Ask around," he said gregariously. "You'll find out."

Caroline finished her drink and got up. "I never want to see or hear from you again," she told him. "I'd advise you to leave now."

Leonard was snickering somewhat drunkenly. "Who the hell do you think you are?" he said.

"Irrelevant," Joseph Spector interrupted. "You have heard what Miss Silvius has to say. Now leave."

The conjuror had entered the bar while the two young people were engrossed in their conversation. Neither had noticed his arrival. Now he was standing directly behind Leonard, who tottered round on his bar stool to look the old man in the eye.

"Spector," he said, "this isn't what it looks like, you know."

"It's exactly what it looks like. Now . . ." he placed the ferrule of his cane in the centre of Leonard's chest and gave him a quick shove, sending him spilling backwards off the stool. Leonard saved himself just in time, but staggered away from the bar. "I'd advise you to do as Miss Silvius says, or else face the consequences."

"From you, old man?"

But Spector was not intimidated. He stood steadfastly as Leonard leaned in close, until they were almost nose to nose.

"Yes," said Spector.

He and Caroline stood side by side and watched as Leonard skulked toward the door.

"Did you hear what he was saying?" Caroline asked urgently. "Do you think *he* might be the one who . . . ?"

"No," said Spector, his gaze still fixed on the retreating Leonard as he passed by the window. "I don't think he murdered Gloria Crain. And as for Ruth Kessler . . . at a guess, I would say she was related to Richmond Kessler."

"Oh," said Caroline, "now I *have* heard of him. The industrialist. But he died years ago . . ."

"Indeed," said Spector, setting the fallen barstool upright and perching on it. "He also happened to be a Tragedian. As is your employer, Horace Tapper."

Caroline sat down beside him. "How did you find out about that?"

"I simply asked Peter Nightingale—that's Leonard's secretary. He told me he drove Leonard out to Horace Tapper's home the day before yesterday. So I spoke with Tapper himself on the telephone, and he filled in the remaining gaps in my knowledge. I also assume that you are the young lady who dined with Leonard the night Sylvester Monkton was killed. In other words, *you* are his alibi."

She thought about this. There was little use in attempting to deny it.

"How do you know Tapper is a Tragedian?" she asked.

Spector smiled. "I didn't. But I do now. Tell me, Miss Silvius, why is it so important to you to be close to the Tragedians? You really think an old boys' drinking club has conspired to keep your brother behind bars for all these years?"

"I don't think it," she answered. "I know it. But there's something else you don't know yet, Mr. Spector. I no longer work for Horace Tapper. I came clean with him this morning about my brother, and he instructed me to pack my bags—which I was only too pleased to do."

Spector nodded. "Perhaps that was for the best. All the same, I wonder if it's wise for you to remain in Benhurst. There have already been two deaths out here. And until I can untangle the threads of this case, I'm afraid there might well be another."

Behind the bar hung an antique oak barometer. Ignoring Spector's last remark, Caroline studied it.

"Pressure is dropping," she said. "It's going to be a cold night. Perhaps you'll excuse me, Mr. Spector."

He simply stood and watched her go.

That was when he sensed that they had not in fact been alone. There came an involuntary rustle of newspaper and Spector realised someone had been keeping himself hidden throughout the entire encounter, and that Leonard's back had been to him.

A man slouched in an armchair by the grate, with his back to the bar. Sensing that he was caught, he angled his head lazily to get a look at Spector. He had grey hair and bushy muttonchops, plus a woollen suit to match.

"Lot of fuss about nothing," he observed.

"You kept well out of it," said Spector.

"Only thing to do," replied the man.

Spector ambled over. "I suppose you know Marchbanks?" he said casually.

"The big house? Hardly." The man fidgeted a little, sensing that he was under close scrutiny, and leaned over to retrieve the newspaper. But before he could start reading, Spector spoke to him again.

"What about The Grange?"

The man didn't answer.

"You know, I thought I recognised you from a description given by a friend of mine. You're Thomas Griffin, aren't you?"

TOM MEAD

"Famous, am I?" said Griffin from behind his paper.

"Waiting for someone?" Spector went on, careful to maintain the slow, hypnotic timbre of his voice that was so useful in eliciting the truth from an unwilling suspect. "Or perhaps . . . the person you were here to meet . . . has already left?"

Griffin screwed up his newspaper and got to his feet. Spector was tall, but the head orderly towered over him. The two men stood still for a moment, and then Griffin brushed past and headed out.

Spector headed after him, but stopped when he got to the front door of the establishment. He watched the orderly traipsing back along the High Street in the direction of The Grange.

Why here? the conjuror wondered. *Why now?*

CHAPTER TWELVE

A TURN ABOUT THE GARDEN

I t was full dark by the time Joseph Spector got back to Marchbanks. In spite of the offer of a lift from Sergeant Hook, he
opted to walk from the village back to the house, just as he had
that morning. Drawing his cloak around him and setting his hat
more firmly on his silver head, he set out into the chilly evening air.

The house was as still as death. Lady Elspeth was in her room.
Leonard and Ambrose smoked cigarettes and played gin rummy.
Neither of the young men said much, instead focusing all their
attention on the cards. They scarcely acknowledged Spector as he
strode past.

At half past eight, and at considerable length, Lady Elspeth
descended the staircase. Evidently Moncrieff's soporific had
worn off.

"Darling," said Sir Giles, rushing over to her.

If he did not know better, Spector would have said it was the
stuff of bad theatre. Husband and wife embraced, and Lady

Elspeth avoided Spector's gaze by burying her face in Sir Giles's shoulder. Then they parted, and normal business swiftly resumed.

"Mr. Spector, my wife and I are going to take our stroll."

"I would strongly advise you not to leave the house," said Spector.

"You think there's a killer lurking in the woods, is that it?" Following his unguarded, maudlin slump in the study, the judge's familiar boisterousness was back. "Well I say, let him have at it."

"Please," Spector persisted. "Don't do anything foolish."

"The foolish thing," said the judge as his wife slipped an arm through his, "would be to remain cooped up here. Not good for the spirit. And besides, Flint has left a horde of constables about the grounds to keep an eye on us. He'd be a bloody fool if he comes back tonight. Which reminds me—Runcible, better arrange for some extra firewood."

"Yes, sir."

Undeterred by Spector's concern, the couple made for the front door.

Spector went through to the salon, and from the French windows he watched Sir Giles and Lady Elspeth, silhouetted in soft moonlight, as they took their evening promenade, just as they had the previous night and the night before that. In other circumstances, it would be such a benign sight. But now he scanned the distant trees for movement.

Spector felt a sense of formless malevolence closing in on him. An invisible killer stalked Marchbanks, and his work was not yet done.

"Care to join us, Spector?" Leonard spoke a little louder than necessary, evidently hoping to make the old man jump—the sort of petulant prank that suited his personality. A fitting revenge, no doubt, for the humiliation he had received from Spector at The Old Ram.

But Spector simply answered, "Thank you, no." He did not take his eyes from the couple in the garden. He lit himself another cigarillo.

The judge and his wife returned within a quarter of an hour, unscathed. Lady Elspeth retreated upstairs without a word, but Sir Giles sidled up to Spector.

"You ought to know," he said, "that I've made a decision. I spoke with the uniformed chaps in the garden. I dismissed them. They have gone back to Benhurst. I do not wish to turn Marchbanks into a fortress."

"May I say, Sir Giles, that I think you're being very foolish?"

"You may," answered the judge, with something like a smile. "But it is my decision. You see, while I was walking with my wife, I thought about what you said earlier. And I am determined now. Determined to conquer my fear of death."

With these portentous words, the judge wished Spector a peaceful night and followed his wife up the stairs.

Feeling restless, Spector went to the music room, where Leonard and Peter Nightingale were going through a heap of correspondence.

"Fan letters," Leonard explained. "I asked Nightingale to bring it from London. Not sure what's afoot with the GPO, but everything seems to be turning up a day late, so we're somewhat behind."

Nightingale was in his shirtsleeves again, smoking one of his fragrant foreign cigarettes and skim-reading a letter. He acknowledged Spector's presence with a friendly nod.

"Where is Ambrose?"

"Gone to bed, poor lamb," Leonard said unsympathetically.

Spector tended to need less sleep than other people, but even he was beginning to feel the aftereffects of the day's grisly travails. Two houseguests dead, and he had been at Marchbanks less than forty-eight hours. The surveillance teams had indeed withdrawn, leaving the grounds of the house conspicuously unguarded. The trees loomed threateningly on all sides. Perhaps, Spector surmised, the judge had placed a telephone call to one of his high-powered Tragedian friends and issued the order. It was the only explanation for the utterly foolhardy withdrawal of that first line of defence. A chilly menace lingered in the darkest corners of Spector's heart.

He made his way through the silent halls of this rambling house, ending up in the study once again. Flint had returned to Marchbanks minutes ago, and was now back behind the judge's desk, and Spector joined him just as Sergeant Hook was detailing the fruits of his inquiries.

"Thought you might like to know, sir, that I did a bit of digging about Thomas Griffin, the orderly at the Grange. Quite a colourful past he has. Served overseas, violent temperament, dishonourable discharge. Did some time for assault and battery. Employed by Dr. Moncrieff about four years ago. Married last spring."

"Married?" This piqued Flint's interest. "And who's the lucky lady?"

"Waiting to hear back from the records office at Gretna Green, sir."

"Gretna Green? So it was an elopement? Most interesting. Well, keep me posted, won't you."

"Yes, sir."

"I see," Spector remarked, "that your theory aligns with my own. You think it's all connected, don't you? Victor Silvius, Gloria Crain, Sylvester Monkton, Jeffrey Flack, Dr. Moncrieff . . ."

Flint exhaled. "I wish I knew. It seems that each path I take leads precisely nowhere."

"Right." In spite of himself, Spector was smiling.

"What are you so happy about?" Flint asked him.

"A pair of paradoxes," said Spector. "Sylvester Monkton, killed in the open air, and yet there was no way the killer could have reached him. And now Jeffrey Flack, killed in a locked room by an invisible killer whom everybody saw."

Flint shook his head, ruminating on this latest distasteful crime. "It's like a jigsaw," he said, "but with all the wrong pieces."

"*There*," said Spector, "is an apt description."

Flint sat with his arms folded at his breast.

Spector, sensing the other fellow's ennui, spoke again. "Here. This will cheer you up. Look," he gestured toward a nearby bookshelf. "Choose a book from that top shelf."

"Spector, I'm not in the mood for magic."

But the conjuror would not be deterred. "You'll find this educational. Now please—choose a book."

Flint studied the top shelf, as instructed, and pointed. "That big green one."

"A fine choice." Spector went over and seized the hefty legal tome, which was bound in lime-green leather. "Now, watch. I am going to skim through the book like so." He demonstrated, holding the book toward Flint and quickly riffling through its pages. "See? And when I skim through the book, I want you to tell me 'stop' at any point. Understand?"

Flint nodded resignedly.

"Right." Spector began the riffle.

"Stop."

Spector did. Holding the book away from him, so that only Flint could see the page, the conjuror said, "Read the top line of the left-hand page. Aloud, if you please."

Flint squinted. "'Accordingly,'" he read, "'we will divide the subject of mortgages of land, not into legal and equitable mortgages, but into mortgages by deed and mortgages by deposit of title deeds, or by memorandum of deposit; or, to put it in other words, mortgages by legal conveyance and mortgages by equitable conveyance.'"

"Marvellous," Spector enthused. "These lawyers have such a wonderful command of the King's English. Enough to make one forget that it's also the language of Shakespeare. Look in the top drawer of the desk."

Flint did, and produced a sealed envelope.

Grinning, Spector instructed him to open it.

Again, Flint obeyed, and unfolded the sheet of paper within. Written at the top in Spector's inimitable, somewhat spidery hand, was the same exact phrase.

Like Leonard Drury before him, Flint was impressed in spite of himself. "All right then," he said, "put me out of my misery. Tell me how it's done."

"Well," Spector replaced the book on the shelf, "it's important to understand that every illusion I perform is illustrative. Nothing is without significance. I wouldn't have done the trick if I didn't think its principle might be applied to the case. Here, it was a question of 'forcing,' also known as the 'magician's choice.' First, look at that top shelf. I count nine books on there—nine dense legal tomes. You might have picked any of them. Yes? Well, it wouldn't have mattered if you had. Pick another."

"The blue one."

Spector removed it from the shelf, and skimmed through it once again. "Your telling me to 'stop' was simply theatre. No matter when you said the word, I should have stopped on the same page. All it took was a hairpin inserted down the spine of the book, invisibly marking that particular page. So with nine hairpins, I could control the outcome depending on your choice." He pointed to the top line of the left-hand page. "And if you open the left-hand drawer of the desk, you'll find an envelope containing this phrase."

"I see," said Flint, "so it's a cheat."

"Of *course* it is. Haven't you learned that by now? It always is. Nine envelopes, nine hiding places, and nine hairpins. That's all it takes."

"So," Flint persisted, "how does this relate to the case?"

"The illusion of control," repeated the conjuror. "You thought you were making a free choice. But you weren't."

With that, Spector replaced the book and resumed his seat.

These abstract little performances were nothing new to Flint. Spector liked to use them to demonstrate certain logical threads he was currently pursuing. But this one was lost on the Scotland Yard man. The illusion of control?

Before he could delve into the trick's implications in further depth, Spector's spell was broken by the sudden jangle of the telephone. It echoed around the dark, death-stalked halls of Marchbanks. Again, Spector thought of literature: of *A Christmas Carol*, and the bells that herald the arrival of Marley's ghost, and the beginning of Scrooge's horror.

He leaned over the desk and grasped the receiver. "Yes?"

"Oh Mr. Spector, thank God it's you."

"Caroline? What is it? Where are you?"

"I'm at The Grange."

"Why? Has something happened to your brother?"

"Yes," she answered. "Yes, it has. He's disappeared."

PART THREE

EQUIVOQUE

December 19-24, 1938

Thus much by wit, a deep revenger can:
When murder's known, to be the clearest man.
—*The Revenger's Tragedy*, act 5, scene 1

"They are blind," the masked man said, "because they
have looked upon my face."
—Jorge Luis Borges, "The Masked Dyer, Hakim of Merv"

CHAPTER THIRTEEN

THE DANCE

I.

On Flint's instruction, Sergeant Hook kept his hobnailed boot flat on the accelerator, sending the car surging through the snow and darkness. The headlamps cast narrow daggers of illumination, and Hook's gloved grip on the wheel was tenuous. Spector was almost supernaturally still in the back seat, while Flint careered from side to side with each bump and turn. Neither man said a word, though Flint grunted irritably with the exertion of staying upright.

The ride, which should have taken thirty minutes, took ten.

With a final, definitive swing of the wheel, Hook turned them onto the driveway of The Grange and brought the car to a skidding stop.

"Dear God," said Flint.

The iron gates hung open.

The three men proceeded toward the clinic on foot; Hook carried a torch and led the way. When they reached the main building, they found it well-lit and curiously devoid of life. The front door, through which Flint had stepped only a week ago, slammed itself open and shut repeatedly, as though beset by a poltergeist. But it was just the wind.

Caroline Silvius appeared from inside, staggering slightly. She came out to meet them, her face a nightmarish Kabuki white and her eyes stunned orbs. She seemed almost elfin in her oversized chinchilla-wool topcoat. Her hands were buried in the pockets, but when she took them out Spector saw the sleeves were a good couple of inches too long. She hunched her body against the cold, shoulder pads brushing her ears. The buttons down the left side were brass, and wouldn't have looked out of place on an old-fashioned army greatcoat.

Instructing her to remain outside with Sergeant Hook, Flint and Spector plunged into the darkened foyer. Flint had the torch now, gripping it like a weapon, and did his best to remember the way.

The place was empty. The footsteps of the two men echoed as Flint led Spector through another open door, along a passageway, and another, final open door to the cells.

Victor Silvius was indisputably gone. But so were the other two patients who had previously occupied those padded rooms. Each door hung open, and each room stood gaping and horrifyingly vacant.

"Where the hell are the guards?" Flint demanded aloud, not expecting an answer.

But Spector said, "There."

Flint spun with the torch, training its beam on the shape at the end of the hallway.

Thomas Griffin—what was left of him—lay in the corner of the room, a mess of tattered rags and ruined flesh. He had been stabbed, beaten and brutalised. The weapon—the point of a needle—now jutted from his neck, where it was encrusted with dried blood.

"Good God," said Flint, sniffing the air. "Spector, I can smell smoke."

"Same here," said Spector. "I believe it's coming under the door."

Following the odour, they went through a door into what had been Thomas Griffin's office. A tin bucket in the middle of the floor churned both smoke and flame. Flint gave a yell, kicking over the bucket and stamping out its blazing contents.

When the scorched mess was finally extinguished, Spector dropped to his haunches and prodded the blackened ashes with the tip of his cane.

"Records," he said. "Someone was burning records. And there's some sort of material here, too."

The far wall was lined with steel filing cabinets, and several of the drawers had been ransacked. While Flint continued his search of the building, Spector strolled over to those filing cabinets. Each drawer was categorised alphabetically, and contained Moncrieff's patient records. The S drawer had been thoroughly rifled, and the Silvius file removed. It seemed a likely conclusion that the document had been used as kindling in that bucket in the middle of the floor. Spector checked a few other drawers and found their contents undisturbed.

But then, to his mild surprise, he saw that the *N* drawer had also been raided. Easing shut the drawer, Spector turned his attention to the one directly above it, which was labelled *M*. This one was unmolested. Spector skimmed its contents, a vague idea beginning to take shape in his mind, and stopped when he reached a familiar name.

II.

Griffin's subordinates, Matkin and Coombs, were eventually found, both unconscious and swathed in straitjackets, behind the locked door of the pharmaceutical dispensary. Neither had any recollection of how they had come to be there, though they bore no visible wounds. It seemed most likely that they had been drugged.

Flint found a switch that restored the electricity, then did his best to question the two surviving orderlies. But they had little to offer. Both men seemed almost delirious, as though still under the influence of some illicit substance. By the time reinforcements arrived, Victor Silvius, the Edgemoor Strangler, and the Ambergate Arsonist had been gone from their cells for almost two hours.

As the night rolled on, the snowstorm worsened. Hastily convened search parties combed the countryside while Flint coordinated proceedings from The Grange's spartan office. In a reversal of their habitual positions, Flint sat at the desk poring over files while Spector paced.

"We must speak with Caroline Silvius," said Spector.

"We will," Flint assured him, "but for now, I want those three missing men found. Hook has instructions to telephone HQ for reinforcements."

"If the phones are working in Benhurst . . ." Spector commented.

"It's not like you to be so pessimistic," observed Flint.

Spector stopped and fixed him with an icy look. "Flint, this is all part of the dance. Everything is proceeding exactly according to plan. Somebody's plan."

"Who?"

Spector perched on the corner of the desk. He threaded his fingers around the handle of his silver-tipped cane. "I don't know."

Flint looked up from the files. In profile, his head hanging, Spector looked despondent. It must have been a particularly difficult admission to make, and a very disturbing one for Flint. Seeing the ageless, deathless old conjuror vulnerable was akin to facing his own mortality for the first time.

"But," Spector eventually said, "I am now convinced that every aspect of this case is connected to everything else. A kind of webwork. Several files have been removed from these cabinets, and presumably burned. But one has not. Tellingly, it was left on the desk, right where you are sitting. You remember the case of the Edgemoor Strangler, don't you?"

Flint did; a publican who, over the course of a year, had throttled the life out of six young women and left their bodies strewn across the barren wastes of Edgemoor.

"But what you may *not* remember," Spector continued, "is the name of the judge who oversaw the Strangler's case. It was Giles Drury."

Now the clinic was flooded with investigators. Dr. Findler stood over the butchered body of Thomas Griffin, shaking his head solemnly. A crime scene photographer's flash flared and briefly illumined what was left of his face in horrifying relief. Even in death Griffin had not lost that supercilious tilt to his chin.

"Well," Flint commented to Sergeant Hook, "at least they can't try and pin this one on Arthur Cosgrove."

"What's that, sir?"

"Nothing. What I really want to know, Hook, is where to find Dr. Moncrieff. This is his clinic, after all."

"He's in Benhurst, sir. At the station."

Flint gave a sharp, humourless laugh. "Then we mustn't keep the good doctor waiting, must we? Warm up the car, Hook."

Before setting off, Flint returned to the bloody corridor, where Spector was now examining each of the three open cells.

"The middle one belonged to Silvius," Flint informed him. "Anyway, Hook tells me Moncrieff is waiting at Benhurst Police Station. There's not much more we can do here, and the manhunt's already underway. Want to tag along?"

"Not yet," answered a distracted Spector, "there's something else I need to do. Tell me, where has Caroline Silvius got to?"

"At the station already, I think. One of the constables took her. She's in shock. Why? You think she's involved?"

"I think," said Spector, "it would be the best if you kept her there for the time being."

Flint and Hook drove into Benhurst at a considerably more leisurely pace than the outward journey.

At long last, the storm had begun to abate. Thick snowdrifts lined the streets of Benhurst, but the snowfall had eased. It was now almost 3:00 in the morning.

When Flint strode into the Benhurst Police Station—which was abuzz with activity, in spite of the ungodly hour—the first person he saw was Caroline Silvius. She came up to him with a pleading look.

"Mr. Flint, have you found him?"

"Not yet, miss. Please wait with Sergeant Hook. I'll be with you presently."

Reluctantly, she withdrew. Flint then proceeded to a corner office—the quietest spot in the building—where Jasper Moncrieff was waiting for him.

Moncrieff and Flint shook hands, and the doctor seemed genuinely appalled by what had transpired in his clinic. Flint looked him up and down; it was the first time he had laid eyes on the man, having missed him by moments the day Jeffrey Flack died. He was as Spector had described him, though: elegant, suave, largely unflappable.

"Mr. Flint, how did this happen?" was his first question.

"That's what I'm hoping you can tell *me*. All three of the permanent inmates at your clinic escaped in one go. An horrific breach of responsibility, wouldn't you say?"

"I'm not a man to shirk responsibility, Mr. Flint, you may be assured of that. The surviving orderlies will be taken care of, and Griffin's widow will be in for a hefty windfall."

"You know Griffin's widow?" Flint asked quickly.

"Never had the pleasure. But we seem to be getting away from the focus of our discussion."

"We do. Where were you this evening, sir?"

"I was in London, at the home of a private patient. I came from there directly as soon as I heard the news."

"Would you be willing to provide the patient's name?"

"I would not."

Flint gave a sigh. "Can anybody confirm this alibi of yours?"

"Yes. The patient."

"Anybody else?"

"No."

"I see. Well, I'm familiar with Victor Silvius's case history, but what can you tell me about the other two escapees, Doctor?"

"Well, they're both male, of course, with violent tendencies. Typically, their medication keeps them docile."

"What medication?"

"Various sedatives. I can provide you with their medical records if you think it will be useful."

"Thank you. And who gives them the medication?"

"As in, actually administers it? Often it was, uh . . . Griffin. Between our sessions, they remain in his care."

"Would it be possible for any of them to stop taking their medication?"

"No! No. At least, I don't think so."

"Then how did any of them manage to orchestrate this elaborate escape?"

"I . . . I wish I knew."

After more questioning that got him precisely nowhere, Flint left the man with his thoughts. He approached Caroline Silvius, who sat wringing a handkerchief on a nearby bench. She was sitting alone, careless strands of hair across her face, still bundled in that unbecoming coat. She was staring into the empty air between them, and it took her a moment to acknowledge that Flint was even there at all.

"Oh," she eventually said, "it's all gone so wrong."

"It must have been a very distressing experience for you."

"Yes," she answered vaguely. "It gives me chills just thinking about it. I'm afraid I shall never feel warm again." And she pulled the coat tighter around herself.

"All right, Miss Silvius," he said, taking a seat beside her, "what have you got to tell me?"

"Mr. Flint," she said, "are you going to find my brother?"

"I shall do my damnedest. But in the meantime I need you to tell me why you were out at The Grange tonight."

"It was a telephone call at The Old Ram. The landlady came to fetch me; she said there was a gentleman wanting to speak to me. And when I picked up the receiver, I recognised the voice on the other end straight away—it was Victor. All he said to me was, 'It's all right now, sis. Everything's going to be all right.' I had no idea what he was referring to, but the very fact that he was using the telephone at all was alarming. I told him to stay where he was; that I'd come and see him. I was in such a panic. But the call disconnected before we could speak further."

"How did he know where you were staying?"

"I don't know."

"So you came traipsing out to The Grange on foot?"

"Yes."

"And when you got there, you found the doors open, the inmates vanished, and Thomas Griffin dead."

Caroline shielded her eyes with her hand. She did not want him to see her cry. "Please, Inspector Flint," she said, "find my brother."

CHAPTER FOURTEEN

AN UNINVITED GUEST

T he man in white approached Marchbanks at a grim trudge. His shoulder-length hair whirled about his head in the bitter wind, and his eyes burned black with hatred. It had taken many hours—seemingly endless hours of torture in the ice and snow—but he had reached the home of his enemy. At last—at long last—justice would be served.

As he drew closer to the house, his heart thundered with rising anticipation.

The front door was impenetrable mahogany, but a quick kick splintered the side entrance, and he was in.

He had not walked on soft carpets for many years, or looked at ancient paintings and cut-glass chandeliers. Marchbanks was another world; an older, kinder world. He sidled from room to room with the polite curiosity of a tourist in a strange and antique land.

The house was largely unlit, and he moved with the quiet celerity of a shadow, his progress occasionally punctuated by a pause to examine some especially captivating antique. Each unoccupied room only augmented his growing anger. It was an anger that had been brewing in him for a long time—he had not even fully realised how angry he was when he was staring at the wall of his cell. But now he knew.

He cracked his knuckles. There was work to be done.

From the hall he passed through the salon, the game room, the music room, the dining room. Each was dark and empty. When he came to the study, he found a slim flicker of amber light emanating from beneath the closed door.

Grasping the brass door handle, he crept into the room.

"Your Honour," he said softly, "I have been waiting for this day . . ." But he trailed off into silence when he saw the man in the armchair waiting for him.

"It's all right," said Joseph Spector, "I'm not going to hurt you."

The Edgemoor Strangler proved surprisingly amenable. Soft-spoken and polite, he accepted Spector's offer of a cup of tea, and the two men sat in the salon and waited for the police to arrive.

Over tea, Spector asked him how he had found the place. With a slight smile, the Edgemoor Strangler produced from the pocket of his trousers a slip of paper.

"It was most easy," he said. "People have been very kind."

Spector took the paper and scrutinised it closely. "Who gave this to you?"

The Strangler shrugged. "A benefactor."

The note was handwritten in blocky capitals. It said simply:

SIR GILES DRURY

MARCHBANKS

NR. BENHURST

"May I keep this?"

"Please," said the Strangler. "I doubt I shall have further use for it."

"I have so many questions to ask you," Spector went on with a smile. The flickering firelight gave it an almost demonic quality.

"Ask away," said the Strangler, sipping his tea.

"I'm a man of singularly morbid curiosity."

"Something we have in common."

Spector's smile grew wider. "You and I, our brains work rather differently to other people's. You might be surprised at how much we have in common. But I'm afraid now is not the time. Your fellow inmates are out there somewhere in the snow."

The Strangler reflected on this. "It is awfully cold out there," he said.

"I understand you often spoke to each other through the walls."

The Strangler shook his head. "Only Victor. He was the only one. The other fellow—some sort of arsonist, I think—was never particularly civilised. Although I must say that Victor has been out of sorts for a while, too. Prone to lengthy silences that make me feel as if I had done something wrong . . ."

"Have you any idea where he might have gone?"

But the Strangler shook his head. He replaced the teacup and saucer on the desk and sat upright, not turning round. He seemed to sense the approaching police officers before he saw them. His body tensed, then slackened. He knew there was no point in resisting.

Sergeant Hook was the one who emerged from the shadows and clipped the cuffs around his wrists. As he was led away, Flint held the door open for him.

"Thank you," said the Strangler.

They took him out through the hall, where the Drurys and other residents had emerged from their sanctuary in the cellar. They all studied the Edgemoor Strangler with varying degrees of morbid curiosity as they filed past him into the salon.

Soon, only Flint and Spector were left in the hall.

"Good work, Spector," said the policeman.

"It struck me that there must have been a reason for releasing the other two prisoners as well as Silvius."

"What *was* the reason?"

"To keep us occupied. Like Silvius, the Edgemoor Strangler had a grudge against Sir Giles. Releasing him—as well as the Ambergate Arsonist—would distract us from our primary task, and give Silvius plenty of time to get away."

"You think he's the mastermind, then?"

But Spector remained noncommittal. "Let's put it this way: I think that whoever was responsible for tonight's audacious escape deemed it expedient to slow our progress. Whether it was Victor Silvius himself or whether it was another faceless criminal remains to be seen."

"What about Caroline Silvius?"

"A good question. *Very* good, I should say. Hook has taken her to the Benhurst Police Station, is that so?"

"Correct."

"Then let's keep her there for a while. Just until we have a better idea of what's going on."

Flint moaned. "How long's it going to take, Spector? The whole thing is like some crazy spider's web. I can't see how it all ties together."

"It's funny you should mention a spider's web. That was my preferred analogy, too. But the thing to remember about a spider's web, Flint, is that there's always a spider at its heart."

"Moncrieff claims he was in London tonight."

Spector smiled. "That doesn't surprise me. No doubt a clutch of Tragedians will spring from the woodwork to vouch for him."

Flint narrowed his eyes. "You think he's involved?"

"I doubt it. Rather, I think our mastermind merely took advantage of Moncrieff's trust in his subordinates. After all it was Griffin, wasn't it, who 'ruled the roost' at The Grange, to borrow your phrase?"

With a shrug, Flint said, "It seemed that way. I didn't like his manner. All the same, nobody deserves to die like that."

"True enough. And what about the Ambergate Arsonist?"

"One of my men found him by the Benhurst road. Frozen to death. Ironic, I suppose. We got no sense out of the Strangler. Reckons he 'didn't see' who it was that let him out of his cell. And claims Griffin was already dead in the corridor."

"I'm inclined to believe him," said Spector. "After all, his clothes were still pristine and white. Whoever killed Griffin must have been doused in blood."

"Hmm. Well, we've got nothing from the other orderlies, either. Seems as though they were doped somehow."

"Ah!" Spector jabbed the air with a skeletal index finger. "A clue at last."

"Where?"

"Well, a clue in the form of a question. But the question itself is telling." As Flint huffed, Spector explained. "The other two orderlies were doped and kept discreetly out of harm's way, but Griffin was butchered in that savage attack. Why?"

"Revenge. I assume he treated all three inmates poorly."

"Yes. But in that case, I should have thought it more likely for all three orderlies to be killed. So the question is not why Griffin was killed, but why the others were spared."

"Incidentally," said Flint, "the handwriting matches." He produced from the pocket of his greatcoat two slips of paper. One was the note that had been slipped under the door of the Strangler's cell. The other was the poisoned pen letter that Lady Elspeth had presented to Spector on the first night of their acquaintance; the note in green ink that read, MURDERER, YOU WILL GET WHATS COMING TO YOU.

Spector looked at each note in turn, then smiled. "It's coming together, Flint. I know it may not seem like it, but you must trust me. This time tomorrow, we will have our killer."

At that moment, Ambrose Drury exploded into the hall.

"That's enough!" he cried. "I can't take all this dreadful whispering and secrecy. It's simply intolerable."

Leonard came out after him. "I must apologise for my brother," he said, "he still hasn't shaken his nasty habit of listening at doors . . ."

And in an instant they were all spilling back into the hall—Sir Giles and Lady Elspeth, with Mrs. Runcible bringing up the rear.

But Ambrose was now the centre of attention.

"I've had it," he yelled, "do you hear me? This whole thing is sheer madness. Why are we still here in this wretched house, just waiting for the killer to pick us off one by one? It's insanity."

"Mr. Drury," said Flint, "please calm down."

"No!" the artist snapped, "I shan't. This whole thing has gone on long enough . . ."

Leonard wrapped an arm around his younger brother's shoulder, but Ambrose wrenched himself away.

"This is *your* fault," he cried. "It's all your fault, Leonard."

Then he placed his hand flat against his brother's chest, shoved him away, and bolted for the front door.

"Quick," snapped Spector, "after him, Flint."

But Flint was already in pursuit. He headed out into the bitter air, following Ambrose's fleeing footprints through the snow. They rounded the house and approached the garage.

Flint reached it just in time to see Ambrose springing into his bold blue Bugatti and firing up the engine with a glorious, animalistic roar. The whipping wheels sent chunks of snow and gravel skittering as the torpedo-like sports car thundered away.

Ambrose spun the steering wheel at the bottom of the drive and, with a shriek, the Bugatti was on the road.

Flint turned, and there was Spector advancing purposefully toward him.

"Here," said the old magician, brandishing a key, "I borrowed it from Leonard. We can't let him get away."

The two men clambered into the Austin and gave chase, headlamps cutting thin swathes through the darkness.

"What the hell's this all about?" Flint demanded over the roar of the engine.

"He's making a run for it, Flint," answered Spector. "He knows he's done for."

CHAPTER FIFTEEN

COLD FEET

I.

"**D**one for? What are you talking about?"

The Bugatti was a good mile or so ahead of them now, its thin tyre tracks visible on the snow-strewn road.

"He knows I'm onto him. He knows that I know."

"For God's sake, *what* do you know?"

"I know that he killed Jeffrey Flack."

Flint was speechless. This was not aided by the fact that he had just reached a perilous chicane in the country road, which took considerable effort and concentration to navigate to prevent the Austin from veering off into a ditch.

"Keep your eyes on the road," said Spector, "and I'll tell you the whole thing."

They were heading back toward London. Apart from that, neither of them had the slightest idea what Ambrose might be planning. But Flint did as he was told. He did not look at Spector at all. He just focused on the road, and let the conjuror's voice wash over him.

"The first clue was the shotgun," Spector began. "When it transpired that the shotgun found in a ditch was *not* the murder weapon, the first question was: Why not? Obviously somebody wanted us to *think* it was. So why not plant the actual weapon? This made me wonder if there was a reason we could not be permitted to find the real weapon, because it would tell us something about the method used by the killer. This led me to the conclusion that a duplicate weapon had to be planted because the real weapon had been modified in some way. That was my first clue.

"My second clue came when I took a stroll around the house in the aftermath of the murder. When I stood beneath the dead man's window, I was surprised to find the snow completely smooth and bereft of footprints. But I wasn't surprised for the reason you might expect—I did not anticipate finding a killer's footprints, but my own. I had previously walked that stretch of grass and left a clear set of footprints behind me.* It hadn't snowed since, so there was no natural way for them to be covered. Which told me the killer had covered them. Perhaps not deliberately, but he had covered them.

"Another clue came when I examined the 'warped' window in the murder room. To my surprise, the wooden frame was in fact perfectly smooth. Not warped at all. So why did the sash refuse to open? We had no way of knowing whether or not the window

---

*   *See page 114*

was in working order *before* the murder, but the absence of the real weapon, coupled with the tampering with the snow beneath the window, led me to believe that it was. Therefore, the likeliest conclusion was that the window was sealed by the killer after the crime. Then it struck me—what if the window was actually *part* of the murder device? What if the shooting took place neither in nor out of the room, but *in-between?*

"Think about it this way: *Why* would the killer want us to think he had vanished into thin air under impossible circumstances? Simple: he wouldn't. The impossibility was unintentional. It was evidence of the killer's lively imagination, coupled with his inexperience. By rights, the window should have remained open. Then we would have simply assumed that the killer climbed out that way and headed across the lawn."

"One moment," said Flint. "Even if the window was open, we'd be able to tell he hadn't escaped that way. There were no prints in the snow."

"Right. You're ahead of me, Flint. This was another flaw in the killer's plan. The crime was timed to perfection, but it was not *plotted* to perfection. Picture the device: a double-barrelled shotgun positioned outside the window, aiming inward, its long barrels protruding into the room. With the window open a couple of inches to admit the barrels, and to hold the weapon in place. Simple enough to set up. But here's the clever part—the killer needed to be able to fire the shot without actually having his hands on the weapon. So how did he do it? Simple enough, he did it from the ground below the window. All he did was prepare the weapon by unscrewing the trigger and tying a length of string to the firing pin. The string would hang down to the ground from the upper window, so that the killer could tug on it to empty both barrels. The recoil would send the weapon flying backward from the window, falling to the ground within a couple of seconds. So all the killer had to do was retrieve it and drop it into a ready-prepared hole, before covering it over and smoothing the snow on top of it. It could be done in a matter of perhaps ten seconds.

"But this is where he made his first mistake. What he should have done was to prop open the upstairs window somehow, so that when the shot was fired the sash did not automatically slam with the force of the recoil. Because the backward force of the weapon, combined with the pull of gravity, caused the jambliner to crack. This meant the sash was no longer fully parallel with the frame, rendering it immobile. And so the window was effectively—and inadvertently—sealed.

"The natural assumption, bearing in mind the weather and the age of the house, was that the frame was warped. In fact, it wasn't. Rather, it was the *sash* within the frame that had been shifted out of sync by the force of the shotgun blast."

"This is all well and good," put in Flint, "but what you haven't said is *why*. Far as I can tell, the only person with a motive to kill Flack was Cosgrove . . ."

"I have a theory. But I don't want to get into specifics yet, Flint, because of the wider implications the theory presents. You have the method. That's enough for now."

Flint managed to resist the immediate urge to curse Spector colourfully. Instead he said, "You haven't given me the whole method. How could he have aimed the shotgun from where he was?"

"He did it by sound."

"What sound?"

"The sound of footsteps overhead. Really, there was only one person the killer could be, and that person was Ambrose. His studio was directly beneath the room in which the murder occurred. That's why it was vital that Jeffrey and Leonard swap rooms, so that Jeffrey would be returning to the room above the studio. When I visited Ambrose, we both heard the creak of a loose board as Doctor Findler examined the window upstairs.* I think he waited until he heard the telltale creak of a footstep, then went out through the French windows and pulled the string, firing the fatal shot. And he did not need to worry about his aim—the close-range shotgun blast would kill whoever got in its way.

"But there was also another clue—the painting Ambrose claimed to have been working on while we were at church. I had seen that painting in its earlier stages when I visited him before we left that morning. But I looked at it closely when I interviewed him after the murder, and I spotted that the paint was completely dry. In other words, it could not be the same painting which I had seen him working on before I left for church. He had completed a painting, and then set about creating a *duplicate* to serve as his alibi. Which means that if he was not painting, then he must have been doing something else while the rest of the family was out. Of course, he was rigging this lethal device, and digging that hole beneath the window.

"Ambrose was capable of bold sweeps of imagination, but he lacked the patience or common sense to see them through. It was

---

*   *See Page 154*

a half-formed murder plot. He rigged his device while we were at church that morning, but of course he'd laid the groundwork beforehand. The only problem was that he had not put enough thought into the variables that might derail his plan. So we find ourselves picking up the pieces of a foolish, half-baked scheme. An impossible crime that never should have been impossible in the first place."

"There's another question, though. Arthur Cosgrove—how did he come to be in Benhurst?"

"Simple enough. He was invited. An anonymous letter, similar to the poisoned pen missives that have been troubling Sir Giles. Cosgrove will never admit it, and I imagine it has long since been destroyed, but I'd wager the letter told him that if he came to Benhurst on the specified date, then he'd find himself face to face with the man responsible for his wife's death. Ambrose couldn't be certain the letter would do the trick, but he was willing to take the risk. I would also imagine that the tip-off received via telephone at the Benhurst police station was his doing."

"Does this mean he's the one behind the poisoned pen letters, too?"

"No, no, no. Far from it, in fact . . ."

Before Spector could comment further, Ambrose swerved into a Soho side street and brought the Bugatti to a screaming halt.

"Quick, Flint!" Spector said sharply, bounding from the Austin with an almost acrobatic swiftness that belied his age.

But instead of clambering from the car in his usual lanky-limbed fashion, Ambrose Drury remained where he sat. Flint and Spector approached the Bugatti, and Ambrose glanced round. A strange look crossed his face—one of sudden and acute discomfort.

"What on earth . . . ?" Flint whispered.

Ambrose's skin began to change colour. It became a deep crimson and his body arched back in his seat like a bucking mule. He was foaming at the mouth.

Flint and Spector watched in horror, but there was nothing to be done. Ambrose Drury was dead. He remained in the driving seat of his prized Bugatti, bolt upright with his head lolling backward.

II.

Findler, the Scotland Yard pathologist, seemed able to exist without sleep. Having spent most of the previous night cataloguing the hideous, bloody wounds inflicted on Thomas Griffin, he now presented himself at this fresh crime scene in Soho looking positively chipper.

Dawn had come and gone, and the sky was the drab grey of old photographs. A crowd of neighbours had taken a fleeting interest in the sizzling Bugatti, but police reinforcements quickly dispelled them and cordoned off both ends of the street.

"Well I can tell you one thing for damn sure, gentlemen," said Findler, "you are very lucky to be alive."

"How so?" asked Flint.

"This lad was killed with a particularly devilish murder device. Electricity. That Bugatti of his was transformed into an electric chair on wheels."

"How is that possible?"

"More simply than you might think. A sheet of metal, slid underneath the floor of the vehicle, connected by wire clips to the auto battery and finally wired to the body of the Bugatti itself, creating a deadly circuit. When Ambrose started up the engine, he unwittingly completed the circuit. As he was already on the inside of the car, he wasn't affected by the voltage surging through its metal body until he came to climb out. Inevitably, his hand touched the side of the door and he was fatally electrocuted. Odd that it should be *here*, though," Findler went on. "We had a suicide at the other end of the street just last night. Chap of about nineteen, same as Drury."

"Oh yes?" said Flint, not particularly interested.

But Spector took a step toward the pathologist. "The same age as Ambrose? What was his name?"

A little nonplussed, Findler blinked a couple of times before replying, "Ludo Quintrell-Webb."

"Quintrell-Webb? Something to do with the MP?"

"His son," Findler nodded. "Why? You think he's involved with the Drurys?"

"What are you getting at, Spector?" asked Flint.

"Tell me, when did the unfortunate Ludo take his own life?"

"Last night, about eleven. Went headfirst off that roof there, and splattered what brains he had onto the pavement."

"Did he have anything in his pockets? A suicide note, for instance?"

"Oh yes. A very verbose suicide note that said very little. He reckoned that he couldn't live with what he'd done, whatever that was."

"I think I know what it was," said Spector.

Findler looked bemusedly from Flint to Spector and back again. "You mean Quintrell-Webb is something to do with that business out at Marchbanks?"

"I think he was the stooge in the murder of Jeffrey Flack. An unwitting stooge in some ways. This morning, on the way to church, I slipped back into Marchbanks to retrieve Lady Elspeth's gloves. That was when I saw the maid moving Leonard's suitcase between rooms. But when I was heading back downstairs, I overheard a telephone conversation between Ambrose and somebody named Ludo. It lasted only seconds, but Ambrose mentioned a 'forfeit.' A gambling debt, perhaps? I think Ambrose was forcing him to impersonate Arthur Cosgrove. Ludo must have been in Benhurst, waiting for his cue. The plan was for him to be seen running away from the house along the southern lawn, and then off into the woods. The shotgun was a prop. Borrowed from Shepperton, maybe.

"I imagine the 'Cosgrove' disguise was a makeshift affair, though of course it was not designed to stand up to any particular scrutiny. The witnesses were only supposed to catch a glimpse. Maybe Ludo thought the whole thing was a big prank. I imagine he thought he was simply framing Cosgrove for robbery, or some equally innocuous crime. I doubt he had as much as an inkling that a real and brutal murder was about to occur. That's why, when he heard the unmistakable sound of a *real* shotgun blast, he took fright and ran back the way he had come, rather than across the south lawn as planned. And when he heard about the death of Jeffrey Flack, the guilt was simply too much for him. He was too afraid to go to the police and face the music . . ."

"So he took the easy way out," Flint finished the thought for him. "I'm still not convinced. I mean, how can you know all this for sure, Spector?"

"I don't. I know some of the key facts, and the rest is inference. But it will not be too difficult to prove. First, you may be able to match Ludo's shoes with the prints left in the snow after Flack's death. And second, I reckon he may have left a fingerprint or two on the discarded shotgun. Even if not, a close look at the suicide note may shed further light on the matter."

Flint yawned and cricked his neck. "Ugly, Spector," he said. "It's all very ugly. So you still think Ambrose killed Jeffrey Flack?"

"I'm positive of it."

"Well, now somebody's killed *him*."

"Indeed they have. And using such an outlandish method! Wouldn't you have thought there would be a simpler means of murdering Ambrose Drury? It's almost as if our killer is deliberately making things difficult for himself."

"To tell you the truth," said Flint, "I'd been thinking the same thing. If they were going to kill him with the car, why not just sever the brake line? Quicker, easier, less risky."

Spector's eyes twinkled. "The right question. *That*, my dear Flint, is the right question."

"Well, what's the answer?" When Spector did not reply—he was now staring thoughtfully at nothing in particular—Flint lapsed into self-pity. "And of course *I'm* the one who has to break it to the family."

"I wouldn't be surprised," said Spector at length, "if there is one of them who already knows."

III.

Before Flint set out once again for Marchbanks, he and Spector decided to have some breakfast at the coffeehouse farther along the street. It was perhaps poor taste to seek warmth and nourishment in an establishment that looked out on the crime scene, but Flint for one had ceased caring. His head ached, his pudgy stomach growled, and if he did not sit down soon he knew he would eventually crumple like one of the many corpses he had faced in the last few days.

Spector sought out the most shadowy corner of the place and Flint ordered a cooked breakfast for him and a black coffee for the conjuror.

Spector sat in thoughtful silence for perhaps two minutes, then he said, "This is a very strange case, Flint."

"There's an understatement if ever I heard one."

"I don't mean 'strange' in the sense of 'inexplicable.' I mean 'strange' in the sense of 'bizarre.' 'Outré.' These are illusions within illusions. It might be likened to Dante's circles of hell; there are different *levels* of illusion at play here. For example, the killing of Ambrose Drury is scarcely an illusion at all. Anyone at Marchbanks might have tampered with the Bugatti to create that rudimentary death device. Any of them.

"The shotgun murder of Jeffrey Flack *was* an illusion, but so badly botched that it took on a different appearance altogether.

"The stabbing of Sylvester Monkton, however, was *not* botched—far from it. I'd say it worked rather beautifully. But if we wish to work out how that particular trick was done, we first need to work out *what* exactly the illusion was. Was it a problem of time or space? Does the trick turn on the fact that a killer committed a crime at a moment when he had a perfect alibi, or on the fact that a corpse was placed in the centre of a frozen lake? Time . . ." He showed an open palm, clicked his fingers, and from the empty air produced a fob watch. "Or space?"

While listening to the conjuror's soliloquy, George Flint felt the world around him gradually dwindle into silence. It was a knack the old man had—not just the mesmeric quality of his voice, but his ability to turn even the dingiest coffeehouse into a temple of magic, and the idlest onlookers into an enraptured audience.

"Personally," Spector continued, "I'm leaning toward the latter. I think the killer used a trick to place the body in the boat *after* the surrounding water was frozen. That demolishes every alibi, and explains how that particular knife came to be used. But how was it done? Perhaps a variation on Harry Kellar's *Levitation of Princess Karnac*? Or . . ."

He paused and seemed to consider something. Flint watched expectantly. Then, from his jacket pocket, Spector produced a small object. Absurdly, it was an egg. He placed it flat on his palm, and held it out to Flint.

"Take it, Flint. Examine it."

Flint did. It was an ordinary egg, white and lightly speckled.

"Now hand it back to me."

Flint placed it back in Spector's palm. Spector tossed it lightly back and forth from hand to hand, as though it were a grenade he was about to let fly. Then, at once, he clapped his hands and the egg was gone. He showed his bare hands so Flint could see there was not a hint of yolk or shell on them.

"Your pocket," he instructed. "The right one."

Flint fished around and emerged with the egg, perfectly intact. "How the hell did you do that? And how did you get it in my pocket?"

"An impossibility," Spector smiled. "Comparatively minor, though no less puzzling. Don't you agree? But like every trick I demonstrate for you, Flint, there's a lesson in it. See if you can spot this one." Suddenly, his expression was gravely serious. "I think we are approaching the end."

"End of what?"

"Of this. Of everything. And if we handle it well, we may yet be able to force the killer's hand."

Impatiently waiting while his bacon and eggs sizzled away in the kitchen, Flint said, "I thought you told me Ambrose was the killer."

"Of Jeffrey Flack, yes. But not of Thomas Griffin. Not of Gloria Crain."

"Then who is?"

"I'm very close to it now. It is one of *them*. One of those residing at Marchbanks. Tell me, Flint, are you heading straight back out there?"

"Yes. I'm going to break the news about Ambrose in person."

Spector nodded thoughtfully. "Very well. But will you do me one favour, my friend?"

"Depends what it is."

"I have a few things I must take care of today. Three visits I need to make, to obtain the answers to some questions. And then I'll come straight back to join you at Marchbanks. In the meantime, I'd like you to wait a little while before you break the news about Ambrose."

"What? Why?"

"Because I want to force the killer's hand."

"I don't see how I can keep it a secret from his parents," Flint protested.

"Just a short while. A matter of hours. And make sure there are plenty of men on duty in the grounds. I've a feeling this business is coming to a head."

With that, Spector produced a gold watch from the pocket of his suit. He held it up, so that its metal case caught the light. Then he snapped his fingers, and it was gone.

While Flint blinked in bemusement, Spector got to his feet. "Until this afternoon, then."

"Just wait a moment! Who are these three people you're visiting?"

"The first is Horace Tapper, film producer. The second is the erstwhile pathologist Professor Keith Valentine . . ."

"You mean you've tracked him down?"

"I do."

"And who's the third?"

"I think I shall keep their identity a secret for the time being," Spector said, offering a conciliatory smile. "But all will be revealed." And with that, he left the coffeehouse.

Flint, who had not slept in close to forty-eight hours, finished a coffee and ordered another. "The strongest you've got," he specified.

CHAPTER SIXTEEN

SOUND CITY

Tuesday, December 20, 1938

Walking through Shepperton Sound City was like traversing a dream landscape—progressing from an Italian taverna to a Parisian bistro to a medieval castle made from plyboard. Stepping through each new door was like stepping into another chamber of a single fractured consciousness. The soundstage itself was an immense, cavernous warehouse laden with cables and lit by the sterile beams of criss-crossing overhead lamps.

Horace Tapper sat in a folding canvas chair with PRODUCER printed on the back. He watched the filming of a scene with a scowl and a scrutinous eye, a cigar hanging damply between too-wet lips.

The setting was King Herod's banquet hall in his Judaean palace. A long wooden table stretched the length of the scene, with high-backed chairs at each end. Overhead hung a chandelier from which a young actor was currently swinging. Tapper studied the scene intently—so intently, in fact, that he failed to notice the gaunt, black-clad creature emerging from the shadows beside him.

When he did, the creature was upon him.

"Good God!" Tapper bellowed, the cigar dropping from his mouth. He clutched his chest, panting. "Good God," he repeated between heaving breaths. "You scared the life out of me. Who the hell are you? What are you doing here?"

Joseph Spector grinned, exposing twin rows of even, sharp teeth. "Do you recognise my voice, Mr. Tapper?"

"It's all right, everyone," Tapper reassured the cast and crew, "false alarm." Then he looked back at the old man whose blue eyes were pale and yet curiously intense. "Your voice? Should I?"

"We spoke on the telephone. My name is Joseph Spector."

Recognition dawned. "Something about Leonard Drury?"

"There, I knew you would remember. Is there somewhere quiet we can talk?"

"No time," said Tapper, not troubling to look at his watch. Instead he returned his attention to the set. "Run it through again," he instructed the cast.

A thin, chilly hand landed on the producer's shoulder. "I would greatly appreciate a moment or two of your time."

Tapper did not resist. "All right," he said eventually. "We can talk while they run through the duel scene."

"The duel scene. Yes. Tell me, who is the gentleman swinging from the chandelier?"

"John the Baptist," Tapper explained in a whisper. "You might say we've taken a few liberties with the tale of Salome."

"And the gentleman with the sword?"

"Herod. We left the duel scene until last because of course it's the trickiest part."

Spector watched as John the Baptist dropped from the chandelier with a thump, then drew his own sword. The two men began to fight, while Tapper looked on, nodding.

"You're lucky to have caught me," he said to Spector, not taking his eyes off the contretemps on set. "We're shutting up shop for Christmas this afternoon. The studio's going to be mothballed until January first. That's why I'm trying desperately to get these last few shots in the can. The editing will take place at our studio offices in the city. What is it you want?"

"Unfortunately, I must be the bearer of bad news."

"Bad news? What bad news?"

Spector informed him of the death of Ambrose Drury.

"How dreadful," said Tapper. "Accident, I suppose?"

"Not at all," answered Spector. "It was murder."

"Murder? Goodness."

"I understand Ambrose was looking to pursue a career as an actor."

"Right enough. He battened on to me at some sort of showbiz shindig at the Palmyra Club in Soho. You know it?"

Spector didn't reply. Instead he persisted, "He auditioned, is that right? You gave him a screen test?"

"That's right." The producer shrugged. "I think he'd have done nicely in *Tarrare*. It was going to be our follow up to *Salome*. These historical pictures are a decent draw, and Ambrose had a certain unconventional quality that would have suited the character. I pictured something akin to Fredric March in *Jekyll and Hyde*. What

I wanted was to bring the atavistic, animalistic nature of the man to the fore and put it on the screen."

"So you *were* planning to offer him the part?"

"Why, yes. Out of Leonard and Ambrose, Ambrose was always my pick. He just had a bit more about him."

"And yet you previously signed Leonard to a motion picture contract."

Tapper shrugged. "Leonard's good at standing where you tell him to, but he's a bit too clipped—too *cold*—to be a leading man."

Spector watched the clatter of swords on the soundstage. "Yesterday," he said, "Ambrose received a letter telling him that the part had been offered elsewhere."

Tapper twisted in his seat to stare at Spector's profile. "He what?"

"He was under the impression that it came from you."

"Well, it didn't. I was all set to sign him up. Just hadn't got around to finalising the contracts. Now of course I'll have to look elsewhere."

"So the letter Ambrose received, it didn't come from your office?"

Tapper shook his head before bellowing at King Herod: "For God's sake man, not like *that*. Do you want me to get up there and do it for you?" When he returned his attention to Spector, he said, "So what do you think all this means then? Somebody conned Ambrose?"

"Well, if you are convinced that the letter didn't come from your office . . ."

"Might have," Tapper conceded, "but not from me."

"I didn't read the letter, but I noticed that it arrived on headed notepaper."

Tapper shrugged. "That doesn't mean anything. There's tons of the stuff floating around at my office. I even keep a batch in my study at home."

"Well, it raises a question," said Spector, watching thoughtfully as John the Baptist arced through the air again from the candle-laden chandelier. "Why would someone play a trick like that on Ambrose?"

"Good question. Beats me. It would have been easy enough to refute. If he'd rung me up then I'd have been able to tell him it was a phoney. Sounds like a stupid prank to me."

"Yes," Spector commented thoughtfully, "it does, doesn't it?"

"You know who my suspect would be? Leonard. He's got rather a warped sense of humour, that lad. One of the reasons I've lost some of my appreciation for him. He has an air about him that everybody else is simply there to amuse him. Louche. Not always a bad trait in an actor, you understand, but not an entirely appealing one either. Tell me this, Spector," Tapper said suddenly, "just what's going *on* out at Marchbanks? Some sort of mad killer picking them off one by one? All sounds a bit *Cat and the Canary* to me."

Spector decided to be candid. "I believe it stems from a single incident which took place ten years ago, almost to the day. A young woman named Gloria Crain was poisoned under Sir Giles's roof. Perhaps you remember the case?"

"Ah," said Tapper, "that caused quite a bit of consternation."

"Did you visit Marchbanks at that time?"

"No. But that was a miserable Christmas, I recall, what with the Crain girl's death, and what happened to Ruth Kessler . . ."

"Ruth Kessler," Spector repeated the name contemplatively. "The daughter of Richmond Kessler, am I right?"

"You've done your research."

"What happened to Ruth Kessler?"

"Well, she died. Nothing suspicious in it, though. Natural causes, before you get excited. Her funeral was out in Cricklewood, near the old Kessler place."

"Richmond Kessler was a Tragedian, wasn't he?"

Tapper grinned and nodded. "Adolescent foolishness, but it keeps us entertained."

"What can you tell me about the other members?"

"Nothing at all, old chum. It's in the bylaws. Punishable by death—or debagging. But there's nothing to stop *you* from telling me about them. And I'll affirm or disaffirm with a quick nod or shake of the head. No harm in that, is there?"

"None," Spector smiled. "Well, I think I'm right in saying that Sir Giles Drury and Dr. Jasper Moncrieff are also members of the club."

Tapper nodded.

"Perhaps you can tell me when Richmond Kessler died?"

Tapper had no qualms about this. "It was . . . 1925, if memory serves. Heart attack. Rather unexpected, I understand. At least, he had always seemed a healthy sort of fellow. Decent chap, too. His daughter was bereft, of course."

"His daughter, the aforementioned Ruth?"

"Yes. She and Kessler's brother had a real hatred for one another. Ruth was in her teens at that time, and was finally becoming cognisant of what a leech Daniel Kessler was to his brother. Richmond was constantly calling in favours from the Tragedians, bailing out his wretched brother."

"What happened to Daniel Kessler when Richmond died?"

Tapper pondered this. "I *believe*, though I may be wrong, that he became Ruth's guardian. Until she turned twenty-one, that is. But of course he'd already stripped the estate clean by then; sold up the property, and moved them into a poky flat in Holborn. Listen, Spector, what's this got to do with the Drurys?"

"Nothing whatsoever," answered the conjuror, "but I'm interested all the same. Tell me, was there much in the way of an inheritance?"

"To be honest, this is a bit beyond my area of expertise. You'd have to talk to a lawyer for the details. But I think I'm right in saying that Richmond's money was held in trust for Ruth."

"With Daniel Kessler in charge of the purse strings, I imagine."

Tapper shrugged. "I would imagine so."

"But then," Spector said slowly and thoughtfully, "Ruth died."

"Indeed. Ruptured appendix; a sorry way to go."

Spector leaned forward with ghoulish fascination. "Was there any suspicion of foul play?"

"Oh no," Tapper chuckled benignly, "nothing like that. It's hard to fake a burst appendix, I understand. Oh for God's sake!" He sprang to his feet and bellowed at John the Baptist, "You're fighting for your life, not dancing the Lindy Hop . . ."

When he looked back, Spector was gone.

CHAPTER SEVENTEEN

A WHEEL,
SPINNING FOREVER

Professor Keith Valentine had lively, darting eyes that belied his age and obvious infirmity. When Spector entered the room he did not stand, but his face was expressive and inquisitive.

"It was most kind of you to pay me a visit," he said, his voice a little slow and ever so slightly slurred—the aftereffect of a recent stroke.

"I hope you don't mind talking a little shop, Professor."

For all the speculation as to what had become of Professor Valentine, he had in fact proved comparatively easy to track down. He had never married, and he'd lived alone at a country cottage for almost sixty years, with a flat in London to be used when required. But a recent fall had seen him confined to hospital for a number of weeks, after which it was determined that he was perhaps not equipped to remain alone. And so he was forced from his self-appointed hermitage into the care of a convalescent home in Cricklewood, where he was attended by starched nurses and cheerful, chattering orderlies. Not all that different from The Grange, Spector reflected as a dour nurse led him along a corridor to Valentine's room.

"Nobody calls me Professor these days," Valentine commented, though he did not seem especially put out by the fact. "The nurses here have no idea who I am. They call me *Mister* Valentine. Better than nothing, I suppose. But they don't know who I am. Who I *was*," he corrected himself. "You know, Mr. Spector, that the papers used to call me the most powerful man in England? My expert testimony could mean the difference between life and death for a defendant."

"Indeed," said Spector. "Quite a responsibility."

"A dreadful, awe-inspiring responsibility. Enough to drive a man mad. Which, in the end," he smiled, "it did."

Spector settled on a wooden chair beside the professor's bed. "I've met some madmen in my time. You don't appear to be one of them."

"You flatter me. But I understand you wish to discuss one of my cases?"

Spector inclined his head. "You can probably guess which one."

Valentine nodded. "Gloria Crain. That was when I knew I was finished. It should have been easy, you see. When I was a young man, I could have cracked it in my sleep. But the inconsistencies were just too jarring. It could not have been suicide, and yet it could not have been murder. Nor could it have been accidental. Like a wheel, spinning forever."

"The case was eventually marked down as a suicide."

"Ha!" A chilly laugh. "That was Findler's conclusion, not mine. I never cared for the fellow, you know. His ambition always outweighed his ability. He couldn't wait to get his grubby hands on my job, but he's a pencil-pusher, nothing more."

"Why were you so convinced Gloria Crain didn't kill herself?"

"If you've read about the case then you already know the answer. Strychnine. Two milligrams of the stuff, that's what I found in her system. While it's not unheard of for an individual to commit suicide with strychnine, it's a comparatively rare occurrence. My initial supposition was that it had been consumed as an abortifacient, and she simply got the dosage wrong. Certain backstreet practitioners have been known to dish it out to unwary, desperate young women.

"But again, it was swiftly ruled out. You see, she wasn't pregnant."

"You still haven't explained why you were so sure it couldn't be suicide."

"It was simply that it did not *feel* like suicide to me. Of the three most easily accessible and commonly used poisons—strychnine, arsenic, and cyanide—I'd have said strychnine would be the least likely candidate. It is the most painful and drawn out, but also the least toxic, which means there is no guarantee of death, and one runs the risk of brain-death instead."

"Gloria Crain may not have known that."

"True—but if she had gone as far as to find out the amount required for a lethal dose she would inevitably have stumbled across details of the agonising symptoms it was bound to induce. The lockjaw, the opisthotonic spasms. I was born in Brighton, you see, and one of the most vivid memories of my childhood is the story of the so-called Chocolate Cream Poisoner, Christiana Edmunds. Fortunately I never came into contact with her tainted confectionery, but her case was the one that got me interested in forensic medicine. Her lover, Charles Beard, was our family doctor, you know.

"And in the early days of my career, my mentor was Athelstan Braxton Hicks, a truly exemplary coroner. One of the first cases I ever worked on was that of Thomas Neill Cream, the Lambeth Poisoner, who murdered several prostitutes with strychnine. So, Mr. Spector, I think it fair to say that I know and understand strychnine."

"Very well," said Spector, "then it was murder."

"The natural conclusion," Valentine conceded, "and yet this, too, was incorrect. Dinner at the Drurys' table concluded at roughly half past nine. The victim retired to bed perhaps fifteen minutes later, citing an upset stomach. Strychnine poisoning takes certainly no more than thirty minutes to display symptoms. This would imply that the poison was in the dessert—and yet, this was a trifle that was served from a single glass bowl with a ladle. The wine, too, was poured into each glass from the same bottle. It was impossible to pinpoint *how* the strychnine was administered. All I knew for certain was that it had been ingested."

"Could the killer have employed sleight of hand to drop a poisoned capsule into her drink?"

"That was my next hypothesis. But several maids, not to mention the housekeeper, were attending the table throughout the meal. And they all swore blind that nobody who was at or near the table had acted suspiciously in any way. The housekeeper in particular was adamant; her statement is on record, I'm sure you've already read it yourself. So . . ." he concluded desolately, "what choice did I have?"

Professor Valentine looked at Spector and was surprised to find the conjuror staring beatifically into the middle distance. "Spector?"

"No choice," Spector answered somewhat dreamily, "no choice at all. Please excuse me, Professor," he continued, getting hastily to his feet. And he was gone as swiftly as he had appeared, leaving the old professor to ponder whether this surreal visitation had really happened at all.

CHAPTER EIGHTEEN

HOW TO GET AHEAD
IN SHOW BUSINESS

I.

"**N**ightingale," whispered a voice. It was Leonard Drury.

The young actor was peering out through the crack in his mahogany bedroom door. But his voice sounded different. Thinner, as though he were under considerable strain.

"Yes, sir?"

Nightingale crept along the landing and found Leonard hastily stuffing shirts into his suitcase, empty sleeves flailing limply over the side of the overpacked case.

"Everything all right, Mr. Drury?"

"What does it look like, Nightingale?" Leonard snapped.

He was not himself. But of course, that was to be expected. Not only was the crisp snow turning to ice, but the house itself now positively seethed with menace. Every voice echoing along the corridor was a cry of terror, every creak of the floorboards an approaching assailant. The place was cursed.

Leonard ceased his frenzy of activity for a moment, and seemed to catch his breath. Then he turned to look at Peter. "I've got to get out of here, Nightingale. There's something very wrong here."

"But there are police on watch twenty-four hours a day, sir. I hardly think . . ."

"Stop talking, Nightingale, or you just might convince me. No, getting away is the only thing for it."

Neither man spoke for a moment. Peter Nightingale looked at his employer, who now seemed little more than a hollowed-out shell of a man. It was almost sad to see.

"Listen, Peter," Leonard continued. He did not often use his secretary's first name, so it was a sign that this was very serious indeed. "You and I get on rather well, don't we? I mean, you're a trustworthy sort. And here you've found yourself suddenly thrust into the midst of all this madness. Must have been a shock to the system, no?"

"Well, I suppose it has rather."

"I can rely on you, can't I? If I tell you something, you won't breathe a word, will you?"

Leonard spoke with mounting desperation, and crystalline gobbets of sweat stood out on his forehead. He seemed on the brink of mania.

To try to maintain control of the situation, Peter spoke calmly. "You can trust me, Mr. Drury."

"All right." Leonard appeared to come to a sudden and drastic decision. He slammed shut the suitcase, leaving a couple of errant sleeves poking out. "I've got to tell someone, and it may as well be you. Yes, in fact I think it's rather fitting. You know all my dirty secrets, don't you? All except one, that is. But first, I need you to do something for me. I need you to call a taxi. Use the telephone in Father's study. Will you do that for me?"

Nightingale seemed sceptical. "Are you sure, sir?"

"Positive. I need a word with Runcible, so go and make the call now. Then, when you come back, I'll tell you the whole thing."

Nightingale could not resist another question. "Tell me *what* exactly, sir?"

Leonard gave a laugh that was slightly hysterical. "Tell you everything. Got to tell someone, or else I shall go mad. I don't care what *you* do with the story. Tell the police, tell whomever you like. You can even tell that wicked old Spector. But there's nothing else for it. Only one thing for me to do now, Nightingale, and that's *confess*."

II.

Flint disembarked from the 12:31 at Benhurst Station, his head buzzing with unanswered questions, loose ends, and outright impossibilities. He wished Spector had accompanied him, and quelled his panic that the case was spinning even further out of control.

He walked the half mile or so from Benhurst to Marchbanks, reflecting that Victor Silvius, the benign-looking painter he had met a couple of days prior, was roaming the countryside somewhere. The last escapee. The one that got away.

As he reached the summit of the hill and Marchbanks came into view, he felt the familiar pangs of disquiet that afflicted him here. There was undeniably *something* about the place. It existed in a vacuum, removed from the real world. Anything might happen here and, what was more, it did.

He walked in the tracks left by Ambrose's Bugatti. He walked past the lake, which was frozen once again. He looked up at the window of the murder room where Jeffrey Flack's guts had been blown out.

This house. This wretched house. It didn't need a detective, he thought, but a priest. He rang the bell, and his palms felt sweaty in spite of the chill as he removed his hat.

Mrs. Runcible answered the door. Flint opened his mouth to begin his prepared excuse, but the housekeeper cut him off.

"Thank God you're here," she said.

"Why? What is it?"

"I can't find the master and mistress. They've gone missing."

She let Flint into the hall and he immediately began a search of the downstairs rooms. Runcible and Becky the maid trailed after him.

"When did you last see them?"

"Perhaps half an hour ago, sir," said the maid.

"Reinforcements are on their way," Flint informed them, peeking into the study. "I just hope to God they're not too late. What happened? Did they say anything to you?"

"Nothing, sir. Nothing at all. They were in the salon, taking tea. Very worried about Master Ambrose, of course. Sir Giles tried telephoning Scotland Yard, but the lines are down."

"I see. What about Leonard and Nightingale?"

"I believe they are upstairs, sir," put in Runcible. "Master Leonard was in his room, and I saw Mr. Nightingale on the staircase perhaps two hours ago."

"Right," said Flint, making for the stairs. Becky and Mrs. Runcible followed him, keeping close behind and peering anxiously about them.

Marchbanks felt very large and very empty—less of a home than a crypt. If Flint hadn't been in such an awful rush as he scurried up the stairs, he would have noticed something missing: one of the scimitars from the central display on the far wall. Its mate now hung there alone, looking almost despondent in the dingy light.

"We'll start with Leonard. Tell me, where's his room?"

"It's this one, sir," said Mrs. Runcible, indicating the mahogany door.

Flint approached and rapped on the wood. Then he paused, waiting. No response. He knocked again.

Again, nothing.

He tried the door handle, throwing a cautious glance at the housekeeper. He expected it to be locked, but to his mild surprise it was not. He eased it open and stepped across the threshold.

Maybe it was the lack of sleep, but what he saw sent him into a kind of paralysis. Rooted to the floor, his eyes wide, he stared for perhaps three, four, five seconds.

That's when Becky screamed.

The body on the bed was stretched out almost peacefully, his hands folded at his midriff. His polished shoes pointed toward the ceiling, and his necktie was as straight as an edge rule. The reason Becky had screamed was the dead man's neck, and what should have been above it.

The head was gone, a blood-soaked pillow taking its place on the white sheets.

"Get her out of here," Flint snapped at the housekeeper.

Runcible's mouth was open, but she did not speak, and simply looked at the body in horrified silence. Her hands were shaking. This death was a shock to her. A *real* shock.

"Out, I said!"

Startled back to reality, Runcible slipped an uncharacteristically tender arm around Becky's shoulders and led her from the room.

When Flint approached the corpse, he touched one of the hands and found it cold. Then he spotted the *other* occupant of that room—an inanimate one, though no less menacing for that. In the centre of the rug gleamed the copper-handled, jade-crusted scimitar, its steel blade now laced with dark black blood.

Mrs. Runcible, her curiosity clearly getting the better of her, reappeared in the doorway.

"It's Nightingale," she said in disbelief. "I recognise his suit."

Flint just nodded. "Spector," he said under his breath, "where the hell are you?"

III.

At the very moment Flint was flinging open the door of Leonard Drury's bedroom, Joseph Spector stood alone in a snowy Cricklewood churchyard, gazing down at an ill-attended gravestone. This was his last stop; the last of the three visits he had planned to make.

"Mr. Spector?" said a soft voice.

Spector turned and smiled. "How did you find me?"

"It was Sergeant Hook," said Caroline.

Spector scoured the misty perimeter of the churchyard and spotted Hook waiting by an idling police car. He waved, and the sergeant waved back a little self-consciously.

Caroline hooked her arm through the crook of Spector's elbow and the two of them made their way toward the car. "Please," she said, "tell me there's been news of my brother."

"No news," answered Spector, "but I doubt we shall have to wait much longer."

"Afternoon, sir," said Sergeant Hook as the pair reached the car. "Inspector Flint gave me a call at the Benhurst Police Station, sir. Told me to come and find you, and to bring Miss Silvius with me. Lucky for us, Dr. Findler had an idea where you might be going."

"Very prescient of him," said Spector, climbing into the back of the car. "Have you heard anything from Marchbanks?"

"Nothing."

"Well, I think you'd better take me there."

"What about me?" asked Caroline, settling in the passenger seat.

Spector ruminated as Hook fired up the engine. "Yes," he eventually said, "I think you ought to come with us."

IV.

When they reached the house it was full dark, but the windows of Marchbanks blazed bright. Every single lamp had been lit, and scores of police officers combed the grounds and nearby woodland.

Flint came down to meet them as the car drew to a halt. He instructed Hook to remain with the car, and with Caroline.

"Spector," he hissed, "where the hell have you been?"

"Obtaining the answers to some questions," said Spector. "I now have everything I need."

"I've been trying to track you down all day. Something hideous has happened. Nightingale's dead. *Decapitated*, for Christ's sake. And the others have gone missing."

"The others? I see," Spector did not seem particularly troubled by the news. "So, by my count, that leaves three unaccounted for."

"Don't forget Victor Silvius."

"No," said Spector, "I wasn't."

"Well, what happens now? What the bloody hell are we supposed to *do*?"

Spector gave him an affable look. "Perhaps we should take a drive."

"Where to?"

"Ah, that would be telling. But I don't think you need worry about Victor Silvius. After all"—he glanced toward Caroline, who stood out of earshot—"we have someone that belongs to him. He won't leave for good until he has her once again."

As though sensing that they were talking about her, Caroline sidled over, hugging herself against the cold.

"Well?" she said. "What happens now?"

Spector spoke first. "I notice," he said, "that you have decided to forego your greatcoat."

Flint opened his mouth to say something else, but a quick look from the conjuror silenced him.

"What do you mean?" Caroline asked bemusedly.

"I should have thought the statement perfectly clear. Never mind. We are about to take a short car ride, Miss Silvius, to find your brother."

"You mean you know where he is?"

"No. But I've a fairly good idea."

"Spector," Flint interrupted, "don't you want to take a look at . . . what's upstairs?"

"I think not. I shall leave the unfortunate fellow in the capable hands of Dr. Findler. Though I doubt there's much he will be able to tell us that we do not already know. I don't suppose anybody has found the head?"

"It looks as though Leonard took it with him."

"Why, I wonder, would he do a thing like that?"

"You've stumped me there."

"I hope that pun was unintentional, Flint," Spector grinned, "or else I'll be concerned you are developing a sense of humour."

Flint just looked at him blankly, then headed for the waiting police car.

Sergeant Hook was a considerably more capable driver than Flint, and he handled the snowy conditions with skill.

"Where to, Mr. Spector?" he inquired.

"Just drive, Hook," said the magician.

"Come now, Spector," put in Flint, "play fair. I've been with you right the way through this, you can't cop out now. You're saying Leonard's the killer, is that it?"

"It seems to be the only conclusion."

"And he's taken his parents off somewhere, has he?"

"Again, a fair assumption."

"Well, where has he taken them?"

"The Kingdom of Judaea," said Spector.

"Don't be foolish," snapped Flint. The effect of that strong coffee had worn off, and aside from a cheese sandwich on the train he had not eaten since breakfast. Under these conditions, he was a dangerous man. "Tell us what you know."

"Mr. Spector," Caroline said, "if you know where my brother is, I think it's your duty to tell us."

Spector nodded. "You want to hear the truth, is that it?"

WHEREIN THE READER'S ATTENTION IS RESPECTFULLY REQUESTED

*T*his has been no ordinary mystery. There have been more bodies, more clues, more deceptions, than even Joseph Spector is accustomed to. And yet there remains only one solution. A single answer to this concatenation of puzzles and impossibilities. Spector has found it.

Have you?

CHAPTER NINETEEN

THE CONFESSION
OF GILES DRURY

I.

There was a hammer in Sir Giles's skull, beating against his brain. He blinked in the blinding light until the room returned to focus. He was propped upright in a hard-backed dining chair. When he tried to move, he found he could not. Nor could he speak. He glanced downward and saw that his arms were tightly tied to the arms of his chair. Some probing with his tongue revealed that he was gagged.

Beside him was Elspeth, similarly bound. They looked at each other, panic in their eyes.

The man, their host, had his back to them. They were in an unfamiliar setting, with spotlights blazing down on them. It was a stage set of some kind; Sir Giles had never seen it before. The last thing he remembered was taking a much-needed sip of brandy in the aftermath of the night's horrors.

"I'm nearly finished now," the man said, "but before I bring this whole horrid affair to an end, there are one or two things I should like you to know." He turned to face them, smiling urbanely. "Do you remember the tale of Salome? Spurned by John the Baptist, she wanted one thing only. His head on a silver charger. And she got it, at the cost of her life and her eternal soul."

He held in his hands a silver charger, just like the one depicted in the various gruesome biblical paintings. He laid it on the table in front of them.

Elspeth squealed through her gag. Sir Giles sat rigid, staring daggers at their captor.

"Who do you think is under there? Would you care to guess? After all, there are not too many candidates *left*, are there? No? You don't feel like playing along? In that case, I had better show you . . ."

The man whisked away the lid. Elspeth screamed. Staring up at them from the silver platter was Leonard.

Peter Nightingale was looking eminently pleased with himself. "I'm going to remove the gag from your mouth," he said. "When I do, I don't want you to cry out. I don't want you to curse me. I don't want you to tell me I'm insane or I'll never get away with this. Because I will. In fact, I already have."

When the gag was removed, Sir Giles simply stared at him.

"There's a good fellow. If you will look over *there* you will see I have set up a motion picture camera and a voice recorder. Understand?"

Sir Giles nodded.

"I brought you here for a reason. As I'm sure you now realise, there's a reason for everything I do. After all, I had nine years of solitude in which to plan my actions very carefully indeed." From inside his jacket, he produced a long carving knife.

"Just get it over with," said the judge.

"Not so fast," Nightingale grinned. "Not until I've finished my film. Once it's done, it will be sent to the relevant authorities. And the truth will be out at last. Of course, I will be condemned as a madman in the press, and perhaps I am. But you will not be able to hide from justice anymore, Sir Giles. You will pay for your crime at last.

"We are going to have a trial," said Peter Nightingale. "*I*, however, am the judge, the jury, and"—he examined the knife, gauging its sharpness—"the executioner."

Then, in a swift motion, he jammed it blade-first into the surface of the table.

"In the case of the Crown versus Sir Giles Drury," he announced, "the court is now in session."

II.

The Sound City Studios lot lay in the countryside between London and the nearby village of Shepperton. As Horace Tapper had claimed, the place was indeed closed up for Christmas. The seventeenth-century mansion at the heart of Littleton Park had been appropriated for administrative and editorial suites, all of which stood in darkness. Taking the mansion as a centrepiece, various garages, canteens, and workshops mushroomed from it, plus wardrobe suites, rehearsal spaces, and storage units.

When Hook drove up to the main entrance, Flint was surprised to see that the lock on the gate had been broken and that the gates themselves bore indentations of a vehicle travelling at speed. But Spector was not surprised at all.

"Drive on," he said.

When they reached the soundstages—which were housed in large, hangar-like warehouses—the car drew to a halt beside a seemingly abandoned vehicle: a police van.

"He must have kept it near Marchbanks," said Spector, "which explains the paint job. He knew the woods and fields would be searched. The only way to ensure his escape vehicle went unnoticed was to disguise it. If your investigators stumbled across it, they wouldn't have given it a second glance. And so he drove away from Marchbanks without attracting attention."

"Why bring them *here* of all places?"

"The decapitation was the clue."

The four of them began crunching their way through the snow toward the largest building. Spector led the way with Flint on his heels. Caroline and Sergeant Hook trailed behind.

As they drew closer to the ominous-looking edifice, Spector slowed his pace.

"When you spoke to Dr. Moncrieff he claimed he was in London last night, didn't he? Visiting a private patient?"

"Yes," answered Flint. "What's that got to do with anything?"

"Maybe nothing, maybe everything. Call it a wild guess, but I think there's every chance Moncrieff's 'private patient' was the explorer Byron Manderby."

"I *do* call that a wild guess," said Flint. "Where the hell did you get the notion from?"

Spector grinned. "Manderby's a Tragedian, after all. I doubt Moncrieff would go so far out of his way for a patient unless they shared that particular clandestine bond."

"How do you know Manderby's a Tragedian?"

"The day we met, Peter Nightingale mentioned that the Javanese junk on which they sailed the Ulanga River was called the *Shamshir*. A shamshir is a Persian sword akin to the scimitar—emblem of the Tragedians. Manderby's expedition was cut short because he contracted malaria. And according to the document I found in the filing cabinet out at The Grange, he's still suffering the aftereffects."

"All right, so Manderby is a Tragedian. So what?"

"Bear with me, Flint. Manderby and Peter Nightingale met when Nightingale was recuperating from injuries sustained in the British Battalion, fighting the Spanish Nationalists. Both men were cared for by the same doctor. At a guess, I'd say it was Moncrieff, though there ought to be documentary evidence one way or the other."

"Spector, you're going round in circles. What if Moncrieff looked after them both? What does it *tell* us?"

"When Moncrieff was administering a sedative to Lady Elspeth after Jeffrey Flack's murder, Nightingale interrupted him. From the way they spoke to each other, it was evident they'd never met before.* If Moncrieff had treated Nightingale in the past, he would have recognised him, wouldn't he?"

"So what?"

"So . . . what if the man we came to know as Nightingale *was not Nightingale at all?*"

Flint took his eyes from the road to give Spector a suspicious sideways look. "Then who was he?"

Spector came to a halt. He turned and stared straight at Caroline. "Perhaps *you* had better tell us that, Miss Silvius."

Like a cornered animal, Caroline ducked low and poised to make a break for it. But Sergeant Hook, who had the youthful advantage over his colleagues, caught her by the elbow.

"Please arrest her," said Spector, "on a charge of murder."

She twisted and struggled as Hook clamped the handcuffs around her wrists.

"But you're not really Caroline Silvius at all, are you? You're Mrs. Caroline Griffin."

"How in the hell did you work *that* out?" said Flint.

"Process of elimination. We know Griffin and his bride eloped to Gretna Green last spring. Gretna Green is a preferred spot for so-called runaway marriages, because the Clandestine Marriages Act of 1753 doesn't apply across the Scottish border. And the Act forbids the marriage of a person under the age of twenty-one without parental consent. Griffin was well over twenty-one, so his betrothed must have been younger. Younger—and with living parents. Another viable suspect might have been Becky, the

---

*   *See Page 153*

housemaid at Marchbanks, but as Mrs. Runcible informed me, she is twenty-six* and therefore the elopement wouldn't have been necessary. Of all the women in this case, only Caroline was the right age. And bearing in mind the fact that her parents only died two months ago, it seems unlikely they would have consented for her to marry Thomas Griffin."

"All the same," said devil's advocate Flint, "couldn't his wife have been anyone?"

"Theoretically. But if so, why keep her identity a secret? Wouldn't she have made herself known in the aftermath of his death—even if only to lay claim to the insurance policy on his life? No, Flint, as soon as we learned that Griffin was married, I began to suspect Caroline. My suspicion was confirmed by a seemingly innocuous encounter in The Old Ram. It wasn't all that unlikely for Griffin to be there. But what *was* unusual was the fact he sat there in stony silence during the encounter between Leonard Drury and Caroline Silvius. And even *more* unusual was the fact Caroline never even mentioned to me that she'd seen him there. But she must have. He was seated behind Leonard's back,** she could hardly have missed him. He was making a show of keeping himself hidden, but really anyone with half-decent eyesight would have spotted him. And with those muttonchops of his he was easy enough to recognise. But she didn't even remark on his presence.

"Now I understand what he was doing there. He'd gone to keep an eye on her when she met with Leonard Drury. He knew

---

*   *See Page 150*
** *See Page 173*

Leonard had designs on her. He was present in case Leonard overstepped the mark. But then I almost ruined everything by appearing unexpectedly, to play the role of the knight in shining armour. It wouldn't have mattered if *Leonard* had seen Griffin. But if *I* saw him, then I might begin to make the kind of cerebral connections that could prove fatal for their plan.

"Add to this the fact Caroline was estranged from her parents when they died, and that they wrote her out of their will. What, I wonder, could she have done that so offended them?"

The question was rhetorical; Spector knew the answer.

"An unsanctioned marriage," he supplied. Then he turned and looked Caroline Silvius full in the face. "It had to be you," he said. "There was nobody else."

To Flint's surprise, Caroline didn't protest. There was no manufactured outrage.

"I suppose," she said, "I had hoped the horror of what I did to him would distract you."

"It did. But there was the inevitable question—if *you* didn't kill Griffin, who did? Whoever it was, they must have been utterly drenched in blood. And there would have been a trail in that pristine white snow. But there was none. Which caused me to wonder—what if the murderer had not left The Grange at all?"

"So *she* killed Griffin?" posited Flint. "And let the lunatics out? What about the other two orderlies, she knocked them out too?"

"No," said Spector. "At least, I doubt it. I'm sure you'll correct me if I'm wrong, Caroline, but I'd wager it was Griffin himself who slipped a sleeping draught into their tea."

Caroline did not correct him.

"You see," Spector continued, "I found it odd that Griffin should be killed in such a violent manner, while the other two orderlies were merely doped and tied up. Two very different approaches, which denoted different assailants. Griffin drugged his colleagues and tied them up. Then, when Caroline arrived, the plan was to stage Victor's escape. Finally, for added verisimilitude, Griffin himself would be knocked unconscious. Of course the entire country would be placed on alert, the countryside would be scoured, but inevitably they would find no trace of him."

"Why not?"

Spector grinned. "*That* is the crux of the entire matter. You see, Victor's sudden flight struck me as being distinctly out of character. And that's when I realised that's just what it was: a character. The Victor you met, the subservient, maligned figure, was a fictional creation of the *real* Victor Silvius: the cold, calculating, vengeful monster.

"It was a question of angles. Typically, a magic trick is 'angly' when it places the audience in a certain position for the optical illusion to work. Levitation tricks are a good example. But so is this identity trick, which required the establishment of two separate identities: Victor Silvius and Peter Nightingale."

"What are you saying? They were the same man?"

Spector nodded. "The fact Caroline and Thomas Griffin were married changes everything. Think about your visit to The Grange, where the objectionable Griffin treated both Victor and Caroline so poorly. It was a performance, Flint. For your benefit."

"So the man in the cell . . ."

"Was Victor Silvius. But he was *also* Peter Nightingale. That's why he made a point of avoiding you at Marchbanks, Flint. Because he knew that if you spoke to him alone, then you might see through his disguise.

"He had an arrangement with Griffin which enabled him to construct a second identity outside the walls of The Grange. News of Byron Manderby's failed expedition along the Ulanga River was widely reported, and most articles referred to Peter Nightingale as Manderby's right-hand man. I believe when Nightingale got back to England at the beginning of December, he really *did* return to his former agency in search of private secretarial work. But Victor and Caroline conspired to remove him from the equation, and to establish Victor as 'Peter' in his place."

"Then where's the real Peter Nightingale?"

"In the care of Dr. Findler."

"What . . . ?" Recognition dawned. "You mean the body in the trunk? The man we fished out of the Thames?"

"That's right. It was a webwork of murder, but there was one man behind it all, playing on the others' weaknesses and exploiting their ruthless, covetous instincts. Honestly, I'm in awe of the sheer audacity of it. The work of a brilliant, demented mind. But he couldn't have done it without *you*, Caroline. I imagine your marriage to Griffin was part of a very long game, with the sole objective of freeing your brother. All along, your only loyalty has been to Victor. Isn't that so? There's no one else."

Tears streamed down Caroline's face as she smiled. But she didn't say a word.

"And he was scheming right till the end," Flint observed. "Why did he swap clothes with Leonard's corpse?"

"To get Nightingale out of the picture, and simultaneously to paint Leonard as the mastermind. He knew the decapitation would lead to a manhunt but thought it expedient to send the authorities looking for the wrong man. That was the reason for the decapitation. Or, I should say, *one* of the reasons . . ."

"And the other?"

"The reason he brought Sir Giles and Lady Elspeth *here*, of all places."

"Which is?"

"He wants Sir Giles to confess, on camera, to the murder of Gloria Crain. *That's* what this has all been about. He spent nine long years brooding over the death of his true love. In all that time, his hatred for the judge has been seething away. The only way for Victor to achieve justice is to force a confession from the judge. The decapitation suggests the story of Salome, which suggests Tapper Productions. And Silvius had detailed knowledge of Horace Tapper's filming schedule thanks to Caroline. That's why he waited until now, when the studio would be closed up for Christmas, and he'd have his pick of the soundstages and equipment. He is going to film a motion picture of his own."

III.

"I don't understand any of this," said Sir Giles, playing for time. "You were behind bars, weren't you? You were locked away."

"I was," said Silvius. "For nine long years. But you forget I have a sister. A beautiful, industrious sister who would do anything to restore my freedom. She seduced an orderly by the name of Thomas Griffin. They cultivated an outward appearance of hostility—even outright enmity. Griffin had a tendency to over-egg the cake with ostentatious displays of disdain and cruelty. But he eventually permitted me to shave and to dye my hair blond, and to dress in a manner befitting a cultured gentleman. And he smuggled me out of the asylum. For days at a time I lived in London, in a room above a pub. I became Peter Nightingale. I read about him, I learned his behaviours, I even developed a taste for his brand of cigarettes. It was in this identity that I first visited Leonard and took on the role of personal secretary."

"You were in the asylum at that time. I know you were."

"You're quite right—I was. Various people came to visit me, not only my sister. I also had your friend Moncrieff, and a few others—including the Scotland Yard man, George Flint. But you see, that was the brilliance of my scheme. Thomas Griffin helped me to escape. But then he helped me to *get back in*. These occasions were carefully arranged in advance. Should anyone turn up to visit me when I was otherwise engaged, Griffin sent them away with a flea in their ear. Visits were planned for times when I could evade Leonard's attention, and Griffin snuck me back into the hospital and helped me don the disguise of the madman. The long wig, the false beard. Underneath it all, I was as you see me now.

"But eventually, when events began to gather pace, I decided to escape for good. So much had already occurred—so many deaths—that I would be an unlikely suspect. And besides, I had convinced Flint that *I* was the wronged party in all this. Which, in many ways, I am. But they would not see me as a murder suspect—rather, a desperate man out to prove his innocence.

"And God help me, it worked. I established Victor Silvius and Peter Nightingale as separate entities. And as soon as my last act of vengeance is completed, I shall disappear for good. Just as soon as you tell the truth."

"I don't know what you want me to say," said Sir Giles. "If it's about the dead girl . . ."

"Gloria. You know full well it's about Gloria."

"But you have it all wrong. I never touched her. I never had anything to do with her. I've no idea how she was poisoned."

"Liar. You might have fooled everyone else, but you can't fool me. I assure you, your band of 'Tragedians' hold no sway over *me*."

"I had no motive! No reason whatever to murder Gloria . . ."

"You used your power and influence to draw her in, didn't you? To seduce her away from me."

"I did nothing of the kind!" the judge protested, glancing sideways at his wife, who watched the proceedings with chilly horror.

"You did. Just as you seduced Esther Monkton and fathered the bastard, Sylvester. Is that why you killed Gloria? You thought she was going to tell your wife? Just too much of a nuisance, wasn't she, to be left alive . . . ?"

"No!" Sir Giles's protest echoed around the soundstage.

For a moment, it silenced Victor. The younger man studied his enemy carefully, cocking his head to one side.

TOM MEAD

"You know," he eventually said, "I almost believe you. But if *you* didn't kill Gloria, then there's only one other person who might have." He smiled at Lady Elspeth.

She shook her head frantically as he inched toward her, blade in hand.

"It had to be one of you," Victor continued. "Either you, Sir Giles, because Gloria was threatening to make things difficult for you. Or you, Lady Elspeth, because you were jealous. Well? Which is it?"

"Neither!" the judge barked. "You're insane!"

Victor's expression grew cold. He spoke in low, measured tones. "I warned you, didn't I, what would happen if you called me insane."

And he raised the knife.

In that instant, like a blinding bolt of lightning, every single light on that soundstage burst into brilliant life. The tableau of the judge and the madman was illuminated in its hideous glory.

"It's over," yelled George Flint. "You may as well drop it."

Victor Silvius stared back at Flint and Spector. "Gentlemen," he said, "you are just in time. The judge has a confession to make."

"No," said Spector, stepping forward. "He doesn't. It'll be best for everyone if you give up now, Victor. Hand over the knife. The place is surrounded, you couldn't hope to get away." Pure bluff.

"An inch closer, Mr. Spector, and I slash the judge's throat."

"You ought to know, Victor," the conjuror vamped, "that we have your sister. Caroline is under arrest for the murder of Thomas Griffin, among other things. If you try to make a run for it now, she will suffer for your crimes."

254

Victor swallowed. "Caroline? I don't believe you."

"But it's true. Hook! Bring Caroline out here!"

And the sergeant appeared with a handcuffed Caroline, emerging from behind a matte painting of King Herod's palace.

Caroline hung her head, looking down at the cuffs around her wrists.

"Caroline," said Victor, "I'm . . . I'm sorry. I never meant for you . . ."

"Just give up," said Flint. "It will be best for everyone. Most of all Caroline."

Hook and Caroline moved slowly toward the banquet table. As they did, Spector noticed Caroline's left foot inching in the direction of a long black cable that stretched across the concrete floor. He narrowed his eyes, sensing she was about to try something foolish. But before he could open his mouth to warn them, she pounced.

All it took was a flick of her foot, and the cable was around her ankle. Then she jerked her leg, wrenching over the tallest of the spotlights. It came spilling sideways, bursting in a shower of sparks on impact with the floor.

It was theatre; a perfect misdirection. Only Spector did not take his eyes from Victor Silvius. Neither Flint nor Hook could help themselves. And though their collective shift in attention lasted only a moment, it was enough.

Victor hurled the knife at Sergeant Hook; it embedded itself in his shoulder. Hook cried out and fell backward, allowing Caroline to break free of his grip.

The pounding footsteps of Victor and Caroline echoed around the soundstage. In an instant they were gone. Flint went after them.

Spector, meanwhile, dashed over to the fallen sergeant. He'd seen wounds like this one before, and he knew it was nothing serious. Nonetheless, he swiftly extricated the blade—prompting a squeal from the sergeant—and produced a blood-red handkerchief from his sleeve, which he used to staunch the wound.

She's done it again, Spector thought, *yet again she's saved her brother's skin.*

It was only a couple of minutes before reinforcements arrived, but plenty of time for Victor and Caroline Silvius to escape. Once he had handed the wounded sergeant over to an ambulanceman, Spector headed toward the banquet table, and set about freeing the prisoners.

Lady Elspeth seemed incapable of speech. Her gaze was rooted on that of her son, who peered lazily at her from the silver charger. Sir Giles just kept saying, "Spector . . . Spector . . ."

"It's over," Spector told him, and meant it.

Flint, meanwhile, oversaw the sacking of the soundstage. By the time every shadowed nook had been searched, both Victor and Caroline Silvius were gone.

"Find them," Flint commanded.

The van was gone too, leaving behind a trail of tyre tracks all the way along the studio driveway. They then turned out onto the main road, whereupon they slithered away and vanished, serpent-like, among the other, innocent tracks.

CHAPTER TWENTY

THE WEBWORK METHOD

Saturday, December 24, 1938

T he whole gloomy business had left Flint thoroughly depressed, though the same could not be said of Spector. When they met on Christmas Eve in the snug of The Black Pig, the old magician was positively buoyant. With a glass of absinthe in front of him, he greeted Flint warmly.

"You're pleased with yourself," the policeman observed.

For a fleeting moment in the immediate aftermath of the Silvius siblings' escape, Flint had thought his job might be on the line. But to his surprise, the superintendent had shaken him by the hand.

"Damn tricky business," he said.

Flint could only agree.

When the superintendent gripped his hand, Flint leaned in, and his superior's tiepin caught the light. Strange, Flint thought, that he had never noticed it before: the silver emblem of the crossed scimitars.

This explained why the case barely made the papers, and then only as a scant half column on page six or seven. It also explained why, in the spring of 1939, Dr. Jasper Moncrieff would very discreetly leave the country for sunnier climes, abandoning altogether his practice at The Grange. The Edgemoor Strangler, the clinic's last surviving patient, would be quietly transferred to Broadmoor. It further explained why Sir Giles Drury and Lady Elspeth withdrew from public life that same spring, sealing up both their Chelsea townhouse and their country seat at Marchbanks. The Tragedians looked after their own.

But all of this was in the future on Christmas Eve, 1938. Flint was still letting himself entertain vague hopes that Victor and Caroline Silvius might yet be caught.

"I suppose I'm enjoying the afterglow of a truly wonderful illusion; one of the best I've ever witnessed," said Spector. "Victor Silvius's scheme was excellent. I'll go further: magnificent. But it was not the scheme of a lunatic. I should say it was the product of a mind that was disturbingly, diabolically sane."

"Then who came up with it? Which of them? I'd have thought they were both as mad as hatters."

Spector considered this with a look of some distaste. "This business has given me occasion to reconsider my preconceived notions of madness. It is not a 'thing.' It's not tangible. Rather, it insinuates itself like smoke." With that, he sighed. "I presume the press will have a jolly time portraying the Silvius siblings as a kind of *folie à deux*. But I think it's more complex than that. I think perhaps in this instance it is better *not* to know the truth."

"Explain it to me," Flint persisted. "As usual, I can't get my head round it."

Spector offered a flicker of a smile. "You're too modest. I think you understand the scheme better than you realise. Nonetheless, here goes . . ."

He drew himself up, his shoulders arching back, and Flint was put in mind of a spider poising to pounce on a trapped fly.

"It's ironic, in a way, that Leonard Drury thought himself an actor, and yet he was utterly outclassed by one of the most convincing performances in the history of the craft. Victor Silvius was a master. But please," he said, "tell me about Sergeant Hook. Is he recovering well?"

"He's fine. Lucky it was just a flesh wound. All the same, he's taking some leave."

Spector nodded. "Good for him. Well, I presume you've come here for a reason, other than to wish me the joys of the festive season."

"As usual, you're right," said Flint. "I want you to tell me *how*."

"With pleasure. Well, Victor Silvius is undeniably a genius, but he could not have achieved his scheme without his sister. Caroline fed him the information he needed, so that when he made his first foray back into the real world, he knew exactly what to do. How did he know about Peter Nightingale? Because Caroline either informed him herself, or else slipped him clippings about the explorer's abandoned expedition. How did he know when Tapper would be closing up the Shepperton soundstage? Because Caroline, Tapper's governess, told him. How did he escape from The Grange? Because Caroline facilitated it.

"She killed Thomas Griffin, then she unlocked the cells. This was to add a fresh layer of confusion. Similarly, it's the reason she slipped the Strangler a note with the judge's address on it.

"Beforehand, she had set up the middle cell so it appeared that Victor had escaped along with the others. In effect, she facilitated two genuine escapes to add authenticity to the fraudulent one. Because by then, Victor was well-established in the Drury household as Peter Nightingale. His only return visits to The Grange were for specific appointments, prearranged with Griffin. The other night, Moncrieff mentioned that he entrusted Griffin with managing the three inmates, while he himself only had sessions with them periodically. *Griffin* was the one in charge. But he was in thrall to Caroline. When she double-crossed him, I bet it came as a complete surprise.

"But time was of the essence. The snow was coming down again, and she wanted police on the scene as soon as possible. The more police were at The Grange, she reasoned, the fewer would be left at Marchbanks. Her own coat was drenched with blood, so she had no choice but to destroy it. That was the reason for the fire. She threw in various case files for kindling, but also to disguise the real, eminently pragmatic rationale behind the conflagration.

"This, of course, left her without a coat, which would naturally arouse suspicion on a winter night. So she simply appropriated Griffin's. I noticed instantly that it was too large for her, and the buttons down the left side of the torso* told me it was in fact designed for a man.

---

*   *See Page 186*

"And if you're looking for real, tangible evidence, then consider those filing cabinets in Griffin's office. It makes sense for the killer to ransack the *S* drawer, as it contained the Silvius file. But why the *N* drawer?"

"Nightingale," said Flint.

"Right. And don't forget, whoever killed the man in the trunk made sure to pulverise the victim's face, to disfigure him, so that no one could identify him by looks alone."

"But how did they make sure Leonard Drury hired 'Nightingale' as his secretary in the first place?"

"It was what we magicians call an 'equivoque'—similar to the trick I showed you in the study at Marchbanks. Silvius forced Peter Nightingale onto Leonard in the same way a conjuror might force a card onto an audience member. The illusion of choice, when in fact there is none. It required careful planning to find the ideal candidate—a man Leonard could not help but be drawn to, someone with a reputation and unquestionable provenance. Leonard mentioned to me that his letters had been arriving a day late.* That was the result of a bribe to the postman, who delivered them to Caroline *first*, so she could steam them open and vet each of the other candidates. Anyone who might be a viable alternative to the formidable Peter Nightingale was swiftly discarded. Only the weakest, most ill-suited candidates made their way to Leonard's letterbox. That way, they could more or less guarantee 'Peter' would fit the bill.

"And once he was in the Drury household, 'Nightingale' worked quickly. He set about exposing and exploiting the weaknesses of

---

*   *See Page 177*

every single member of the Drury family. Fortunately for him, there were plenty to choose from. One of his first moves was to reveal to Leonard that Sylvester and Lady Elspeth were having an affair. Leonard tried blackmailing Sylvester, only for Sylvester to counter with the fact that *he* had witnessed Leonard taking a potshot at Sir Giles outside the Chelsea townhouse. Sylvester *had* to have seen Leonard taking that shot. The more I thought about it, about the placement of those footprints in the snow, and about the time at which Sylvester must have reached the townhouse, the more convinced I was that Sylvester had seen his half brother taking that shot. And so Leonard and Sylvester were at an impasse, which is why Leonard decided to murder his half brother. But he couldn't do it alone. He needed Ambrose's help. Between them, they killed Sylvester Monkton."

"How?"

"All in good time. No sooner had they killed Sylvester than Ambrose received the following morning a letter from Horace Tapper informing him that he would *not* after all be playing the lead in *Tarrare*. Needless to say, no such letter was sent. It was Victor's doing. I spoke to Tapper, and he informed me that he keeps a stock of headed studio notepaper in his office at home. Caroline was governess to his two young children, so it makes sense that *she* was the one to procure the paper, while Victor forged the note.

"I don't know exactly what was said in the letter—Ambrose destroyed it—but it was evidently part of Victor's plan to cause a rift between the brothers. It might have worked, if they had not been already bound by murderous conspiracy. A shot in the dark, you might say, that went wide of its target. But the letter he wrote to *Leonard* was lethally effective."

"What letter?"

"Now, I've no proof as to its existence," said Spector, "because I'm sure Leonard burned it. But it makes sense, does it not, for Victor to have written to *both* brothers, rather than just the one? He forged a letter to Ambrose, ostensibly from Horace Tapper. But he *also* forged a letter to Leonard. While the Tapper letter missed its mark, this other one was almost too perfect. It accused Leonard of murdering Sylvester Monkton."

"How the hell can you know that for sure?"

"Think about it, my friend. Silvius had already informed Leonard that Sylvester Monkton and Lady Elspeth were having an affair. When Monkton turned up dead, it would be all too obvious who was responsible. So Silvius wrote another of his poisoned pen missives, and this one really put the cat among the pigeons. Leonard knew well enough about Jeffrey Flack's propensity for blackmail—the death of Ida Cosgrove is fresh in all our minds. So he jumped to a false conclusion. He decided it was Flack who had written the letter. When you think about it, the idea makes sense. Why suspect 'Nightingale,' whom he perceived as an ally? And why suspect Ambrose, who was complicit in the crime? It's ironic, really, that the crime for which Jeffrey Flack was executed was the one crime he did *not* commit. But the fact remains: Victor Silvius *tricked* Leonard into murdering Jeffrey."

"But wait a moment," said Flint. "I thought you said *Ambrose* killed Jeffrey Flack?"

"Literally speaking, he did. He was the one who pulled the trigger, using the method I've already explained. But you see now why I was unwilling to outline my theory about the motive. There was so much more that I needed to unravel. Now I can tell you definitively that the murders of Sylvester Monkton *and* Jeffrey Flack were perpetrated by both brothers, Leonard and Ambrose, working together. Leonard was the one who stabbed Sylvester, and Ambrose was the one who pulled the trigger on Jeffrey Flack from his studio. But the ice trick couldn't be done without Ambrose, and the shotgun trick couldn't be done without Leonard's insistence that he and Flack swap rooms. They planned the murders together, and each brother had his part to play.

"Just before Flack was killed, Leonard escorted me into the music room—next door to the studio. In a curiously loud voice (obviously a signal for Ambrose) he told me there was something he wanted to discuss. This was presumably the prearranged vantage point from which I was *supposed* to see Ludo Quintrell-Webb fleeing the scene disguised as Arthur Cosgrove. But as we know, that part of their plan failed when Ludo took fright. So you see, the brothers were equally guilty."

Flint had taken his pipe from his pocket and clamped his teeth around it. "So the brothers committed the first two murders, and then *they* were murdered by Victor Silvius."

"Let me run through the remainder of the chronology," said Spector. "Ambrose set up his crime while the rest of us were at church in Benhurst. That morning, you and Caroline travelled out to The Grange for your visit with Victor Silvius. It had been arranged for the Sunday in the full knowledge that the family would most likely be attending the local church service. This gave Victor the chance to eschew his 'Nightingale' identity and drive back out to the sanatorium to re-establish his identity as the inmate. A wig and false beard were sufficient. But he took the Austin Seven, so that when I interviewed him in the aftermath of Jeffrey Flack's death the engine was still warm."*

Flint was awestruck at the sheer audacity of the whole scheme. "But there's no way Silvius could have predicted everything that would happen."

"You're right. And he didn't. The forged Horace Tapper letter, for instance, was a failure. But you forget, his *real* quarrel is with Sir Giles. The deaths of the judge's sons were all part of the perverse game he was playing, as were the poisoned pen letters. It was psychological warfare. He was determined to rob the judge of everything he had, just as he, Victor, had been robbed. So he played puppetmaster, pulling strings here and there, and playing on the covert enmities between the young men."

"All right," said Flint, "I've just about got my head around that part of it. But one thing you *haven't* explained is the poisoned pen letters."

"True," said Spector, "and that's because there is not very much to explain. The letters were written by Victor and delivered by Caroline. They did it knowing full well they would lead investigators back to the Gloria Crain case and expose the unanswered questions surrounding it. They *also* knew that it would seem impossible for Victor to have been the author of those letters.

---

* *See Page 143*

"However, they decided between them to add another layer to the puzzle. That was why Caroline sought *you* out, Flint. Your involvement in the judge's last high-profile case, the Dean affair, was well-reported. You knew Sir Giles professionally. So, by bringing you into the Crain case and coopting you against him, she hoped to hasten his downfall."

Flint was nodding. "And Victor took advantage of the invitation to Marchbanks to begin his campaign against the judge's sons."

"It was pure malice," Spector agreed. "He wanted Sir Giles to feel the loss that he himself had felt. As though the world was crumbling around him. So he played on each of the sons' weaknesses. He turned them against each other."

"You've explained how Leonard and Ambrose killed Flack. But you *haven't* explained how they killed Monkton, and got him out into the middle of that lake."

"You're right, I haven't. It was a decent scheme in itself, but not as ambitious as anything Victor Silvius cooked up. And yet there's still something to admire in it. That's the interesting thing about Leonard and Ambrose. Individually, they lacked the wit to pull off a truly ingenious impossible murder. But together . . .

"So, you want to know how they did it? You'll like this one, Flint. Personally, I've never come across one like it. But as you'll see, there is no way either of them could have accomplished it solo.

"Do you remember the egg trick I showed you at the Soho coffeehouse after Ambrose's murder?"

Flint thought for a second. It seemed such a long time ago now. Some little sleight of hand with an egg . . . yes, that was it! He had somehow slipped it into Flint's pocket in a matter of seconds. "I remember."

"Did you divine its significance?"

"Funnily enough, I had more important things on my mind that day."

"Ah . . ." Spector wagged a long, thin finger. "There's meaning in every trick, Flint. And it was a transportation trick, wasn't it? How did the egg get into your pocket—that was the insoluble question. And really, is that so different from getting a body into a boat?" Now the old conjuror was feeling playful. "I'd better put you out of your misery, hadn't I? Well, of course there were two eggs. I pinched them from the kitchen at Marchbanks, because I was planning to show you the trick earlier in the day. Two real eggs, and a third false egg made from rubber. You can buy them at any magic shop. And I decorated them by hand, with a pencil, to ensure the speckles were identical. I slipped a real egg into your pocket, I gave you another real egg to examine, and then when you handed it back to me I made a little show of 'weighing' it in both hands. That's when I swapped it for the rubber egg. Clapped once to flatten the rubber and make the egg disappear. But by then, the hard work had already been done. The second egg was in your pocket, waiting for you to discover it."

Flint was frowning. "I don't understand that at all. It's got nothing to do with the body on the lake. And besides, when did you slip the egg in my pocket? Don't tell me it was while we were watching Ambrose sizzling to death in his Bugatti?"

"No, no. I may be a ghoul, but I'm not as tasteless as all that. No, I slipped the egg into your pocket several hours earlier.

While we were still at Marchbanks. Before the atrocity out at the Grange."

"So you mean I had it in my pocket the whole time?"

"Yes. That's why I was so keen for you to keep your eyes on the road during that mad flight across country in pursuit of Ambrose. Didn't want to crack the egg and give the game away, did I?"

Flint was still frowning. "You went to all that ridiculous effort for a little parlour trick?"

Spector grinned, baring his sharp, white teeth. "And there's the lesson, Flint. It's that any conjuror worth his salt will go to whatever lengths are necessary to achieve even the most rudimentary effect. You'd be amazed at the effort that goes into creating the simplest illusion."

"But what if I had found the egg? Or if it broke?"

"You're missing the point. If you found it, or it broke, the trick was ruined. But the egg *didn't* break. That was pure serendipity. It was as if the fates *wanted* me to perform that trick for you. There's a magician in the United States whose name is Max Malini. Ever heard of him? Yes, I thought you might have. There's a tale told about him, to the effect that when he goes out to dine in New York City, he often finds himself ambushed by admirers demanding a trick. He will be gracious, he will tell them he's sorry, but he cannot perform on an empty stomach. And so his fellow diners wait until he has finished his meal. And then, with a sudden flourish of his cloak, he reveals a huge, heavy block of ice produced from nowhere; from thin air. Everyone is amazed, he receives a standing ovation. But the trick is simple: the ice is there all along, Malini arrived at the restaurant with it concealed in the folds of his cloak. It has been there the entire time he was calmly eating his meal. You see, he *knew* he would be asked for a trick, and he prepared accordingly. But he *also* knew that his audience would never expect him to go to such lengths for a simple, impromptu parlour trick.

"There's your lesson, Flint. Never underestimate the lengths to which an illusionist will go in pursuit of applause.

"Or, in the case of our homicidal brothers, in pursuit of a perfect crime.

"One of them—at a guess I would say Ambrose, on his way to the pub with Jeffrey—had taken a moment to cut the rope which tethered the boat to the jetty, then given it a hefty shove out toward the centre of the lake. It didn't matter if it was not precisely in the centre; just that it was away from the shore. He knew the temperature would soon drop below freezing point, so they made sure they were covered up until that point with flawless alibis. We would assume the murder must have taken place *before* the freeze, and thus rule them both out.

"Ambrose spent the evening at The Old Ram in the company of Jeffrey Flack. But all the time he was in clear sight of a barometer,* so he would be able to estimate when the lake would begin to freeze.

"And Leonard needed a witness who was whiter than white. Somebody whose testimony would never, ever be brought into question. So he found a young woman who hated his guts but who, when interviewed, would have to admit that he had been

---

*   *See Page 173*

in her company until after midnight. Ironically, that woman was Caroline Silvius. Once their rendezvous was over, he *then* drove out to Marchbanks alone, where he met with Ambrose in the garden and readied himself for what they were about to do. Ambrose had pinched the knife from the kitchen after Becky and Mrs. Runcible retired.

"They had already arranged to meet Sylvester at the sycamore. Which, incidentally, explains his haste in his encounter with Lady Elspeth at the Eros statue. You see, it really *was* Sylvester she met out there. But little did she know he had a second appointment that night, and one which would prove fatal."

"Yes, I can just about get my head around all that," Flint commented, "but what you haven't told me is *how* they did it. Got Monkton out into the lake, I mean."

"All right. Here goes. They met Sylvester by the sycamore tree, most likely having promised to pay him off. Instead, they killed him. The tree, you'll remember, is about a hundred yards from the edge of the lake and, crucially, directly opposite the jetty. Keep that image in your mind, and consider *this*."

Spector produced from his pocket a cricket ball. Flint took it from him and peered through the hole that had been drilled through its centre.

"I found this in the garage at Marchbanks and immediately saw it for what it was: a botched first attempt."

"First attempt at what?"

Spector grinned. "Note how narrow the hole is. About a third of an inch too narrow."

"For *what*, for heaven's sake?"

But Spector was not quite ready to play this hand. "When I first went to dinner at the Drury townhouse, it emerged that Ambrose was a cricketer. I was able to work out from the way he spoke that he was a bowler.* And Leonard Drury made a great deal of his knack for tying knots.** Bearing those two details in mind, the scheme comes into clearer focus, does it not? No? Well, think about *this*. When I first visited the garage at Marchbanks, I noticed a lengthy coil of rope among the miscellanea. Any ideas now?"

Evidently Flint had none and was not too happy about it. Spector decided at last to put him out of his misery.

"Combining Ambrose's bowling skill with Leonard's ropework, the two brothers came up with a nifty means of moving Sylvester Monkton's body across the frozen lake. It began with the drilling of a hole in an ordinary cricket ball, a hole that was just the right size for a length of rope to be fed through. Procuring the coil of rope, they did just that, and Leonard put his hard-won knot-tying skill to use. The other end they anchored on the shore opposite the sycamore using something innocuous like a croquet hoop. *Where* they anchored it would depend entirely on how far the boat had drifted—but they needed a straight line across the boat to the tree. That was essential.

"Next, Ambrose took the ball (with the rope threaded through it) and flung it from the jetty across the surface of the water. A bowler as skilled as he was would have the strength and accuracy to send it the 100 feet across to the other side of the lake. Leonard,

---

*   *See Page 49*
**   *See Page 50*

waiting in position, picked up the ball and fed it along the dead man's right shirt sleeve, across his back and out the left. Pulling the rope through after it, he then chucked the ball up and across an overhanging branch, which he and Ambrose used to hoist Sylvester's body up into the tree. When the cadaver was secure, they fixed the end of the rope to the ground with another croquet hoop. This gave them a makeshift rope-slide all the way across the surface of the water. Thus, by manipulating the rope from opposite sides of the lake they could slowly and gradually move the corpse out, and position it directly above the boat.

"Then it was simply a matter of untying the rope and lowering the body. All of this they accomplished without once setting foot on the ice. And you recall Sylvester's curious pose when he was found, his almost crucifixion-like attitude? That was necessary, to enable them to reel the rope back in again without disturbing the body too much. Once it had been fully retrieved, Sylvester was left exactly as we found him; on his back in the rowing boat, the knife protruding from his chest, his arms outstretched in a curious T shape, his knuckles just resting on the surface of the icy water."

Flint could not help but chuckle, in spite of the thoroughly macabre plot that had just been explained to him. "I swear I don't know how you do it, Spector."

"A chain of logical inferences. It also explains why they were not able to return the rope to the garage—I noted the following day that it was missing. Having fed it through the corpse's clothes, it must have been laced with blood. They had no choice but to burn it at the first opportunity, presumably first thing the following morning. Same goes for the cricket ball. Fortunately for us, they neglected their first, botched attempt. Otherwise I might never have pieced together their crude but effective pulley device."

Flint scratched his chin. "So Leonard and Ambrose killed Sylvester Monkton because he witnessed Leonard trying to shoot the judge. Next, they killed Flack because Silvius convinced them that he'd seen them murdering Monkton . . ."

Spector nodded.

"And once Ambrose was dead Silvius decided to frame Leonard for the whole lot."

"Right. Which naturally meant Leonard himself had to die. So Silvius decapitated him, planning to disguise the corpse as Nightingale's. It would have worked."

Flint huffed noisily. "The whole thing would have worked. Like a sort of daisy-chain of murder, one thing leading to the next."

"He came so far," said Spector with a melancholic lilt, "Silvius, I mean. He spilt so much blood. And at the last instant, he failed to complete his final task."

There was a long, heavy silence which hung between the two men like a corpse from a noose.

"It pains me," Spector finally said, "to see genius thwarted."

"Not me," said Flint.

"Though even Victor Silvius wasn't quite as clever as he thought himself to be, you know. In our very first meeting, in fact, he mentioned traversing the Ulanga River from the Eastern Rift to the mouth of the Atlantic.* Considering the fact the Ulanga eventually reaches the *Indian* and not the Atlantic Ocean, I'd say that was a

---

*   *See Page 113*

rather glaring error, wouldn't you? Perhaps if I'd spotted it at the time, I might have been able to prevent some of this bloodshed."

A moment of solemn silence passed before Spector spoke again.

"There's one last question, you know. A final mystery to be solved."

"Which is?" Flint was in no mood.

"The question at the very centre of the web. Who killed Gloria Crain? I rather think that has been neglected in light of everything else."

Flint blinked a few times and ferreted in his pocket for some matches to light his pipe. It was true—nobody had yet come up with a satisfactory answer to the mystery. None that satisfied him, anyway.

"Whoever killed her has a lot to answer for," he observed. "Not only *her* murder, but the other murders it led to."

"I agree. In many ways her death is the centre of the web. Everything else spun directly from it."

"And I presume you have an answer you're just waiting to spring on me? Who was it? Who murdered Gloria Crain ten years ago?"

Spector sipped his absinthe. "Nobody."

"What the hell are you talking about? Is this going to be some sort of trick, where you tell me she's not even dead, and she's going to come walking into the snug any moment . . . ?"

"You heard me. Gloria Crain is most definitely dead. And yet nobody killed her. The 'murder' of Gloria Crain never happened at all."

"For God's sake," Flint huffed, "then how did she *die?*"

"At a guess, I'd say complications from a ruptured appendix. Maladies of that nature are always dangerous, and require immediate medical attention. By the time a doctor arrived on the scene, the only thing to do was issue a death certificate." Spector shook his head slowly and solemnly. "A pointless death. Such a waste."

"If you're trying to be funny, Spector, I'd advise against it. I'm too tired, cold, and miserable for that."

"No joke, my friend."

"Then what about the poison? How the hell did the poison get into her system?"

Spector took a deep breath and issued a thoughtful sigh. "It didn't. That's the tragedy of this whole case. A fundamental misconception that destroyed countless other lives. All because of one man's ambition."

Flint sat, waiting.

"I'm talking about Doctor Findler." Spector took another sip of absinthe. "But of course you must have guessed by now. Findler has always had a bloated opinion of his own importance, wouldn't you say? It's difficult to imagine him as anyone's subordinate. And yet for many years, he was Professor Valentine's right-hand man. By 1928, this situation had become intolerable to him, as he himself admitted.* And so he began his subtle campaign, undermining Valentine at every opportunity. But he was careful to disguise these strategic blunders as lapses in Valentine's own conduct. He fostered the notion that it was *Valentine* who was losing his grip."

"What's this got to do with Gloria Crain?"

---

* *See Page 35*

"I never told you about the third visit I made while you were on your way back to Marchbanks. I stopped by a certain church-yard, to visit the grave of a woman named Ruth Kessler. I had a suspicion based on certain other statements, but when I got a look at her grave, I was able to confirm it. It was the date of her death: December 24th, 1928. Ten years ago this very night. Ruth Kessler died within twenty-four hours of Gloria Crain. A sheer coincidence—the only *real* coincidence in this entire case. Two young women, the same age and approximate in appearance. One died by strychnine poisoning, the other from a ruptured appendix. And Findler, for the sake of devilment, swapped their records before the postmortems were performed."

"My God," said Flint, "that's a hell of an accusation. Are you sure?"

"As sure as I can be. The only evidence is circumstantial, but I rather think it's too late to do anything about it now anyway. You see, when you and I met with Findler in the mortuary, he practi-cally confessed, didn't he? Do you remember? He pointed out the toe tags, and observed how difficult it could be to keep track of his guests' identities?* He practically *handed* us the solution. Findler was the one who swapped the names, and created an impossible murder where there was none, and turned a very real murder into an untimely yet natural death. I imagine his intention was for the blunder to seem like Valentine's doing, so he could build up a case for forcing his mentor into retirement and taking the top job for himself. But when Valentine got so wrapped up in trying to unravel the puzzle of Gloria Crain's poisoning, he opted to keep

---

*　*See Page 35*

shtum and let the old professor dig his own grave. And it worked, didn't it? This chink in Valentine's armour proved fatal, and saw his breakdown followed by a forced retirement within the year."

Flint curled his fingers into a fist and pounded the table. "That bastard. So you're saying he created a fake murder, and let a real killer get away with it?"

"Unfortunately, yes. There were of course questions around Ruth Kessler's death, but the apparently irrefutable verdict of natural causes quickly put them to rest. Ruth was dead, her father Richmond was dead; there was simply nobody else to kick up much of a fuss."

"Then who killed Ruth Kessler?"

"At a guess, I would say Daniel Kessler—her uncle. Leonard Drury claimed responsibility when he confronted Caroline Silvius at The Old Ram, but that was mere braggadocio. I have since gathered that while Leonard and Ruth Kessler were indeed childhood playmates, there was never anything romantic between them. Daniel Kessler, however, was Ruth's guardian, and her father's estate was held in trust for her until she turned twenty-one. With her out of the way, any money and property would go to Daniel, the last surviving Kessler. The irony of course is that if not for Findler's little piece of skulduggery, Kessler would have been caught almost immediately. He had the means, the motive, *and* the opportunity. Really, he was the only person with a vested interest in seeing Ruth Kessler dead. And I imagine he was pleasantly surprised when the death was written off as natural, enabling him to enjoy what he saw as his rightful inheritance in peace."

Flint had finished his beer, and was now giving the foamy bottom of his glass melancholy scrutiny. "I don't see how

Valentine can have missed the fact he was looking at the wrong woman . . ."

"Well, both deaths occurred on Christmas night, did they not? Though I don't know what Ruth Kessler ate that night, there's a decent likelihood it was more or less the same menu as the one at Marchbanks. English cuisine, after all, is not noted for its creativity. So, with the similar age and appearance, as well as the same or similar contents of their stomachs, I find Valentine's mistake rather more credible than it might initially seem."

"Findler," Flint said again. "I can't believe *he's* the one responsible for all this . . ."

"Well, naturally he had no way of knowing it would lead to a string of deaths a decade later. But he didn't care. That's what irks me, Flint. He simply *didn't care.*"

The two men sat in silence for a moment, listening to the crackling fireplace and the sound of the wind beyond the windows. It had begun to snow again.

"What are you going to do?" Spector asked, finishing the last of his absinthe.

"I'm going home to my wife," came the answer, "and I'm going to enjoy a peaceful Christmas. I imagine I'll eat and drink too much. And then I'll go back to work."

"I mean, what are you going to do about Findler?"

There was a long silence between the two men.

"I don't know," Flint eventually confessed.

"For what it's worth," said Spector, "this case has caused me to reevaluate my perception of 'justice.' There's no use waiting for divine retribution, Flint, because it simply doesn't happen."

"That's true enough," Flint said with a thoughtful nod.

"Sometimes, one has to take matters into one's own hands."

This was met with more silence.

Not long after that, Flint began the lengthy process of swathing himself in coat and scarves before donning his too-large bowler. Then he held out his hand, which Spector gratefully shook.

"Good night to you, my friend," he said, "and Merry Christmas."

"And to you," answered Flint.

THE MYSTERY OF COLOUR

I.

"I thought he'd never leave," said Spector's guest, resuming her seat. "Why didn't you tell him the truth?"

"And what truth would that be?" asked Spector with every semblance of sincerity.

Mrs. Runcible's expression was chilly, but all the same she seemed somehow *lighter* than before, as though she had suffered a great ordeal that was finally approaching its end.

"I believe you know well enough."

"I had my suspicions. But your presence here confirms them. You must have gone to a considerable effort to find me."

"You are perhaps not such an enigma as you like to think," said the housekeeper.

Spector ignored this. "Flint is a good fellow," he expounded, "and he works hard, but he's damnably short on imagination sometimes. It never occurred to him that there might be *two* revengers at Marchbanks, bearing two very different grudges. Care for a cigarillo?"

She took one and he lit it for her. While they smoked, Spector began to speak.

"I admire you, you know. I think you're a remarkable woman. The name 'Runcible'—where does it come from?"

"My mother's maiden name."

"I see. Would you like to tell the story, or shall I?"

She gave a desultory flap of her hand. "You do it. You're a better talker than I am."

"I won't dispute the point," said Spector, "though I'd appreciate it if you'd correct me when I go wrong."

She nodded curtly.

"You are Esther Monkton's mother, are you not? And the unfortunate Sylvester was your grandson?"

Mrs. Runcible's jaw clenched, but otherwise she remained motionless.

"You entered Sir Giles's service soon after the death of your daughter, didn't you? Your aim was to establish a relationship with your grandson, but also to avenge poor Esther. And over the years, you made yourself indispensable at Marchbanks, and when Sylvester came of age, you informed him of your real identity. You did it out of hatred for Sir Giles, but also out of guilt. You knew that you could have done more to save Esther, and that you failed her. This must have been a source of bitter regret. And the young Sylvester became your confidant. But the grief and bitterness never goes away. You were overheard on the telephone, you know. Talking to Sylvester, I presume."

"Damn that Becky," Runcible snapped, "nosy little cow."

"Becky leapt to a conclusion. She was aware of only one dead female—Gloria Crain. And so she interpreted what she heard as a tacit admission that *you* were the one who killed Gloria. In fact you were speaking rhetorically about your role in Esther's death. Isn't that so? I noted with interest your sudden, unanticipated sympathy for Lady Elspeth in the aftermath of Jeffrey Flack's murder. That was because you know full well what it's like to lose a child. But also because you knew she was about to lose two more. You were planning it then, weren't you? You knew that Ambrose and Leonard would have to die. To atone for *your* daughter and *your* grandson. You and Sylvester came up with a plan for him to seduce Lady Elspeth, to murder Sir Giles, and claim the inheritance. But it never made sense to me how an educated and intelligent man like Sylvester could be so naive as to trust Elspeth Drury. It seemed obvious that she would double-cross him as soon as her husband was out of the way. But *you* were his insurance, weren't you? You would have protected him no matter what the cost. You would have lied for him, or killed for him.

"But you never got the chance. Sylvester was killed before your plan came to fruition. And so you were back where you started. Unlike Scotland Yard, *you* knew immediately that Leonard and Ambrose were responsible for his murder, and for the murder of Jeffrey Flack. How did you know? Because Sylvester confided in you before he died that the brothers were trying to blackmail him, didn't he?"

She nodded.

"But he didn't tell you that he had turned the tables on them by virtue of what he saw at the Chelsea townhouse. If you had known *that*, you might have realised that his life was in danger. The brothers murdered Sylvester, and then they murdered Jeffrey Flack. But they would not go unpunished for long.

"I thought it odd at the time that Ambrose should be killed by an elaborate electrocution device when simply cutting the brakes on his Bugatti would have accomplished the same effect. But you had a reason for it, didn't you? You couldn't cut the brake line for the simple reason that you couldn't *see* the brake line. That's something your grandson inherited from his mother, isn't it? And she inherited it from you. Colour-blindness. I knew Sylvester was colour-blind because his father told me. And I surmised you were as well, on account of a couple of little incidents at Marchbanks. *Your* colour-blindness, however, was considerably more intrusive than Sylvester's. I would hazard a guess that you suffer from achromatopsia, which enables you to distinguish only between black, white, and shades of grey. You were unable to identify Lady Elspeth's emerald brooch,* and you served me with sherry instead of the absinthe I had ordered.** Minor occurrences in themselves, but useful illustrations nonetheless. And the coincidence of *two* people under the same roof with the same deficiency of vision was just too great. You had to be related—and closely related at that.

"The rest was logical inference. If you were colour-blind, you couldn't cut the brake line because you couldn't *see* the brake line. As I saw when I glimpsed the open bonnet of the Bugatti, its brake line is green.*** So you had no choice but to improvise. Hence

---

*   *See Page 115*
** *See Page 105*
*** *See Page 144*

the elaborate means of execution for the unfortunate, misguided Ambrose. When we first met, you claimed you were the one who single-handedly keeps the fires lit and the lamps burning at Marchbanks. And I can well believe it. I don't doubt you have taught yourself a thing or two about circuitry, necessity being the mother of invention, as the saying has it."

Mrs. Runcible had been listening closely, and her expression had now become one of mild amusement. "And what of the 'unfortunate, misguided' Leonard?"

"Well, this is pure hearsay from Flint. I wasn't there, and I didn't examine the crime scene. But he was a little surprised at your reaction when the body in Leonard's room was found. True, it was a particularly brutal and bloody crime. But for what it was, there was a curious *absence* of blood. By rights, the walls and ceiling ought to have been awash with the stuff. But they weren't, were they? Which indicates to me that when Leonard Drury was decapitated, he had in fact already been dead for some time. Because you had already killed him, hadn't you?"

She gave a little nod. "Leonard always thought of himself as the genius of the family. In that, as in most other things, he was mistaken. He summoned me to his room and told me outright that he knew I was Sylvester's grandmother. It was the colour-blindness, Mr. Spector. He had spotted it, the same as you."

She paused thoughtfully, and then stubbed out what remained of her cigarillo with a curious stabbing motion.

"I used a letter opener," she said. "It was the closest thing to hand. On his bureau, where he'd been opening fan letters. I grabbed it and I stuck it in his throat."

"And then left the room to carry on with your duties as normal. Yes, that makes sense. And when Victor Silvius stumbled on the scene, he decided to play a macabre little prank of his own, swapping clothes with the corpse and severing its head with the scimitar. No wonder you were shocked when the body was discovered. It was not the death but the *condition* of the body that shocked you. You must have thought you were going mad."

Again she smiled at him. "But I'm not, Mr. Spector. I'm as sane as you are. Which is why I'm curious to know what you intend to do with this information. Is it to be blackmail?"

Spector chuckled. "I see no reason for anyone to know what we have talked about this evening. It shall remain our secret. But what I would also like to know is what *you* are planning to do next."

"My daughter was taken from me. Now his sons are taken from him."

"So your revenge is complete?"

She glanced toward the window. "It's snowing," she observed.

"So it is," said Spector, not taking his eyes off her icily intractable face.

II.

What an agreeable couple they made, thought the waiter as he ushered them into the great ballroom. They strode arm in arm, and in perfect step. Newlyweds, from the look of them.

The husband was a fair-haired Aryan type, tall and rather thin, but he spoke and carried himself with the utmost panache—even down to the way he smoked those fragrant, foreign cigarettes. And she was just beautiful. Positively luminous in a chiffon gown, with platinum blonde hair neatly bobbed like a Jean Harlow or a Carole Lombard.

And the way they looked at one another—it was enough to make the waiter's heart sing. The husband was some sort of explorer; at least that's what the waiter had gathered from the gossip among his colleagues. That was how the fellow had inveigled an invitation to the captain's table the previous evening. How splendidly the couple had danced, how wittily they had impressed the various dignitaries. But what was so wonderful about this loving couple was not the way in which they behaved around other people, but the way they behaved around each other. It was as if they were two halves of the same whole. You could tell just by looking at them.

The husband went to the bar and fetched a couple of cocktails, while the wife gazed longingly after him. Soon the band would strike up once again. Then they would head out on deck to enjoy the music, to dance when the mood took them, and to watch the water rolling ahead of them as wide and dark as the sky.

ACKNOWLEDGEMENTS

Cabaret Macabre was an admittedly ambitious undertaking—a locked-room mystery retelling of *The Revenger's Tragedy*—and as before, I spent my time diving into the world of the classic Golden Age mystery. The usual suspects were all present and correct: John Dickson Carr, Ellery Queen, Agatha Christie, Edmund Crispin, Nicholas Blake, Christianna Brand, Freeman Wills Crofts, et al. This time around, I was also particularly drawn to the splendid eccentricity of Gladys Mitchell and Michael Innes, as well as the byzantine complexity of various great Japanese mystery novels: *The Tokyo Zodiac Murders*, *The Decagon House Murders*, *Death on Gokumon Island*.

Unlike the first two Spector books, this one does not include a dedication to my mum and dad—that's because I wanted to write a more substantial acknowledgement here. They've been a constant source of support throughout the writing of the series. I quite literally couldn't have done it without them.

Thank you to my wonderful long-distance friends—many of whom were also "beta readers": Steve Barge, Gabriele Crescenzi, Michael Dahl, Douglas Greene, Jeff Marks, Dan Napolitano, Gigi Pandian, Ana Teresa Pereira, and Rob Reef.

Thank you to Fiona Erskine and Paul Gitsham for answering certain technical questions.

Thank you to the mystery fiction community, of which I am proud to be a part. It's been my pleasure getting to know many readers, bloggers, interviewers, and reviewers during the promotion of my first two books. I'm especially grateful to Tony R. Cox, Gary Nathan, Pietro de Palma, Lenny Picker, Risto M.K. Raitio—to name only a few.

Certain authors have gone out of their way to support my work when they didn't have to, and that means a great deal to me. Specifically, these are Jenny Blackhurst, M. W. Craven, Victoria Dowd, Steven Dunne, Martin Edwards, A. J. Hawley, Ragnar Jonasson, Barbara Nadel, T. A. Willberg, and Marian Womack. Thank you all.

Thank you to my good friends Michael Pritchard, Milan Gurung, Charlotte Lunn, Amy Louise Smith, Alice Hunter, Sian Burton, James Cornall, Joel Murphie, Harriet Mallard, Sam, Steph, and Ted Hancock.

Thank you to Otto Penzler, Charles Perry, and Julia O'Connell for their continued championing of my books. Special thanks to Luisa Smith for her diligent and astute editorial work on *Cabaret Macabre*.

Thank you to Lorella Belli and her team at LBLA, particularly Laura Darpetti and Flick Hemming.

ACKNOWLEDGEMENTS

Thank you to Greg Rees and Polly Grice at Head of Zeus, and to Sophie Ransom.

Thank you to the libraries and bookshops that have hosted me, made me welcome, and promoted my books. And thanks to you, the reader, for making it this far. I hope you've had fun, and I hope to see you again.